FIRST

In this masterful selection of science fiction stories, author/editor Damon Knight makes contact with the leading minds of speculative fiction. Such celebrated writers as Theodore Sturgeon, Isaac Asimov, and H. G. Wells ask us to explore our reactions to man's first meetings with alien beings.

ENCOUNTERS!

From unknown creatures to unexplained mechanical interferences, from spacecraft sightings to shining structures—how will you respond?

Damon Knight

FIRST CONTACT

PINNACLE BOOKS • LOS ANGELES

This is a work of fiction. All the characters and events portrayed in this book are fictional, and any resemblance to real people or incidents is purely coincidental.

FIRST CONTACT

A reissue of the original Pinnacle Books edition, first published November 1971

Second printing, March 1973
Third printing, August 1978

ISBN: 0-523-40354-2

Cover illustration by Paul Stinson

Printed in the United States of America

PINNACLE BOOKS, INC.
2029 Century Park East
Los Angeles, California 90067

TABLE OF CONTENTS

ACKNOWLEDGEMENTS

This constitutes an extension of the copyright page. Grateful acknowledgment is made to the following holders of copyright for permission to reprint the stories in this anthology.

"First Contact" by Murray Leinster, copyright © 1945 by Street and Smith Publications, Inc., reprinted by permission of the author.

"Doomsday Deferred" by Will F. Jenkins, copyright © 1949 by Curtis Publishing Company, Inc., reprinted by permission of the author.

"The Hurkle Is a Happy Beast" by Theodore Sturgeon, copyright © 1949 by Mercury Press, Inc., reprinted by permission of the author and Robert P. Mills, Ltd.

"Not Final!" by Isaac Asimov, copyright © 1941 by Street and Smith Publications, Inc., reprinted by permission of the author.

"The Blind Pilot" by Charles Henneberg, copyright © 1959 by Mercury Press, Inc., reprinted by permission of the author's estate.

"The Silly Season" by C. M. Kornbluth, copyright © 1950 by Mercury Press, Inc., reprinted by permission of Robert P. Mills, Ltd.

"Goldfish Bowl" by Robert A. Heinlein, copyright © 1942 by Street and Smith Publications, Inc., reprinted by permission of Lurton Blassingame.

"In Value Deceived" by H. B. Fyfe, copyright © 1950 by Street and Smith Publications, Inc., reprinted by permission of the author.

"The Waveries" by Fredric Brown, copyright © 1944 by Street and Smith Publications, Inc., reprinted by permission of Scott Meredith Literary Agency, Inc.

INTRODUCTION

Certain science fiction stories stand out in the mind from all others—brilliantly inventive stories, which either present an idea for the first time in fiction, or embody it more compactly and ingeniously than has ever been done before. High on the list of such stories is one called "First Contact," by Murray Leinster. The plot of the story is simply this: two starships, one from Earth, the other alien, meet far out in space. The captain of each ship realizes that he cannot trust the other, and dares not go home for fear of revealing the location of his home planet to a possible destroyer. What can each do? The answer is absorbing; I won't spoil it for you.

It has been a pleasure to gather the stories in this book in order to honor Murray Leinster and to illustrate other aspects of the "first contact" situation. Two or three of these stories were published before "First Contact"—in the case of the Wells story, forty-one years before. One or two deal with contacts that take place, like Leinster's, in deep space; others are closer to home, and several (again including the Wells) take place on our own Earth.

One of these, "Doomsday Deferred," deserves special mention because it is by Will F. Jenkins—and "Murray Leinster" is his pseudonym, the one he has been using to write superior science fiction since 1918.

DAMON KNIGHT

FIRST CONTACT

BY MURRAY LEINSTER

Tommy Dort went into the captain's room with his last pair of stereophotos and said:

"I'm through, sir. These are the last two pictures I can take."

He handed over the photographs and looked with professional interest at the visiplates which showed all space outside the ship. Subdued, deep-red lighting indicated the controls and such instruments as the quartermaster on duty needed for navigation of the spaceship *Llanvabon*. There was a deeply cushioned control chair. There was the little gadget of oddly angled mirrors—remote descendant of the back-view mirrors of twentieth-century motorists—which allowed a view of all the visiplates without turning the head. And there were the huge plates which were so much more satisfactory for a direct view of space.

The *Llanvabon* was a long way from home. The plates which showed every star of visual magnitude and could be stepped up to any desired magnification, portrayed stars of every imaginable degree of brilliance, in the startlingly different colors they show outside of atmosphere. But every one was unfamiliar. Only two constellations could be recognized as seen from Earth, and they were shrunken and distorted. The Milky Way seemed vaguely out of place. But even such oddities were minor compared to a sight in the forward plates.

There was a vast, vast mistiness ahead. A luminous mist. It seemed motionless. It took a long time for any appreciable nearing to appear in the vision plates, though the spaceship's velocity indicator showed an incredible speed. The mist was the Crab Nebula, six light-years long, three and a half light-years thick, with outward-reaching members that in the telescopes of Earth gave it some resemblance to the creature for which it was named. It was a cloud of gas, infinitely tenuous, reaching half again as far as from Sol to its nearest neighbor-sun. Deep within it burned two stars; a double star; one component the familiar yellow of the sun of Earth, the other an unholy white.

Tommy Dort said meditatively:

"We're heading into a deep, sir?"

The skipper studied the last two plates of Tommy's taking, and put them aside. He went back to his uneasy contemplation of the vision plates ahead. The *Llanvabon* was decelerating at full force. She was a bare half light-year from the nebula. Tommy's work was guiding the ship's course, now, but the work was done. During all the stay of the exploring ship in the nebula, Tommy Dort would loaf. But he'd more than paid his way so far.

He had just completed a quite unique first—a complete photographic record of the movement of a nebula during a period of four thousand years, taken by one individual with the same apparatus and with control exposures to detect and record any systematic errors. It was an achievement in itself worth the journey from Earth. But in addition, he had also recorded four thousand years of the history of a double star, and four thousand years of the history of a star in the act of degenerating into a white dwarf.

It was not that Tommy Dort was four thousand years old. He was, actually, in his twenties. But the Crab Nebula is four thousand light-years from Earth, and the last two pictures had been taken by light which would not reach Earth until the sixth millennium A.D. On the way here—at speeds incredible multiples of the speed of light—Tommy Dort had recorded each aspect of the nebula by the light which had left it from forty centuries since to a bare six months ago.

The *Llanvabon* bored on through space. Slowly, slowly, slowly, the incredible luminosity crept across the vision plates. It blotted out half the universe from view. Before was glowing mist, and behind was a star-studded emptiness. The mist shut off three-fourths of all the stars. Some few of the brightest shone dimly through it near its edge, but only a few. Then there was only an irregularly shaped patch of darkness astern against which stars shone unwinking. The *Llanvabon* dived into the nebula, and it seemed as if it bored into a tunnel of darkness with walls of shining fog.

Which was exactly what the spaceship was doing. The most distant photographs of all had disclosed structural features in the nebula. It was not amorphous. It had form. As the *Llanvabon* drew nearer, indications of structure grew more distinct, and Tommy Dort had argued for a curved approach for photographic reasons. So the spaceship had come up to the nebula on a vast logarithmic curve, and Tommy had been able to take successive photographs from slightly different angles and get stereopairs which showed the nebula in three dimensions; which disclosed billowings and hollows and an actually complicated shape. In places, the nebula displayed convolutions like those of a human brain. It was into one of those hollows that the spaceship now plunged. They had been called "deeps" by analogy with crevasses in the ocean floor. And they promised to be useful.

The skipper relaxed. One of a skipper's functions, nowadays, is to think of things to worry about, and then to worry about them. The skipper of the *Llanvabon* was conscientious. Only after a certain instrument remained definitely nonregistering did he ease himself back in his seat.

"It was just hardly possible," he said heavily, "that those deeps might be nonluminous gas. But they're empty. So we'll be able to use overdrive as long as we're in them."

It was a light-year-and-a-half from the edge of the nebula to the neighborhood of the double star which was its heart. That was the problem. A nebula is a gas. It is so thin that a comet's tail is solid by comparison, but a ship traveling on overdrive—above the speed of light—does not want to hit even a merely hard vacuum. It needs pure emptiness, such as exists between the stars. But the *Llanvabon* could not do much in this expanse of mist if it was limited to speeds a merely hard vacuum would permit

The luminosity seemed to close in behind the spaceship, which slowed and slowed and slowed. The overdrive went off with the sudden *pinging* sensation which goes all over a person when the overdrive field is released.

Then, almost instantly, bells burst into clanging, strident uproar all through the ship. Tommy was almost deafened by the alarm bell which rang in the captain's room before the quartermaster shut it off with a flip of his hand. But other bells could be heard ringing throughout the rest of the ship, to be cut off as automatic doors closed one by one.

Tommy Dort stared at the skipper. The skipper's hands clenched. He was up and staring over the quartermaster's shoulder. One indicator was apparently having convulsions. Others strained to record their findings. A spot on the diffusedly bright mistiness of a bow-quartering visiplate grew brighter as the automatic scanner focused on it. That was the direction of the object which had sounded collision-alarm. But the object locator itself—according to its reading, there was one solid object some eighty thousand miles away—an object of no great size. But there was another object whose distance varied from extreme range to zero, and whose size shared its impossible advance and retreat.

"Step up the scanner," snapped the skipper.

The extra-bright spot on the scanner rolled outward, obliterating the undifferentiated image behind it. Magnification increased. But nothing appeared. Absolutely nothing. Yet the radio locator insisted that something monstrous and invisible made lunatic dashes toward the *Llanvabon*, at speeds which inevitably implied collision, and then fled coyly away at the same rate.

The visiplate went up to maximum magnification. Still nothing. The skipper ground his teeth. Tommy Dort said meditatively:

"D'you know, sir, I saw something like this on a liner of the Earth-Mars run once, when we were being located by another ship. Their locator beam was the same frequency as ours, and every time it hit, it registered like something monstrous, and solid."

"That," said the skipper savagely, "is just what's happening now. There's something like a locator beam on us. We're getting that beam and our own echo besides. But the other ship's invisible! Who is out here in an invisible ship with locator devices? Not men, certainly!"

He pressed the button in his sleeve communicator and snapped:

"Action stations! Man all weapons! Condition of extreme alert in all departments immediately!"

His hands closed and unclosed. He stared again at the visiplate which showed nothing but a formless brightness.

"Not men?" Tommy Dort straightened sharply. "You mean—"

"How many solar systems in our galaxy?" demanded the skipper bitterly. "How many planets fit for life? And how many kinds of life could there be? If this ship isn't from Earth—and it isn't—it has a crew that isn't human. And things that aren't human but are up to the level of deepspace travel in their civilization could mean anything!"

The skipper's hands were actually shaking. He would

not have talked so freely before a member of his own crew, but Tommy Dort was of the observation staff. And even a skipper whose duties include worrying may sometimes need desperately to unload his worries. Sometimes, too, it helps to think aloud.

"Something like this has been talked about and speculated about for years," he said softly. "Mathematically, it's been an odds-on bet that somewhere in our galaxy there'd be another race with a civilization equal to or further advanced than ours. Nobody could ever guess where or when we'd meet them. But it looks like we've done it now!"

Tommy's eyes were very bright.

"D'you suppose they'll be friendly, sir?"

The skipper glanced at the distance indicator. The phantom object still made its insane, nonexistent swoops toward and away from the *Llanvabon*. The secondary indication of an object at eighty thousand miles stirred ever so slightly.

"It's moving," he said curtly. "Heading for us. Just what we'd do if a strange spaceship appeared in our hunting grounds! Friendly? Maybe! We're going to try to contact them. We have to. But I suspect this is the end of this expedition. Thank God for the blasters!"

The blasters are those beams of ravening destruction which take care of recalcitrant meteorites in a spaceship's course when the deflectors can't handle them. They are not designed as weapons, but they can serve as pretty good ones. They can go into action at five thousand miles, and draw on the entire power output of a whole ship. With automatic aim and a traverse of five degrees, a ship like the *Llanvabon* can come very close to blasting a hole through a small-sized asteroid which gets in its way. But not on overdrive, of course.

Tommy Dort had approached the bow-quartering visiplate. Now he jerked his head around.

"Blasters, sir? What for?"

The skipper grimaced at the empty visiplate.

"Because we don't know what they're like and can't take a chance! I know!" he added bitterly. "We're going to make contacts and try to find out all we can about them—especially where they come from. I suppose we'll try to make friends—but we haven't much chance. We can't trust them a fraction of an inch. We daren't! They've locators. Maybe they've tracers better than any we have. Maybe they could trace us all the way home without our knowing it! We can't risk a nonhuman race knowing where Earth is unless we're sure of them! And how can we be sure? They could come to trade, of course—or they could swoop down on overdrive with a battle fleet that could wipe us out before we knew what happened. We wouldn't know which to expect, or when!"

Tommy's face was startled.

"It's all been thrashed out over and over, in theory," said the skipper. "Nobody's ever been able to find a sound answer, even on paper. But you know, in all their theorizing, no one considered the crazy, rank impossibility of a deep-space contact, with neither side knowing the other's home world! But we've got to find an answer in fact! What are we going to do about them? Maybe these creatures will be aesthetic marvels, nice and friendly and polite—and underneath with the sneaking brutal ferocity of a Japanese. Or maybe they'll be crude and gruff as a Swedish farmer—and just as decent underneath. Maybe they're something in between. But am I going to risk the possible future of the human race on a guess that it's safe to trust them? God knows it would be worthwhile to make friends with a new civilization! It would be bound to stimulate our own, and maybe we'd gain enormously. But I can't take chances. The one thing I won't risk is having them know how to find Earth! Either I know they can't follow me, or I don't go home! And they'll probably feel the same way!"

He pressed the sleeve-communicator button again.

"Navigation officers, attention! Every star map on this ship is to be prepared for instant destruction. This includes photographs and diagrams from which our course or starting point could be deduced. I want all astronomical data gathered and arranged to be destroyed in a split second, on order. Make it fast and report when ready!"

He released the button. He looked suddenly old. The first contact of humanity with an alien race was a situation which had been foreseen in many fashions, but never one quite so hopeless of solution as this. A solitary Earth-ship and a solitary alien, meeting in a nebula which must be remote from the home planet of each. They might wish peace, but the line of conduct which best prepared a treacherous attack was just the seeming of friendliness. Failure to be suspicious might doom the human race—and a peaceful exchange of the fruits of civilization would be the greatest benefit imaginable. Any mistake would be irreparable, but a failure to be on guard would be fatal.

The captain's room was very, very quiet. The bow-quartering visiplate was filled with the image of a very small section of the nebula. A very small section indeed. It was all diffused, featureless, luminous mist. But suddenly Tommy Dort pointed.

"There, sir!"

There was a small shape in the mist. It was far away. It was a black shape, not polished to mirror-reflection like the hull of the *Llanvabon*. It was bulbous—roughly pear-shaped. There was much thin luminosity between, and no details could be observed, but it was surely no natural object. Then Tommy looked at the distance indicator and said quietly:

"It's headed for us at very high acceleration, sir. The odds are that they're thinking the same thing, sir, that neither of us will dare let the other go home. Do you think they'll try a contact with us, or let loose with their weapons as soon as they're in range?"

The *Llanvabon* was no longer in a crevasse of emptiness in the nebula's thin substance. She swam in luminescence. There were no stars save the two fierce glows in the nebula's heart. There was nothing but an all-enveloping light, curiously like one's imagining of underwater in the tropics of Earth.

The alien ship had made one sign of less than lethal intention. As it drew near the *Llanvabon*, it decelerated. The *Llanvabon* itself had advanced for a meeting and then come to a dead stop. Its movement had been a recognition of the nearness of the other ship. Its pausing was both a friendly sign and a precaution against attack. Relatively still, it could swivel on its own axis to present the least target to a slashing assault, and it would have a longer firing-time than if the two ships flashed past each other at their combined speeds.

The moment of actual approach, however, was tenseness itself. The *Llanvabon's* needle-pointed bow aimed unwaveringly at the alien bulk. A relay to the captain's room put a key under his hand which would fire the blasters with maximum power. Tommy Dort watched, his brow wrinkled. The aliens must be of a high degree of civilization if they had spaceships, and civilization does not develop without the development of foresight. These aliens must recognize all the implications of this first contact of two civilized races as fully as did the humans on the *Llanvabon.*

The possibility of an enormous spurt in the development of both, by peaceful contact and exchange of their separate technologies, would probably appeal to them as to man. But when dissimilar human cultures are in contact, one must usually be subordinate or there is war. But subordination between races arising on separate planets could not be peacefully arranged. Men, at least, would never consent to subordination, nor was it likely that any highly developed race would agree. The benefits to be derived from commerce could never make up for a condition of inferiority. Some races—men, perhaps—would prefer commerce to conquest. Perhaps—perhaps!—these aliens would also. But some types even of human beings would have craved red war. If the alien ship now approaching the *Llanvabon* returned to its home base with news of humanity's existence and of ships like the *Llanvab*on, it would give its race the choice of trade or battle. They might want trade, or they might want war. But it takes two to make trade, and only one to make war. They could not be sure of men's peacefulness, or could men be sure of theirs. The only safety for either civilization would lie in the destruction of one or both of the two ships here and now.

But even victory would not be really enough. Men would need to know where this alien race was to be found, for avoidance if not for battle. They would need to know its weapons, and its resources, and if it could be a menace and how it could be eliminated in case of need. The aliens would feel the same necessities concerning humanity.

So the skipper of the *Llanvabon* did not press the key which might possibly have blasted the other ship to nothingness. He dared not. But he dared not not fire either. Sweat came out on his face.

A speaker muttered. Someone from the range room.

"The other ship's stopped, sir. Quite stationary. Blasters are centered on it, sir."

It was an urging to fire. But the skipper shook his head, to himself. The alien ship was no more than twenty miles away. It was dead-black. Every bit of its exterior was an abysmal, nonreflecting sable. No details could be seen except by minor variations in its outline against the misty nebula.

"It's stopped dead, sir," said another voice. "They've sent a modulated short wave at us, sir. Frequency modulated. Apparently a signal. Not enough power to do any harm."

The skipper said through tight-locked teeth:

"They're doing something now. There's movement on the outside of their hull. Watch what comes out. Put the auxiliary blasters on it."

Something small and round came smoothly out of the oval outline of the black ship. The bulbous hulk moved.

"Moving away, sir," said the speaker. "The object they let out is stationary in the place they've left."

Another voice cut in:

"More frequency modulated stuff, sir. Unintelligible."

Tommy Dort's eyes brightened. The skipper watched the visiplate, with sweat-droplets on his forehead.

"Rather pretty, sir," said Tommy, meditatively. "If they sent anything toward us, it might seem a projectile or a bomb. So they came close, let out a lifeboat, and went away again. They figure we can send a boat or a man to make contact without risking our ship. They must think pretty much as we do."

The skipper said, without moving his eyes from the plate:

"Mr. Dort would you care to go out and look the thing over? I can't order you, but I need all my operating crew for emergencies. The observation staff—"

"Is expendable. Very well, sir," said Tommy briskly. "I won't take a lifeboat, sir. Just a suit with a drive in it. It's smaller and the arms and legs will look unsuitable for a bomb. I think I should carry a scanner, sir."

The alien ship continued to retreat. Forty, eighty, four hundred miles. It came to a stop and hung there, waiting. Climbing into his atomic-driven spacesuit just within the *Llanvabon's* air lock, Tommy heard the reports as they went over the speakers throughout the ship. That the other ship had stopped its retreat at four hundred miles was encouraging. It might not have weapons effective at a greater distance than that, and so felt safe. But just as the thought formed itself in his mind, the alien retreated precipitately still farther. Which, as Tommy reflected as he emerged from the lock, might be because the aliens had realized they were giving themselves away, or might be because they wanted to give the impression that they had done so.

He swooped away from the silvery-mirror *Llanvabon*, through a brightly glowing emptiness which was past any previous experience of the human race. Behind him, the *Llanvabon* swung about and darted away. The skipper's voice came in Tommy's helmet phones.

"We're pulling back, too, Mr. Dort. There is a bare possibility that they've some explosive atomic reaction they can't use from their own ship, but which might be destructive even as far as this. We'll draw back. Keep your scanner on the object."

The reasoning was sound, if not very comforting. An explosive which would destroy anything within twenty miles was theoretically possible, but humans didn't have it yet. It was decidedly safest for the *Llanvabon* to draw back.

But Tommy Dort felt very lonely. He sped through emptiness toward the tiny black speck which hung in incredible brightness. The *Llanvabon* vanished. Its polished hull would merge with the glowing mist at a relatively short distance, anyhow. The alien ship was not visible to the naked eye, either. Tommy swam in nothingness, four thousand light-years from home, toward a tiny black spot which was the only solid object to be seen in all of space.

It was a slightly distorted sphere, not much over six feet in diameter. It bounced away when Tommy landed on it, feet-first. There were small tentacles, or horns, which projected in every direction. They looked rather like the detonating horns of a submarine mine, but there was a glint of crystal at the tip-end of each.

"I'm here," said Tommy into his helmet phone.

He caught hold of a horn and drew himself to the object. It was all metal, dead-black. He could feel no texture through his space gloves, of course, but he went over and over it, trying to discover its purpose.

"Deadlock, sir," he said presently. "Nothing to report that the scanner hasn't shown you."

Then, through his suit, he felt vibrations. They translated themselves as clankings. A section of the rounded hull of the object opened out. Two sections. He worked his way around to look in and see the first nonhuman civilized beings that any man had ever looked upon.

But what he saw was simply a flat plate on which dim red glows crawled here and there in seeming aimlessness. His helmet phones emitted a startled exclamation. The skipper's voice:

"Very good, Mr. Dort. Fix your scanner to look into that plate. They dumped out a robot with an infra-red visiplate for communication. Not risking any personnel. Whatever we might do would damage only machinery. Maybe they expect us to bring it on board—and it may have a bomb charge that can be detonated when they're ready to start for home. I'll send a plate to face one of its scanners. You return to the ship."

"Yes, sir," said Tommy. "But which way is the ship, sir?"

There were no stars. The nebula obscured them with its light. The only thing visible from the robot was the double star at the nebula's center. Tommy was no longer oriented. He had but one reference point.

"Head straight away from the double star," came the order in his helmet phone. "We'll pick you up."

He passed another lonely figure, a little later, headed for the alien sphere with a vision plate to set up. The two spaceships, each knowing that it dared not risk its own race by the slightest lack of caution, would communicate with each other through this small round robot. Their separate vision systems would enable them to exchange all the information they dared give, while they debated the most practical way of making sure that their own civilization would not be endangered by this first contact with another. The truly most practical method would be the destruction of the other ship in a swift and deadly attack—in self-defense.

The *Llanvabon*, thereafter, was a ship in which there were two separate enterprises on hand at the same time. She had come out from Earth to make close-range observations on the smaller component of the double star at the nebula's center. The nebula itself was the result of the most titanic explosion of which men have any knowledge. The explosion took place some time in the year 2946 B. C., before the first of the seven cities of long-dead Ilium was even thought of. The light of that explosion reached Earth in the year 1054 A. D., and was duly recorded in ecclesiastical annals and somewhat more reliably by Chinese court astronomers. It was bright enough to be seen in daylight for twenty-three successive days. Its light—and it was four thousand light-years away—was brighter than that of Venus.

From these facts, astronomers could calculate nine hundred years later the violence of the detonation. Matter blown away from the center of the explosion would have traveled outward at the rate of two million three hundred thousand miles an hour; more than thirty-eight thousand miles a minute; something over six hundred thirty-eight miles per second. When twentieth-century telescopes were turned upon the scene of this vast explosion, only a double star remained—and the nebula. The brighter star of the doublet was almost unique in having so high a surface temperature that it showed no spectrum lines at all. It had a continuous spectrum. Sol's surface temperature is about 7,000° Absolute. That of the hot white star is 500,000 degrees. It has nearly the mass of the sun, but only one fifth its diameter, so that its density is one hundred seventy-three times that of water, sixteen times that of lead, and eight times that of iridium—the heaviest substance known on Earth. But even this density is not that of a dwarf white star like the companion of Sirius. The white star in the Crab Nebula is an incomplete dwarf; it is a star still in the act of collapsing. Examination—including the survey of a four-thousand-year column of its light—was worthwhile. The *Llanvabon* had come to make that examination. But the finding of an alien spaceship upon a similar errand had implications which over-overshadowed the original purpose of the expedition.

A tiny bulbous robot floated in the tenuous nebular gas. The normal operating crew of the *Llanvabon* stood at their posts with a sharp alertness which was productive of tense nerves. The observation staff divided itself, and a part went half-heartedly about the making of the observations for which the *Llanvabon* had come. The other half applied itself to the problem the spaceship offered.

It represented a culture which was up to space travel on an interstellar scale. The explosion of a mere five thousand years since must have blasted every trace of life out of existence in the area now filled by the nebula. So the aliens of the black spaceship came from another solar system. Their trip must have been, like that of the Earth ship, for purely scientific purposes. There was nothing to be extracted from the nebula.

They were, then, at least near the level of human

civilization, which meant that they had or could develop arts and articles of commerce which men would want to trade for, in friendship. But they would necessarily realize that the existence and civilization of humanity was a potential menace to their own race. The two races could be friends, but also they could be deadly enemies. Each, even if unwillingly, was a monstrous menace to the other. And the only safe thing to do with a menace is to destroy it.

In the Crab Nebula the problem was acute and immediate. The future relationship of the two races would be settled here and now. If a process for friendship could be established, one race, otherwise doomed, would survive and both would benefit immensely. But that process had to be established, and confidence built up, without the most minute risk of danger from treachery. Confidence would need to be established upon a foundation of necessarily complete distrust. Neither dared return to its own base if the other could do harm to its race. Neither dared risk any of the necessities to trust. The only safe thing for either to do was destroy the other or be destroyed.

But even for war, more was needed than mere destruction of the other. With interstellar traffic, the aliens must have atomic power and some form of overdrive for travel above the speed of light. With radio location and visiplates and short-wave communication they had, of course, many other devices. What weapons did they have? How widely extended was their culture? What were their resources? Could there be a development of trade and friendship, or were the two races so unlike that only war could exist between them? If peace was possible, how could it be begun?

The men on the *Llanvabon* needed facts—and so did the crew of the other ship. They must take back every morsel of information they could. The most important information of all would be of the location of the other civilization, just in case of war. That one bit of information might be the decisive factor in an interstellar war. But other facts would be enormously valuable.

The tragic thing was that there could be no possible information which could lead to peace. Neither ship could stake its own race's existence upon any conviction of the good will or the honor of the other.

So there was a strange truce between the two ships. The alien went about its work of making observations, as did the *Llanvabon*. The tiny robot floated in bright emptiness. A scanner from the *Llanvabon* was focussed upon a vision plate from the alien. A scanner from the alien regarded a vision plate from the *Llanvabon*. Communication began.

It progressed rapidly. Tommy Dort was one of those who made the first progress report. His special task on the expedition was over. He had now been assigned to work on the problem of communication with the alien entities. He went with the ship's solitary psychologist to the captain's room to convey the news of success. The captain's room, as usual, was a place of silence and dull-red indicator lights and the great bright visiplates on every wall and on the ceiling.

"We've established fairly satisfactory communication, sir," said the psychologist. He looked tired. His work on the trip was supposed to be that of measuring personal factors of error in the observation staff, for the reduction of all observations to the nearest possible decimal to the absolute. He had been pressed into service for which he was not especially fitted, and it told upon him. "That is, we can say almost anything we wish to them, and can understand what they say in return. But of course we don't know how much of what they say is the truth."

The skipper's eyes turned to Tommy Dort.

"We've hooked up some machinery," said Tommy, "that amounts to a mechanical translator. We have vision plates, of course, and then shortwave beams direct. They use frequency-modulation plus what is probably variation in wave forms—like our vowel and consonant sounds in speech. We've never had any use for anything like that before, so our coils won't handle it, but we've developed a sort of code which isn't the language of either set of us. They shoot over short-wave stuff with frequency-modulation, and we record it as sound. When we shoot it back, it's reconverted into frequency-modulation."

The skipper said, frowning:

"Why wave-form changes in short waves? How do you know?"

"We showed them our recorder in the vision plates, and they showed us theirs. They record the frequency-modulation direct. I think," said Tommy carefully, "they don't use sound at all, even in speech. They've set up a communication room, and we've watched them in the act of communicating with us. They made no perceptible movement of anything that corresponds to a speech organ. Instead of a microphone, they simply stand near something that would work as a pick-up antenna. My guess, sir, is that they use microwaves for what you might call person-to-person conversation. I think they make short-wave trains as we make sounds."

The skipper stared at him:

"That means they have telepathy?"

"M-m-m. Yes, sir," said Tommy. "Also it means that we have telepathy too, as far as they are concerned. They're probably deaf. They've certainly no idea of using sound waves in air for communication. They simply don't use noises for any purpose."

The skipper stored the information away.

"What else?"

"Well, sir," said Tommy doubtfully, "I think we're all set. We agreed on arbitrary symbols for objects, sir, by the way of the visiplates, and worked out relationships and verbs and so on with diagrams and pictures. We've a couple of thousand words that have mutual meanings. We set up an analyzer to sort out their short-wave groups, which we feed into a decoding machine. And then the coding end of the machine picks out recordings to make the wave groups we want to send back. When you're ready to talk to the skipper of the other ship, sir, I think we're ready."

"H-m-m. What's your impression of their psychology?" The skipper asked the question of the psychologist.

"I don't know, sir," said the psychologist harassedly. "They seem to be completely direct. But they haven't let slip even a hint of the tenseness we know exists. They act as if they were simply setting up a means of communication for friendly conversation. But there is . . . well . . . an overtone—"

The psychologist was a good man at psychological mensuration, which is a good and useful field. But he was not equipped to analyze a completely alien thought-pattern.

"If I may say so, sir—" said Tommy uncomfortably.

"What?"

"They're oxygen brothers," said Tommy, "and they're not too dissimilar to us in other ways. It seems to me, sir, that parallel evolution has been at work. Perhaps intelligence evolves in parallel lines, just as . . . well . . . basic bodily functions. I mean," he added conscientiously, "any living being of any sort must ingest, metabolize, and excrete. Perhaps any intelligent brain must perceive, apperceive, and find a personal reaction. I'm sure I've detected irony. That implies humor, too. In short, sir, I think they could be likable."

The skipper heaved himself to his feet.

"H-m-m," he said profoundly, "we'll see what they have to say."

He walked to the communications room. The scanner for the vision plate in the robot was in readiness. The skipper walked in front of it. Tommy Dort sat down at the coding machine and tapped at the keys. Highly improbable noises came from it, went into a microphone, and governed the frequency-modulation of a signal sent through space to the other spaceship. Almost instantly the vision screen which with one relay—in the robot—showed the interior of the other ship lighted up. An alien came before the scanner and seemed to look inquisitively out of the plate. He was extraordinarily manlike, but he was not human. The impression he gave was of extreme baldness and a somehow humorous frankness.

"I'd like to say," said the skipper heavily, "the appropriate things about this first contact of two dissimilar civilized races, and of my hopes that a friendly intercourse between the two peoples will result."

Tommy Dort hesitated. Then he shrugged and tapped expertly upon the coder. More improbable noises.

The alien skipper seemed to receive the message. He made a gesture which was wryly assenting. The decoder on the *Llanvabon* hummed to itself and word-cards dropped into the message frame. Tommy said dispassionately:

"He says, sir, 'That is all very well, but is there any way for us to let each other go home alive? I would be happy to hear of such a way if you can contrive it. At the moment it seems to me that one of us must be killed.' "

The atmosphere was of confusion. There were too many questions to be answered all at once. Nobody could answer any of them. And all of them had to be answered.

The *Llanvabon* could start for home. The alien ship might or might not be able to multiply the speed of light by one more unit than the Earth vessel. If it could, the *Llanvabon* would get close enough to Earth to reveal its destination—and then have to fight. It might or might not win. Even if it did win, the aliens might have a communication system by which the *Llanvabon's* destination might have been reported to the aliens' home planet before battle was joined. But the *Llanvabon* might lose in such a fight. If she were to be destroyed, it would be better to be destroyed here, without giving any clue to where human beings might be found by a forewarned, forearmed alien battle fleet.

The black ship was in exactly the same predicament. It too, could start for home. But the *Llanvabon* might be faster, and an overdrive field can be trailed, if you set to work on it soon enough. The aliens, also, would not know whether the *Llanvabon* could report to its home base without returning. If the alien were to be destroyed, it also would prefer to fight it out here, so that it could not lead a probably enemy to its own civilization.

Neither ship, then, could think of flight. The course of the *Llanvabon* into the nebula might be known to the black ship, but it had been the end of a logarithmic curve, and the aliens could not know its properties. They could not tell from that from what direction the Earth ship had started. As of the moment, then, the two ships were even. But the question was and remained, "What now?"

There was no specific answer. The aliens traded information for information—and did not always realize what information they gave. The humans traded information for information—and Tommy Dort sweated blood in his anxiety not to give any clue to the whereabouts of Earth.

The aliens saw by infrared light, and the vision plates and scanners in the robot communication-exchange had to adapt their respective images up and down an optical octave each, for them to have any meaning at all. It did not occur to the aliens that their eyesight told that their sun was a red dwarf, yielding light of greatest energy just below the part of the spectrum visible to human eyes. But after that fact was realized on the *Llanvabon*, it was realized that the aliens, also, should be able to deduce the Sun's spectral type by the light to which men's eyes were best adapted.

There was a gadget for the recording of short-wave trains which was as casually in use among the aliens as a sound-recorder is among men. The humans wanted that badly. And the aliens were fascinated by the mystery of sound. They were able to perceive noise, of course, just as a man's palm will perceive infrared light by the sensation of heat it produces, but they could no more differentiate pitch or tone-quality than a man is able to distinguish between two frequencies of heat-radiation even half an octave apart. To them, the human science of sound was a remarkable discovery. They would find uses for noises which humans had never imagined—if they lived.

But that was another question. Neither ship could leave without first destroying the other. But while the flood of information was in passage, neither ship could afford to destroy the other. There was the matter of the outer coloring of the two ships. The *Llanvabon* was mirror-bright exteriorly. The alien ship was dead-black by visible light. It absorbed heat to perfection, and should radiate it away again as readily. But it did not. The black coating was not a "black body" color or lack of color. It was a perfect reflector of certain infrared wave lengths while simultaneously it fluoresced in just those wave bands. In practice, it absorbed the higher frequencies of heat, converted them to lower frequencies it did not radiate—and stayed at the desired temperature even in empty space.

Tommy Dort labored over his task of communications. He found the alien thought-processes not so alien that he could not follow them. The discussion of technics reached the matter of interstellar navigation. A star map was needed to illustrate the process. It would not have been logical to use a star map from the chart room—but from a star map one could guess the point from which the map was projected. Tommy had a map made specially, with imaginary but convincing star images upon it. He translated directions for its use by the coder and decoder. In return, the aliens presented a star map of their own before the visiplate. Copied instantly by photograph, the Nav officers labored over it, trying to figure out from what spot in the galaxy the stars and Milky Way would show at such an angle. It baffled them.

It was Tommy who realized finally that the aliens had made a special star map for their demonstration too, and that it was a mirror-image of the faked map Tommy had shown them previously.

Tommy could grin, at that. He began to like these aliens. They were not humans, but they had a very human sense of the ridiculous. In course of time Tommy essayed a mild joke. It had to be translated into code numerals, these into quite cryptic groups of short-wave, frequency-modulated impulses, and these went to the other ship and into heaven knew what to become intelligible. A joke which went through such formalities would not seem likely to be funny. But the alien did see the point.

There was one of the aliens to whom communication became as normal a function as Tommy's own code-handlings. The two of them developed a quite insane friendship, conversing by coder, decoder, and short-wave trains. When technicalities in the official messages grew too involved, that alien sometimes threw in strictly nontechnical interpolations akin to slang. Often, they cleared up the confusion. Tommy, for no reason whatever, had filed a code-name of "Buck" which the decoder picked out regularly when this particular one signed his own symbol to a message.

In the third week of communication, the decoder suddenly presented Tommy with a message in the message frame:

You are a good guy. It is too bad we have to kill each other.—BUCK.

Tommy had been thinking much the same thing. He tapped off the rueful reply:

We can't see any way out of it. Can you?

There was a pause, and the message frame filled up again:

If we could believe each other, yes. Our skipper would like it. But we can't believe you, and you can't believe us. We'd trail you home if we got a chance, and you'd trail us. But we feel sorry about it.—BUCK.

Tommy Dort took the messages to the skipper.

"Look here, sir!" he said urgently. "These people are almost human, and they're likable cusses."

The skipper was busy about his important task of thinking things to worry about, and worrying about them. He said tiredly:

"They're oxygen breathers. Their air is twenty-eight percent oxygen instead of twenty, but they could do very well on Earth. It would be a highly desirable conquest for them. And we still don't know what weapons they've got or what they can develop. Would you tell them how to find Earth?"

"N-no," said Tommy, unhappily.

"They probably feel the same way," said the skipper dryly. "And if we did manage to make a friendly contact, how long would it stay friendly? If their weapons were inferior to ours, they'd feel that for their own safety they had to improve them. And we, knowing they were planning to revolt, would crush them while we could—for our own safety! If it happened to be the other way about, they'd have to smash us before we could catch up to them."

Tommy was silent, but he moved restlessly.

"If we smash this black ship and get home," said the skipper, "Earth Government will be annoyed if we don't tell them where it came from. But what can we do? We'll be lucky enough to get back alive with our warning. It isn't possible to get out of those creatures any more information than we give them, and we surely won't give them our address! We've run into them by accident. Maybe—if we smash this ship—there won't be another contact for thousands of years. And it's a pity, because trade could mean so much! But it takes two to make a peace, and we can't risk trusting them. The only answer is to kill them if we can, and if we can't, to make sure that when they kill us they'll find out nothing that will lead them to Earth. I don't like it," added the skipper tiredly, "but there simply isn't anything else to do!"

On the *Llanvabon*, the technicians worked frantically in two divisions. One prepared for victory, and the other for defeat. The ones working for victory could do little. The main blasters were the only weapons with any promise. Their mountings were cautiously altered so that they were no longer fixed nearly dead ahead, with only a 5° traverse. Electronic controls which followed a radio-locator master-finder would keep them trained with absolute precision upon a given target regardless of its maneuverings. More, a hitherto unsung genius in the engine room devised a capacity-storage system by which the normal full-output of the ship's engines could be momentarily accumulated and released in surges of stored power far above normal. In theory, the range of the blasters should be multiplied and their destructive power considerably stepped up. But there was not much more that could be done.

The defeat crew had more leeway. Star charts, navigational instruments carrying telltale notations, the photographic record Tommy Dort had made on the six-months' journey from Earth, and every other memorandum offering clues to Earth's position, were prepared for destruction. They were put in sealed files, and if any one of them was opened by one who did not know the exact, complicated process, the contents of all the files would flash into ashes and the ash be churned past any hope of restoration. Of course, if the *Llanvabon* should be victorious, a carefully not-indicated method of reopening them in safety would remain.

There were atomic bombs placed all over the hull of the ship. If its human crew should be killed without complete destruction of the ship, the atomic-power bombs should detonate if the *Llanvabon* was brought alongside the alien vessel. There were no ready-made atomic bombs on board, but there were small spare atomic-power units on board. It was not hard to trick them so that when they were turned on, instead of yielding a smooth flow of power they would explode. And four men of the earth ship's crew remained always in spacesuits with closed helmets, to fight the ship should it be punctured in many compartments by an unwarned attack.

Such an attack, however, would not be treacherous. The alien skipper had spoken frankly. His manner was that of one who wryly admits the uselessness of lies. The skipper and the *Llanvabon*, in turn, heavily admitted the virtue of frankness. Each insisted—perhaps truthfully—that he wished for friendship between the two races. But neither could trust the other not to make every conceivable effort to find out the one thing he needed most desperately to conceal—the location of his home planet. And neither dared believe that the other was unable to trail him and find out. Because each felt it his own duty to accomplish that unbearable—to the other—act, neither could risk the possible existence of his race by trusting the other. They must fight because they could not do anything else.

They could raise the stakes of the battle by an exchange of information beforehand. But there was a limit to the stake either would put up. No information on weapons, population, or resources would be given by either. Not even the distance of their home bases from the Crab Nebula would be told. They exchanged information, to be sure, but they knew a battle to the death must follow, and each strove to represent his own civilization as powerful enough to give pause to the other's ideas of possible conquest—and thereby increased its appearance of menace to the other, and made battle more unavoidable.

It was curious how completely such alien brains could mesh, however. Tommy Dort, sweating over the coding and decoding machines, found a personal equation emerging from the at first stilted arrays of word-cards which arranged themselves. He had seen the aliens only in the vision screen, and then only in light at least one octave removed from the light they saw by. They, in turn, saw him very strangely, by transposed illumination from what to them would be the far ultra-violet. But their brains worked alike. Amazingly alike. Tommy Dort felt an actual sympathy and even something close to friendship for the gill-breathing, bald, and dryly ironic creatures of the black space vessel.

Because of that mental kinship he set up—though hopelessly—a sort of table of the aspects of the problem before them. He did not believe that the aliens had any instinctive desire to destroy man. In fact, the study of communications from the aliens had produced on the *Llanvabon* a feeling of tolerance not unlike that between enemy soldiers during a truce on Earth. The men felt no enmity, and probably neither did the aliens. But they had to kill or be killed for strictly logical reasons.

Tommy's table was specific. He made a list of objectives the men must try to achieve, in the order of their importance. The first was the carrying back of news of the existence of the alien culture. The second was the location of that alien culture in the galaxy. The third was the carrying back of as much information as possible about that culture. The third was being worked on, but the second was probably impossible. The first—and all—would depend on the result of the fight which must take place.

The aliens' objectives would be exactly similar, so that the men must prevent, first, news of the existence of Earth's culture from being taken back by the aliens, second, alien discovery of the location of Earth, and third, the acquiring by the aliens of information which would help them or encourage them to attack humanity. And again the third was in train, and the second was probably taken care of, and the first must await the battle.

There was no possible way to avoid the grim necessity of the destruction of the black ship. The aliens would see no solution to their problems but the destruction of the *Llanvabon*. But Tommy Dort, regarding his tabulation ruefully, realized that even complete victory would not be a perfect solution. The ideal would be for the *Llanvabon* to take back the alien ship for study. Nothing less would be a complete attainment of the third objective. But Tommy realized that he hated the idea of so complete a victory, even if it could be accomplished. He would hate the idea of killing even nonhuman creatures who understood a human fitting out a fleet of fighting ships to destroy an alien culture because its existence was dangerous. The pure accident of this encounter, between peoples who could like each other, had created a situation which could only result in wholesale destruction.

Tommy Dort soured on his own brain which could find no answer which would work. But there had to be an answer! The gamble was too big! It was too absurd that two spaceships should fight—neither one primarily designed for fighting—so that the survivor could carry back news which would set one race to frenzied preparation for war against the unwarned other.

If both races could be warned, though, and each knew that the other did not want to fight, and if they could communicate with each other but not locate each other until some grounds for mutual trust could be reached—

It was impossible. It was chimerical. It was a daydream. It was nonsense. But it was such luring nonsense that Tommy Dort ruefully put it into the coder to his gill-breathing friend Buck, then some hundred thousand miles off in the misty brightness of the nebula.

"Sure," said Buck, in the decoder's word-cards flicking into place in the message frame. "That is a good dream. But I like you and still won't believe you. If I said that first, you would like me but not believe me, either. I tell you the truth more than you believe, and maybe you tell me the truth more than I believe. But there is no way to know. I am sorry."

Tommy Dort stared gloomily at the message. He felt a very horrible sense of responsibility. Everyone did, on the *Llanvabon*. If they failed in this encounter, the human race would run a very good chance of being exterminated in time to come. If they succeeded, the race of the aliens would be the one to face destruction, most likely. Millions or billions of lives hung upon the actions of a few men.

Then Tommy Dort saw the answer.

It would be amazingly simple, if it worked. At worst it might give a partial victory to humanity and the *Llanvabon*. He sat quite still, not daring to move lest he break the chain of thought that followed the first tenuous idea. He went over and over it, excitedly finding objections here and meeting them, and overcoming impossibilities there. It was the answer! He felt sure of it.

He felt almost dizzy with relief when he found his way to the captain's room and asked leave to speak.

It is the function of a skipper, among others, to find things to worry about. But the *Llanvabon's* skipper did not have to look. In the three weeks and four days since the first contact with the alien black ship, the skipper's face had grown lined and old. He had not only the *Llanvabon* to worry about. He had all of humanity.

"Sir," said Tommy Dort, his mouth rather dry because of his enormous earnestness, "may I offer a method of attack on the black ship? I'll undertake it myself, sir, and if it doesn't work our ship won't be weakened."

The skipper looked at him unseeingly.

"The tactics are all worked out, Mr. Dort," he said heavily. "They're being cut on tape now, for the ship's handling. It's a terrible gamble, but it has to be done."

"I think," said Tommy carefully, "I've worked out a way to take the gamble out. Suppose, sir, we send a message to the other ship, offering—"

His voice went on in the utterly quiet captain's room, with the visiplates showing only a vast mistiness outside and the two fiercely burning stars in the nebula's heart.

The skipper himself went through the air lock with Tommy. For one reason, the action Tommy had suggested would need his authority behind it. For another, the skipper had worried more intensely than anybody else on the *Llanvabon*, and he was tired of it. If he went with Tommy, he would do the thing himself, and if he failed he would be the first one killed—and the tape for the Earth ship's maneuvering was already fed into the control board and correlated with the master-timer. If Tommy and the skipper were killed, a single control pushed home would throw the *Llanvabon* into the most furious possible all-out attack, which would end in the complete destruction of one ship or the other—or both. So the skipper was not deserting his post.

The outer air lock door swung wide. It opened upon that shining emptiness which was the nebula. Twenty miles away, the little round robot hung in space, drifting in an incredible orbit about the twin central suns, and floating ever nearer and nearer. It would never reach either of them, of course. The white star alone was so much hotter than Earth's sun that its heat-effect would produce Earth's temperature on an object five times as far from it as Neptune is from Sol. Even removed to the distance of Pluto, the little robot would be raised to cherry-red heat by the blazing white dwarf. And it could not possibly approach to the ninety-odd million miles which is the Earth's distance from the sun. So near, its metal would melt and boil away as vapor. But, half a light-year out, the bulbous object bobbed in emptiness.

The two spacesuited figures soared away from the *Llanvabon*. The small atomic drives which made them minute spaceships on their own had been subtly altered, but the change did not interfere with their functioning. They headed for the communication robot. The skipper, out in space, said gruffly:

"Mr. Dort, all my life I have longed for adventure. This is the first time I could ever justify it to myself."

His voice came through Tommy's space-phone receivers. Tommy wet his lips and said:

"It doesn't seem like adventure to me, sir. I want terribly for the plan to go through. I thought adventure was when you didn't care."

"Oh, no," said the skipper. "Adventure is when you toss your life on the scales of chance and wait for the pointer to stop."

They reached the round object. They clung to its short, scanner-tipped horns.

"Intelligent, those creatures," said the skipper heavily. "They must want desperately to see more of our ship than the communication room, to agree to this exchange of visits before the fight."

"Yes, sir," said Tommy. But privately, he suspected that Buck—his gill-breathing friend—would like to see him in the flesh before one or both of them died. And it seemed to him that between the two ships had grown up an odd tradition of courtesy, like that between two ancient knights before a tourney, when they admired each other wholeheartedly before hacking at each other with all the contents of their respective armories.

They waited.

Then, out of the mist, came two other figures. The alien spacesuits were also power-driven. The aliens themselves were shorter than men, and their helmet openings were coated with a filtering material to cut off visible and ultraviolet rays which to them would be lethal. It was not possible to see more than the outline of the heads within.

Tommy's helmet phone said, from the communication room on the *Llanvabon*:

"They say that their ship is waiting for you, sir. The air lock door will be open."

The skipper's voice said heavily:

"Mr. Dort, have you seen their spacesuits before? If so, are you sure they're not carrying anything extra, such as bombs?"

"Yes, sir," said Tommy. "We've showed each other our

space equipment. They've nothing but regular stuff in view, sir."

The skipper made a gesture to the two aliens. He and Tommy Dort plunged on for the black vessel. They could not make out the ship very clearly with the naked eye, but directions for change of course came from the communication room.

The black ship loomed up. It was huge, as long as the *Llanvabon* and vastly thicker. The air lock did stand open. The two spacesuited men moved in and anchored themselves with magnetic-soled boots. The outer door closed. There was a rush of air and simultaneously the sharp quick tug of artificial gravity. Then the inner door opened.

All was darkness. Tommy switched on his helmet light at the same instant as the skipper. Since the aliens saw by infrared, a white light would have been intolerable to them. The men's helmet lights were, therefore, of the deep-red tint used to illuminate instrument panels so there will be no dazzling of eyes that must be able to detect the minutest specks of white light on a navigating vision plate. There were aliens waiting to receive them. They blinked at the brightness of the helmet lights. The space-phone receivers said in Tommy's ear:

"They say, sir, their skipper is waiting for you."

Tommy and the skipper were in a long corridor with a soft flooring underfoot. Their lights showed details of which every one was exotic.

"I think I'll crack my helmet, sir," said Tommy.

He did. The air was good. By analysis it was thirty percent oxygen instead of twenty for normal air on Earth, but the pressure was less. It felt just right. The artificial gravity, too, was less than that maintained on the *Llanvabon*. The home planet of the aliens would be smaller than Earth, and—by the infrared data—circling close to a nearly dead, dull-red sun. The air had smells in it. They were utterly strange, but not unpleasant.

An arched opening. A ramp with the same soft stuff underfoot. Lights which actually shed a dim, dull-red glow about. The aliens had stepped up some of their illuminating equipment as an act of courtesy. The light might hurt their eyes, but it was a gesture of consideration which made Tommy even more anxious for his plan to go through.

The alien skipper faced them with what seemed to Tommy a gesture of wryly humorous deprecation. The helmet phones said:

"He says, sir, that he greets you with pleasure, but he has been able to think of only one way in which the problem created by the meeting of these two ships can be solved."

"He means a fight," said the skipper. "Tell him I'm here to offer another choice."

The *Llanavabon's* skipper and the skipper of the alien ship were face to face, but their communication was weirdly indirect. The aliens used no sound in communication. Their talk, in fact, took place on microwaves and approximated telepathy. But they could not hear, in any ordinary sense of the word, so the skipper's and Tommy's speech approached telepathy, too, as far as they were concerned. When the skipper spoke, his space phone sent his words back to the *Llanvabon*, where the words were fed into the coder and short-wave equivalents sent back to the black ship. The alien skipper's reply went to the *Llanvabon* and through the decoder, and was retransmitted by space phone in words read from the message frame. It was awkward, but it worked.

The short and stocky alien skipper paused. The helmet phones relayed his translated, soundless reply.

"He is anxious to hear, sir."

The skipper took off his helmet. He put his hands at his belt in a belligerent pose.

"Look here!" he said truculently to the bald, strange creature in the uneartly red glow before him. "It looks like we have to fight and one batch of us get killed. We're ready to do it if we have to. But if you win, we've got it fixed so you'll never find out where Earth is, and there's a good chance we'll get you anyhow! If we win, we'll be in the same fix. And if we win and go back home, our government will fit out a fleet and start hunting your planet. And if we find it we'll be ready to blast it to hell! If you win, the same thing will happen to us! And it's all foolishness! We've stayed here a month, and we've swapped information, and we don't hate each other. There's no reason for us to fight except for the rest of our respective races!"

The skipper stopped for breath, scowling. Tommy Dort inconspicuously put his own hands on the belt of his spacesuit. He waited, hoping desperately that the trick would work.

"He says, sir," reported the helmet phones, "that all you say is true. But that his race has to be protected, just as you feel that yours must be."

"Naturally," said the skipper angrily, "but the sensible thing to do is to figure out how to protect it! Putting its future up as a gamble in a fight is not sensible. Our races have to be warned of each other's existence. That's true. But each should have proof that the other doesn't want to fight, but wants to be friendly. And we shouldn't be able to find each other, but we should be able to communicate with each other to work out grounds for a common trust. If our governments want to be fools, let them! But we should give them the chance to make friends, instead of starting a space war out of mutual funk!"

Briefly, the space phone said:

"He says that the difficulty is that of trusting each other now. With the possible existence of his race at stake, he cannot take any chance, and neither can you, of yielding an advantage."

"But my race," boomed the skipper, glaring at the alien captain, "my race has an advantage now. We came here to your ship in atom-powered spacesuits! Before we left, we altered the drives! We can set off ten pounds of sensitized fuel apiece, right here in this ship, or it can be set off by remote control from our ship! It will be rather remarkable if your fuel store doesn't blow up with us! In other words, if you don't accept my proposal for a commonsense approach to this predicament, Dort and I blow up in an atomic explosion, and your ship will be wrecked if not destroyed—and the *Llanvabon* will be attacking with everything it's got within two seconds after the blast goes off!"

The captain's room of the alien ship was a strange scene, with its dull-red illumination and the strange, bald, gill-breathing aliens watching the skipper and waiting for the inaudible translation of the harangue they could not hear. But a sudden tensity appeared in the air. A sharp, savage feeling of strain. The alien skipper made a gesture. The helmet phones hummed.

"He says, sir, what is your proposal?"

"Swap ships!" roared the skipper. "Swap ships and go on home! We can fix our instruments so they'll do no trailing, he can do the same with his. We'll each remove our star maps and records. We'll each dismantle our weapons. The air will serve, and we'll take their ship and they'll take ours, and neither one can harm or trail the other, and each will carry home more information than can be taken otherwise! We can agree on this same Crab Nebula as a rendezvous when the double-star has made another circuit, and if our people want to meet them they can do it, and if they are scared they can duck it! That's my proposal! And he'll take it, or Dort and I blow up their ship and the *Llanvabon* blasts what's left!"

He glared about him while he waited for the translation to reach the tense small stocky figures about him. He could tell when it came because the tenseness changed. The figures stirred. They made gestures. One of them made convulsive movements. It lay down on the soft floor and kicked. Others leaned against its walls and shook.

The voice in Tommy Dort's helmet phones had been strictly crisp and professional, before, but now it sounded blankly amazed.

"He says, sir, that it is a good joke. Because the two crew members he sent to our ship, and that you passed on the way, have their spacesuits stuffed with atomic explosive too, sir, and he intended to make the very same offer and threat! Of course he accepts, sir. Your ship is worth more to him than his own, and his is worth more to you than the *Llanvabon*. It appears, sir, to be a deal."

Then Tommy Dort realized what the convulsive movements of the aliens were. They were laughter.

It wasn't quite as simple as the skipper had outlined it. The actual working-out of the proposal was complicated. For three days the crews of the two ships were intermingled, the aliens learning the workings of the *Llanvabon's* engines, and the men learning the controls of the black spaceship. It was a good joke—but it wasn't all a joke. There were men on the black ship, and aliens on the *Llanvabon*, ready at an instant's notice to blow up the vessels in question. And they would have done it in case of need, for which reason the need did not appear. But it was, actually, a better arrangement to have two expeditions return to two civilizations, under the current arrangement, than for either to return alone.

There were differences, though. There was some dispute about the removal of records. In most cases the dispute was settled by the destruction of the records. There was more trouble caused by the *Llanvabon's* books, and the alien equivalent of a ship's library, containing works which approximated the novels of Earth. But those items were valuable to possible friendship, because they would show the two cultures, each to the other, from the viewpoint of normal citizens and without propaganda.

But nerves were tense during those three days. Aliens unloaded and inspected the foodstuffs intended for the men on the black ship. Men transshipped the foodstuffs the aliens would need to return to their home. There were endless details, from the exchange of lighting equipment to suit the eyesight of the exchanging crews, to a final check-up of apparatus. A joint inspection party of both races verified that all detector devices had been smashed but not removed, so that they could not be used for trailing and had not been smuggled away. And of course, the aliens were anxious not to leave any useful weapon on the black ship, nor the men upon the *Llanvabon*. It was a curious fact that each crew was best qualified to take exactly the measures which made an evasion of the agreement impossible.

There was a final conference before the two ships parted, back in the communication room of the *Llanvabon.*

"Tell the little runt," rumbled the *Llanvabon's* former skipper, "that he's got a good ship and he'd better treat her right."

The message frame flicked word-cards into position.

"I believe," it said on the alien skipper's behalf, "that your ship is just as good. I will hope to meet you here when the double star has turned one turn."

The last man left the *Llanvabon.* It moved away into the misty nebula before they had returned to the black ship. The vision plates in that vessel had been altered for human eyes, and human crewmen watched jealously for any trace of their former ship as their new craft took a crazy, evading course to a remote part of the nebula. It came to a crevasse of nothingness, leading to the stars. It rose swiftly to clear space. There was the instant of breathlessness which the overdrive field produces as it goes on, and then the black ship whipped away into the void at many times the speed of light.

Many days later, the skipper saw Tommy Dort poring over one of the strange objects which were the equivalent of books. It was fascinating to puzzle over. The skipper was pleased with himself. The technicians of the *Llanvabon's* former crew were finding out desirable things about the ship almost momently. Doubtless the aliens were as pleased with their discoveries in the *Llanvabon.* But the black ship would be enormously worth while—and the solution that had been found was by any standard much superior even to combat in which the Earthmen had been overwhelmingly victorious.

"Hm-m-m. Mr. Dort," said the skipper profoundly. "You've no equipment to make another photographic record on the way back. It was left on the *Llanvabon.* But fortunately, we have your record taken on the way out, and I shall report most favorably on your suggestion and your assistance in carrying it out. I think very well of you, sir."

"Thank you, sir," said Tommy Dort.

He waited. The skipper cleared his throat.

"You . . . ah . . . first realized the close similarity of

mental processes between the aliens and ourselves," he observed. "What do you think of the prospects of a friendly arrangement if we keep a rendezvous with them at the nebula as agreed?"

"Oh, we'll get along all right, sir," said Tommy. "We've got a good start toward friendship. After all, since they see by infrared, the planets they'd want to make use of wouldn't suit us. There's no reason why we shouldn't get along. We're almost alike in psychology."

"Hm-m-m. Now just what do you mean by that?" demanded the skipper.

"Why, they're just like us, sir!" said Tommy. "Of course they breathe through gills and they see by heat waves, and their blood has a copper base instead of iron and a few little details like that. But otherwise we're just alike! There were only men in their crew, sir, but they have two sexes as we have, and they have families, and . . . er . . . their sense of humor— In fact—"

Tommy hesitated.

"Go on, sir," said the skipper.

"Well— There was the one I call Buck, sir, because he hasn't any name that goes into sound waves," said Tommy. We got along very well. I'd really call him my friend, sir. And we were together for a couple of hours just before the two ships separated and we'd nothing in particular to do. So I became convinced that humans and aliens are bound to be good friends if they have only half a chance. You see, sir, we spent those two hours telling dirty jokes."

DOOMSDAY DEFERRED

BY WILL F. JENKINS

If I were sensible, I'd say that somebody else told me this story, and then cast doubts on his veracity. But I saw it all. I was part of it. I have an invoice of a shipment I made from Brazil, with a notation on it, "José Ribiera's stuff." The shipment went through. The invoice, I noticed only today, has a mashed *soldado* ant sticking to the page. There is nothing unusual about it as a specimen. On the face of things, every element is irritatingly commonplace. But if I were sensible, I wouldn't tell it this way.

It began in Milhao, where José Ribiera came to me. Milhao is in Brazil, but from it the Andes can be seen against the sky at sunset. It is a town the jungle unfortunately did not finish burying when the rubber boom collapsed. It is so far up the Amazon basin that its principal contacts with the outer world are smugglers and fugitives from Peruvian justice who come across the mountains, and nobody at all goes there except for his sins. I don't know what took José Ribiera there. I went because one of the three known specimens of *Morpho andiensis* was captured nearby by Böhler in 1911, and a lunatic millionaire in Chicago was willing to pay for a try at a fourth for his collection.

I got there after a river steamer refused to go any farther, and after four days more in a canoe with paddlers who had lived on or near river water all their lives without once taking a bath in it. When I got to Milhao, I wished myself back in the canoe. It's that sort of place.

But that's where José Ribiera was, and in back-country Brazil there is a remarkable superstition that *os Senhores Norteamericanos* are honest men. I do not explain it. I simply record it. And just as I was getting settled in a particularly noisome inn, José knocked on my door and came in. He was a small brown man, and he was scared all the way down deep inside. He tried to hide that. The things I noticed first was that he was clean. He was barefoot, but his tattered duck garments were immaculate, and the rest of him had been washed, and recently. In a town like Milhao, that was startling.

"*Senhor,*" said José in a sort of apologetic desperation, "you are a *Senhor Norteamericano*. I—I beg your aid."

I grunted. Being an American is embarrassing, sometimes and in some places. José closed the door behind him and fumbled inside his garments. His eyes anxious, he pulled out a small cloth bundle. He opened it with shaking fingers. And I blinked. The lamplight glittered and glinted on the most amazing mass of tiny gold nuggets I'd ever seen. I hadn't a doubt it was gold, but even at first glance I wondered how on earth it had been gathered. There was no flour gold at all—that fine powder which is the largest part of any placer yield. Most of it was gravelly particles of pinhead size. There was no nugget larger than a half pea. There must have been five pounds of it altogether, though, and it was a rather remarkable spectacle.

"*Senhor*, said José tensely, "I beg that you will help me turn this into cattle! It is a matter of life or death."

I hardened my expression. Of course, in thick jungle like that around Milhao, a cow or a bull would be as much out of place as an Eskimo, but that wasn't the point. I had business of my own in Milhao. If I started gold buying or cattle dealing out of amiability, my own affairs would suffer. So I said in polite regret, "I am not a businessman, *Senhor*, do not deal in gold or cattle either. To buy cattle, you should go down to São Pedro"—that was four days' paddle downstream, or considering the current perhaps three—"and take this gold to a banker. He will give you money for it if you can prove that it is yours. You can then buy cattle if you wish."

José looked at me desperately. Certainly half the population of Milhao—and positively the Peruvian-refugee half—would have cut his throat for a fraction of his hoard. He almost panted: "But, *senhor!* This would be enough to buy cattle in São Pedro and send them here, would it not?"

I agreed that at a guess it should buy all the cattle in São Pedro, twice over, and hire the town's wheezy steam launch to tow them up river besides. José looked sick with relief. But, I said, one should buy his livestock himself, so he ought to go to São Pedro in person. And I could not see what good cattle would be in the jungle anyhow.

"Yet—it would buy cattle!" said José, gulping. "That is what I told—my friends. But I cannot go farther than Milhao, *senhor*. I cannot go to São Pedro. Yet I must—I need to buy cattle for—my friends! It is life and death! How can I do this, *senhor?*"

Naturally, I considered that he exaggerated the emergency.

"I am not a businessman," I repeated. "I would not be able to help you." Then at the terrified look in his eyes I explained, "I am here after butterflies."

He couldn't understand that. He began to stammer, pleading. So I explained.

"There is a rich man," I said wryly, "who wishes to possess a certain butterfly. I have pictures of it. I am sent to find it. I can pay one thousand milreis for one butterfly of a certain sort. But I have no authority to do other business, such as the purchase of gold or cattle."

José looked extraordinarily despairing. He looked numbed by the loss of hope. So, merely to say or do something, I showed him a color photograph of the specimen of *Morpho andiensis* which is in the Goriot collection in Paris. Bug collectors were in despair about it during the war. They were sure the Nazis would manage to seize it. Then José's eyes lighted hopefully.

"*Senhor!*" he said urgently. "Perhaps my—friends can find you such a butterfly! Will you pay for such a butterfly in cattle sent here from São Pedro, *senhor?*"

I said rather blankly that I would, but—then I was talking to myself. José had bolted out of my room, leaving maybe five pounds of gravelly gold nuggets in my hands. That was not usual.

I went after him, but he'd disappeared. So I hid his small fortune in the bottom of my collection kit. A few drops of formaldehyde, spilled before closing up a kit of collection bottles and insects, is very effective in chasing away piferers. I make use of it regularly.

Next morning I asked about José. My queries were greeted with shrugs. He was a very low person. He did not live in Milhao, but had a clearing, a homestead, some miles upstream, where he lived with his wife. They had one child. He was suspected of much evil. He had bought pigs, and taken them to his clearing and behold he had no pigs there! His wife was very pretty, and a Peruvian had gone swaggering to pay court to her, and he had never come back. It is notable, as I think of it, that up to this time no ant of any sort had come into my story. Butterflies, but no ants. Especially not *soldados*—army ants. It is queer.

I learned nothing useful about José, but I had come to Milhao on business, so I stated it publicly. I wished a certain butterfly, I said. I would pay one thousand milreis for a perfect specimen. I would show a picture of what I wanted to any interested person, and I would show how to make a butterfly net and how to use it, and how to handle butterflies without injuring them. But I wanted only one kind, and it must not be squashed.

The inhabitants of Milhao became happily convinced that I was insane, and that it might be profitable insanity for them. Each person leaped to the nearest butterfly and blandly brought it to me. I spent a whole day explaining to bright-eyed people that matching the picture of *Morpho andiensis* required more than that the number of legs and wings should be the same. But, I repeated, I would pay one thousand milreis for a butterfly exactly like the picture. I had plenty of margin for profit and loss, at that. The last time a *Morpho andiensis* was sold, it brought $25,000 at auction. I'd a lot rather have the money, myself.

José Ribiera came back. His expression was tense beyond belief. He plucked at my arm and said, "*Senhor,*" and I grabbed him and dragged him to my inn.

I hauled out his treasure. "Here!" I said angrily. "This is not mine! Take it!"

He paid no attention. He trembled. "*Senhor,*" he said, and swallowed. "My friends—my friends do not think they can catch the butterfly you seek. But if you will tell them—" He wrinkled his brows. "*Senhor*, before a butterfly is born, is it a little soft nut with a worm in it?"

That could pass for a description of a cocoon. José's friends—he was said not to have any—were close observers. I said so. José seemed to grasp at hope as at a straw.

"My—friends will find you the nut which produces the butterfly," he said urgently, "if you tell them which kind it is and what it looks like."

I blinked. Just three specimens of *Morpho andiensis* had ever been captured, so far as was known. All were adult insects. Of course nobody knew what the cocoon was like. For that matter, any naturalist can name a hundred species—and in the Amazon valley alone—of which only the adult forms have been named. But who would hunt for cocoons in jungle like that outside of Milhao?

"My friend," I said skeptically, "there are thousands of different such things. I will buy five of each different kind you can discover, and I will pay one milreis apiece. But only five of each kind, remember!"

I didn't think he'd even try, of course. I meant to insist that he take back his gold nuggets. But again he was gone before I could stop him. I had an uncomfortable impression that when I made my offer, his face lighted as if he'd been given a reprieve from a death sentence. In the light of later events, I think he had.

I angrily made up my mind to take his gold back to him next day. It was a responsibility. Besides, one gets interested in a man—especially of the half-breed class—who can unfeignedly ignore five pounds of gold. I arranged to be paddled up to his clearing next morning.

It was on the river, of course. There are no footpaths in Amazon-basin jungle. The river flowing past Milhao is a broad deep stream perhaps two hundred yards wide. Its width seems less because of the jungle walls on either side. And the jungle is daunting. It is trees and vines and lianas as seen from the stream, but it is more than that. Smells come out, and you can't identify them. Sounds come out, and you can't interpret them. You cut your way into its mass, and you see nothing. You come out, and you have learned nothing. You cannot affect it. It ignores you. It made me feel insignificant.

My paddlers would have taken me right on past José's clearing without seeing it, if he hadn't been on the river bank. He shouted. He'd been fishing, and now that I think, there were no fish near him, but there were some picked-clean fish skeletons. And I think the ground was very dark about him when we first saw him, and quite normal when we approached. I know he was sweating, but he looked terribly hopeful at the sight of me.

I left my two paddlers to smoke and slumber in the canoe. I followed José into the jungle. It was like walking in a tunnel of lucent green light. Everywhere there were tree trunks and vines and leaves, but green light overlay everything. I saw a purple butterfly with crimson wing tips, floating abstractedly in the jungle as if in an undersea grotto.

Then the path widened, and there was José's dwelling. It was a perfect proof that man does not need civilization to live in comfort. Save for cotton garments, an iron pot and a machete, there was literally nothing in the clearing or the house which was not of and from the jungle, to be replaced merely by stretching out one's hand. To a man who lives like this, gold has no value. While he keeps his wants at this level, he can have no temptations. My thoughts at the moment were almost sentimental.

I beamed politely at José's wife. She was a pretty young girl with beautifully regular features. But, disturbingly, her eyes were as panic-filled as José's. She spoke, but she seemed tremblingly absorbed in the contemplation of some crawling horror. The two of them seemed to live with terror. It was too odd to be quite believable. But their child—a brown-skinned three-year-old quite innocent of clothing—was unaffected. He stared at me, wide-eyed.

"*Senhor*," said José in a trembling voice, "here are the things you desire, the small nuts with worms in them."

His wife had woven a basket of flat green strands. He put it before me. And I looked into it tolerantly, expecting nothing. But I saw the sort of thing that simply does not happen. I saw a half bushel of cocoons!

José had acquired them somehow in less than twenty-four hours. Some were miniature capsules of silk which would yield little butterflies of wing spread no greater than a mosquito's. Some were sturdy fat cocoons of stout brown silk. There were cocoons which cunningly mimicked the look of bird droppings, and cocoons cleverly concealed in twisted leaves. Some were green—I swear it—and would pass for buds upon some unnamed vine. And—

It was simply, starkly impossible. I was stupefied. The Amazon basin has been collected, after a fashion, but the pupa and cocoon of any reasonably rare species is at least twenty times more rare than the adult insect. And these cocoons were fresh! They were alive! I could not believe it, but I could not doubt it. My hands shook as I turned them over.

I said, "This is excellent, José! I will pay for all of them at the rate agreed on—one milreis each. I will send them to São Pedro today, and their prices will be spent for cattle and the bringing of the cattle here. I promise it!"

José did not relax. I saw him wipe sweat off his face.

"I—beg you to command haste, *senhor,*" he said thinly.

I almost did not hear. I carried that basket of cocoons back to the river bank. I practically crooned over it all the way back to Milhao. I forgot altogether about returning the gold pellets. And I began to work frenziedly at the inn.

I made sure, of course, that the men who would cart the parcel would know that it contained only valueless objects like cocoons. Then I slipped in the parcel of José's gold. I wrote a letter to the one man in São Pedro who, if God was good, might have sense enough to attend to the affair for me. And I was almost idiotically elated.

While I was making out the invoice that would carry my shipment by refrigerated air express from the nearest airport it could be got to, a large ant walked across my paper. One takes insects very casually in back-country Brazil. I mashed him, without noticing what he was. I went blissfully to start the parcel off. I had a shipment that would make history among bug collectors. It was something that simply could not be done!

The fact of the impossibility hit me after the canoe with the parcel started downstream. How the devil those cocoons had been gathered—

The problem loomed larger as I thought. In less than one day, José had collected a half bushel of cocoons, of at least one hundred different species of moths and butterfies. It could not be done! The information to make it possible did not exist! Yet it had happened. How?

The question would not down. I had to find out. I bought a pig for a present and had myself ferried up to the clearing again. My paddlers pulled me upstream with languid strokes. The pig made irritated noises in the bottom of the canoe. Now I am sorry about that pig. I would apologize to its ghost if opportunity offered. But I didn't know.

I landed on the narrow beach and shouted. Presently José came through the tunnel of foliage that led to his house. He thanked me, dry-throated, for the pig. I told him I had ordered cattle sent up from São Pedro. I told him humorously that every ounce of meat on the hoof the town contained would soon be on the way behind a wheezing steam launch. José swallowed and nodded numbly. He still looked like someone who contemplated pure horror.

We got the pig to the house. José's wife sat and rocked her child, her eyes sick with fear. I probably should have felt embarrassed in the presence of such tragedy, even if I could not guess at its cause. But instead, I thought about the questions I wanted to ask. José sat down dully beside me.

I was obvious of the atmosphere of doom. I said blandly, "Your friends are capable naturalists, José. I am much pleased. Many of the 'little nuts' they gathered are quite new to me. I would like to meet such students of the ways of nature."

José's teeth clicked. His wife caught her breath. She looked at me with an oddly despairing irony. It puzzled me. I looked at José, sharply. And then the hair stood up on my head. My heart tried to stop. Because a large ant walked on José's shoulder, and I saw what kind of ant it was.

"My God" I said shrilly. "*Soldados!* Army ants!"

I acted through pure instinct. I snatched up the baby from its mother's arms and raced for the river. One does not think at such times. The *soldado* ant, the army ant, the driver ant, is the absolute and undisputed monarch of all jungles everywhere. He travels by millions of millions, and nothing can stand against him. He is ravening ferocity and inexhaustible number. Even man abandons his settlements when the army ant marches in, and returns only after he has left—to find every bit of flesh devoured to the last morsel, from the earwigs in the thatch to a horse that may have been tethered too firmly to break away. The army ant on the march can and does kill anything alive, by tearing the flesh from it in tiny bites, regardless of defense. So—I grabbed the child and ran.

José Ribiera screamed at me, "*No! Senhor! No!*"

He sat still and he screamed. I'd never heard such undiluted horror in any man's voice.

I stopped. I don't know why. I was stunned to see José and his wife sitting frozen where I'd left them. I was more stunned, I think, to see the tiny clearing and the house unchanged. The army ant moves usually on a solid front.

The ground is covered with a glistening, shifting horde. The air is filled with tiny clickings of limbs and mandibles. Ants swarm up every tree and shrub. Caterpillars, worms, bird nestlings, snakes, monkeys unable to flee—anything living becomes buried under a mass of ferociously rending small forms which tear off the living flesh in shreds until only white bones are left.

But José sat still, his throat working convulsively. I had seen *soldados* on him. But there were no *soldados*. After a moment José got to his feet and came stumbling toward me. He looked like a dead man. He could not speak.

"But look!" I cried. My voice was high-pitched. "I saw *soldado* ants! I saw them!"

José gulped by pure effort of will. I put down the child. He ran back to his mother.

"S-si. Yes," said José, as if his lips were very stiff and his throat without moisture. "But they are—special *soldados*. They are—pets. Yes. They are tame. They are my—friends. They—do tricks, *senhor*. I will show you!"

He held out his hand and made sucking noises with his mouth. What followed is not to be believed. An ant—a large ant, an inch or more long—walked calmly out of his sleeve and onto his outstretched hand. It perched there passively while the hand quivered like an aspen leaf.

"But yes!" said José hysterically. "He does tricks *senhor!* Observe! He will stand on his head!"

Now, this I saw, but I do not believe it. The ant did something so that it seemed to stand on its head. Then it turned and crawled tranquilly over his hand and wrist and up his sleeve again.

There was silence, or as much silence as the jungle ever holds. My own throat went dry. And what I have said is insanity, but this is much worse. I felt Something waiting to see what I would do. It was, unquestionably, the most horrible sensation I had ever felt. I do not know how to describe it. What I felt was—not a personality, but a mind. I had a ghastly feeling that Something was looking at me from thousands of pairs of eyes, that it was all around me.

I shared, for an instant, what that Something saw and thought. I was surrounded by a mind which waited to see what I would do. It would act upon my action. But it was not a sophisticated mind. It was murderous, but innocent. It was merciless, but naïve.

That is what I felt. The feeling doubtless has a natural explanation which reduces it to nonsense, but at the moment I believed it. I acted on my belief. I am glad I did.

"Ah, I see!" I said in apparent amazement. "That is clever, José! It is remarkable to train an ant! I was absurd to be alarmed. But—your cattle will be on the way, José! They should get here very soon! There will be many of them!"

Then I felt that the mind would let me go. And I went.

My canoe was a quarter mile downstream when one of the paddlers lifted his blade from the water and held it there, listening. The other stopped and listened too. There was a noise in the jungle. It was mercifully far away, but it sounded like a pig. I have heard the squealing of pigs at slaughtering time, when instinct tells them of the deadly intent of men and they try punily to fight. This was not that sort of noise. It was worse; much worse.

I made a hopeless spectacle of myself in the canoe. Now, of course, I can see that, from this time on, my actions were not those of a reasoning human being. I did not think with proper scientific skepticism. It suddenly seemed to me that Norton's theory of mass consciousness among social insects was very plausible. Bees, says Norton, are not only units in an organization. They are units of an organism. The hive or the swarm is a creature—one creature—says Norton. Each insect is a body cell only, just as the corpuscles in our blood stream are individuals and yet only parts of us. We can destroy a part of our body if the welfare of the whole organism requires it, though we destroy many cells. The swarm or the hive can sacrifice its members for the hive's defense. Each bee is a mobile body cell. Its consciousness is a part of the whole intelligence, which is that of the group. The group is the actual creature. And ants, says Norton, show the fact more clearly still; the ability of the creature which is an ant colony to scarifice a part of itself for the whole. . . . He gives illustrations of what he means. His book is not accepted by naturalists generally, but there in the canoe, going down-river from José's clearing, I believed it utterly.

I believed that an army-ant army was as much a single creature as a sponge. I believed that the Something in José's jungle clearing—its body cells were *soldado* ants—had discovered that other creatures perceived and thought as it did. Nothing more was needed to explain everything. An army-ant creature, without physical linkages, could know what its own members saw and knew and felt. It should need only to open its mind to perceive what other creatures saw and knew and felt.

The frightening thing was that when it could interpret such unantish sensations, it could find its prey with a terrible infallibility. It could flow through the jungle in a streaming, crawling tide of billions of tiny stridulating bodies. It could know the whereabouts and thoughts of every living thing around it. Nothing could avoid it, as nothing could withstand it. And if it came upon a man, it could know his thoughts too. It could perceive in his mind vast horizons beyond its former ken. It could know of food—animal food—in quantities never before imagined. It could, intelligently, try to arrange to secure that food.

It had.

But if so much was true, there was something else it could do. The thought made the blood seem to cake in my veins. I began frantically to thrust away the idea. The Something in José's clearing hadn't discovered it yet. But pure terror of the discovery had me drenched in sweat when I got back to Milhao.

All this, of course, was plainly delusion. It was at least a most unscientific attitude. But I'd stopped being scientific. I even stopped using good sense. Believing what I did, I should have got away from there as if all hell were after me. But the Something in José's clearing may already have been practicing its next logical step without knowing it. Maybe that's why I stayed.

Because I did stay in Milhao. I didn't leave the town again, even for José's clearing. I stayed about the inn, half-heartedly dealing with gentry who tried every known device, except seeking the *Morpho andiensis*, to extract a thousand milreis from me. Mostly they offered mangled corpses which would have been useless for my purpose even if they'd been the butterfly I was after. No argument would change their idea that I was insane, nor dash their happy hope of making money out of my hallucination that butterflies were worth money. But I was only half-hearted in these dealings, at best. I waited feverishly for the cattle from São Pedro. I was obsessed.

I couldn't sleep. By day I fought the thought that tried to come into my head. At night I lay in the abominable inn—in a hammock, because there are no beds in back-country Brazilian inns, and a man would be a fool to sleep in them if there were—and listened to the small, muted, unidentifiable noises from the jungle. *And* fought away the thought that kept trying to come into my mind. It was very bad.

I don't remember much about the time I spent waiting. It was purest nightmare. But several centuries after the shipment of the cocoons, the launch from São Pedro came puffing asthmatically up the reaches of the river. I was twitching all over, by that time, from the strain of not thinking about what the Something might discover next.

I didn't let the launch tie up to shore. I went out to meet it in a canoe, and I carried my collection kit with me, and an automatic pistol and an extra box of cartridges. I had a machete too. It was not normal commercial equipment for consummating a business deal, but I feverishly kept my mind on what I was going to do. The Something in José's clearing wouldn't be made suspicious by that. It was blessedly naïve.

The launch puffed loudly and wheezed horribly, going past Milhao between tall banks of jungle. It towed a flatboat on which were twenty head of cattle—poor, dispirited, tick-infested creatures. I had them tethered fast. My teeth chattered as I stepped on the flatboat. If the Something realized what it could do— But my hands obeyed me. I shot a dull-eyed cow through the head. I assassinated an emaciated steer. I systematically murdered every one. I was probably wild-eyed and certainly fever-thin and positively lunatic in the eyes of the Brazilian launch crew. But to them *os Senhores Norteamericanos* are notoriously mad.

I was especially close to justifying their belief because of the thought that kept trying to invade my mind. It was, baldly, that if without physical linkage the Something knew what its separate body cells saw, then without physical linkage it also controlled what they did. And if it could know what deer and monkeys saw and knew, then by the same process it could control what *they* did. It held within itself, in its terrifying innocence, the power to cause animals to march docilely and blindly to it and into the tiny maws of its millions of millions of parts. As soon as it realized the perfectly inescapable fact, it could increase in number almost without limit by this fact alone. More, in the increase its intelligence should increase too. It should grow stronger, and be able to draw its prey from greater distances. The time should come when it could incorporate men into its organism by a mere act of will. They would report to it and be controlled by it. And of course they would march to it and drive their livestock to it so it could increase still more and grow wiser and more powerful still.

I grew hysterical, on the flatboat. The thought I'd fought so long wouldn't stay out of my mind any longer. I slashed the slain animals with the machete until the flatboat was more gruesome than any knacker's yard. I sprinkled everywhere a fine white powder from my collection kit—which did not stay white where it fell, but turned red—and pictured the Amazon basin taken over and filled with endlessly marching armies of *soldado* ants. I saw the cities emptied of humanity, and the jungle of all other life. And then, making whimpering noises to myself, I pictured all the people of all the world loading their ships with their cattle and then themselves—because that was what the Something would desire—and all the ships coming to bring food to the organism for which all earth would labor and die.

José Ribiera screamed from the edge of the jungle. The launch and the flatboat were about to pass his clearing. The reek of spilled blood had surrounded the flatboat with a haze of metallic-bodied insects. And José, so weakened by long terror and despair that he barely tottered, screamed at me from the shore line, and his wife added her voice pipingly to echo his cry.

Then I knew that the Something was impatient and eager and utterly satisfied, and I shouted commands to the launch, and I got into the canoe and paddled ashore. I let the bow of the canoe touch the sand. I think that, actually, everything was lost at that moment, and that the Something knew what I could no longer keep from thinking. It knew its power as I did. But there were thousands of flying things about the flatboat load of murdered cattle, and they smelled spilt blood, and the Something in the jungle picked their brains of pure ecstasy. Therefore, I think, it paid little heed to José or his wife or me. It was too eager. And it was naïve.

"José," I said with deep cunning, "get into the canoe with your wife and baby. We will watch our friends at their banquet."

There were bellowings from the launch. I had commanded that the flatboat be beached. The Brazilians obeyed, but they were upset. I looked like a thing of horror from the butchering I had done. I put José and his family on the launch, and I tried to thrust out my hand to the Something in the jungle. I imagined a jungle tree undermined—a little tree, I specified—to fall in the river.

The men of the launch had the flatboat grounded when a slender tree trunk quivered. It toppled slowly outward, delayed in its fall by lianas that had to break. But it fell on the flatboat and the carcasses of slaughtered cattle. The rest was automatic. Army ants swarmed out the thin tree trunk. The gory deck of the flatboat turned black with them. Cries of "*Soldados!*" arose in the launch. The towline was abandoned instantly.

I think José caused me to be hauled up into the launch, but I was responsible for all the rest. We paused at Milhao, going downstream, exactly long enough to tell that there were *soldados* in the jungle three miles upstream. I got my stuff from the inn. I paid. I hysterically brushed aside the final effort of a whiskery half-breed to sell me an unrecognizable paste of legs and wings as a *Morpho andiensis*. Then I fled.

After the first day or so I slept most of the time, twitching. At São Pedro I feverishly got fast passage on a steamer going downstream. I wanted to get out of Brazil, and nothing else, but I did take José and his family on board.

I didn't talk to him, though. I didn't want to. I don't even know where he elected to go ashore from the steamer, or where he is now. I didn't draw a single deep breath until I had boarded a plane at Belem and it was airborne and I was on the way home.

Which was unreasonable. I had ended all the danger from the Something in José's clearing. When I slaughtered the cattle and made that shambles on the flatboat's deck, I spread the contents of a three-pound, formerly airtight can of sodium arsenate over everything. It is wonderful stuff. No mite, fungus, mold or beetle will attack specimens preserved by it. I'd hoped to use a fraction of a milligram to preserve a *Morpho andiensis*. I didn't. I poisoned the carcasses of twenty cattle with it. The army ants which were the Something would consume those cattle to bare white bones. Not all would die of the sodium arsenate, though. Not at first.

But the Something was naïve. And always, among the army ants as among all other members of the ant family, dead and wounded members of the organism are consumed by the sound and living. It is like the way white corpuscles remove damaged red cells from our human blood stream. So the corpses of army ants—*soldados*—that died of sodium arsenate would be consumed by those that survived, and they would die, and their corpses in turn would be consumed by others that would die. . . .

Three pounds of sodium arsenate will kill a lot of ants anyhow, but in practice not one grain of it would go to waste. Because no *soldado* corpse would be left for birds or beetles to feed on, so long as a single body cell of the naïve Something remained alive.

And that is that. There are times when I think the whole thing was a fever dream, because it is plainly unbelievable. If it is true—why, I saved a good part of South American civilization. Maybe I saved the human race, for that matter. Somehow, though, that doesn't seem likely. But I certainly did ship a half bushel of cocoons from Milhao, and I certainly did make some money out of the deal.

I didn't get a *Morpho andiensis* in Milhao, of course. But I made out. When those cocoons began to hatch, in Chicago, there were actually four beautiful *andiensis* in the crop. I anesthetized them with loving care. They were mounted under absolutely perfect conditions. But there's an ironic side light on that. When there were only three known specimens in the collections of the whole world, the last *andiensis* sold for $25,000. But with four new ones perfect and available, the price broke, and I got only $6800 apiece! I'd have got as much for one!

Which is the whole business. But if I were sensible I wouldn't tell about it this way. I'd say that somebody else told me this story, and then I'd cast doubts on his veracity.

THE HURKLE IS A HAPPY BEAST

BY THEODORE STURGEON

Lirht is either in a different universal plane or in another island galaxy. Perhaps these terms mean the same thing. The fact remains that Lirht is a planet with three moons (one of which is unknown) and a sun, which is as important in its universe as is ours.

Lirht is inhabited by gwik, its dominant race, and by several less highly developed species which, for purposes of this narrative, can be ignored. Except, of course, for the hurkle. The hurkle are highly regarded by the gwik as pets, in spite of the fact that a hurkle is so affectionate that it can have no loyalty.

The prettiest of the hurkle are blue.

Now, on Lirht, in its greatest city, there was trouble, the nature of which does not matter to us, and a gwik named

Hvov, whom you may immediately forget, blew up a building which was important for reasons we cannot understand. This event caused great excitement, and gwik left their homes and factories and strubles and streamed toward the center of town, which is how a certain laboratory door was left open.

In times of such huge confusion, the little things go on. During the "Ten Days that Shook the World" the cafes and theaters of Moscow and Petrograd remained open, people fell in love, sued each other, died, shed sweat and tears; and some of these were tears of laughter. So on Lirht, while the decisions on the fate of the miserable Hvov were being formulated, gwik still fardled, funted, and fupped. The great central hewton still beat out its mighty pulse, and in the anams the corsons grew . . .

Into the above-mentioned laboratory, which had been left open through the circumstances described, wandered a hurkle kitten. It was very happy to find itself there; but then, the hurkle is a happy beast. It prowled about fearlessly—it could become invisible if frightened—and it glowed at the legs of the tables and at the glittering, racked walls. It moved sinuously, humping its back and arching along on the floor. Its front and rear legs were stiff and straight as the legs of a chair; the middle pair had two sets of knees, one bending forward, one back. It was engineered as ingeniously as a scorpion, and it was exceedingly blue.

Occupying almost a quarter of the laboratory was a huge and intricate machine, unhoused, showing the signs of development projects the galaxies over—temporary hookups from one component to another, cables terminating in spring clips, measuring devices standing about on small tables near the main work. The kitten regarded the machine with curiosity and friendly intent, sending a wave of radiations outward which were its glow or purr. It arched daintily around to the other side, stepping delicately but firmly on a floor switch.

Immediately there was a rushing, humming sound, like small birds chasing large mosquitoes, and parts of the machine began to get warm. The kitten watched curiously, and saw, high up inside the clutter of coils and wires, the most entrancing muzziness it had ever seen. It was like heat-flicker over a fallow field; it was like a smoke-vortex; it was like red neon lights on a wet pavement. To the hurkle kitten's senses, that red-orange flicker was also like the smell of catnip to a cat, or anise to a terrestrial terrier.

It reared up toward the glow, hooked its forelegs over a busbar—fortunately there was no ground potential—and drew itself upward. It climbed from transformer to power-pack, skittered up a variable condenser—the setting of which was changed thereby—disappeared momentarily as it felt the bite of a hot tube, and finally teetered on the edge of the glow.

The glow hovered in midair in a sort of cabinet, which was surrounded by heavy coils embodying tens of thousands of turns of small wire and great loops of bus. One side, the front, of the cabinet was open, and the kitten hung there fascinated, rocking back and forth to the rhythm of some unheard music it made to contrast this sourceless flame. Back and forth, back and forth it rocked and wove, riding a wave of delicious, compelling sensation. And once, just once, it moved its center of gravity too far from its point of support. Too far—far enough. It tumbled into the cabinet, into the flame.

One muggy, mid-June day a teacher, whose name was Stott and whose duties were to teach seven subjects to forty moppets in a very small town, was writing on a blackboard. He was writing the word Madagascar, and the air was so sticky and warm that he could feel his undershirt pasting and unpasting itself on his shoulder blade with each round "a" he wrote.

Behind him there was a sudden rustle from the moist seventh-graders. His schooled reflexes kept him from turning from the board until he had finished what he was doing, by which time the room was in a young uproar. Stott about-faced, opened his mouth, closed it again. A thing like this would require more than a routine reprimand.

His forty-odd charges were writhing and squirming in an extraordinary fashion, and the sound they made, a sort of whimpering giggle, was unique. He looked at one pupil after another. Here a hand was busily scratching a nape; there a boy was digging guiltily under his shirt; yonder a scrubbed and shining damsel violently worried her scalp.

Knowing the value of individual attack, Stott intoned, "Hubert, what seems to be the trouble?"

The room immediately quieted, though diminished scrabblings continued. "Nothin', Mister Stott," quavered Hubert.

Stott flicked his gaze from side to side. Wherever it rested, the scratching stopped and was replaced by agonized control. In its wake was rubbing and twitching. Stott glared, and idly thumbed a lower left rib. Someone snickered. Before he could identify the source, Stott was suddenly aware of an intense itching. He checked the impulse to go after it, knotted his jaw, and swore to himself that he wouldn't scratch as long as he was out there, front and center. "The class will—" he began tautly, and then stopped.

There was a—a *something* on the sill of the open window. He blinked and looked again. It was a translucent, bluish cloud which was almost nothing at all. It was less than a something should be, but it was indeed more than a nothing. If he stretched his imagination just a little, he might make out the outlines of an arched creature with too many legs; but of course that was ridiculous.

He looked away from it and scowled at his class. He had had two unfortunate experiences with stink bombs, and in the back of his mind was the thought of having seen once, in a trick-store window, a product called "itching powder." Could this be it, this terrible itch? He knew better, however, than to accuse anyone yet; if he were wrong, there was no point in giving the little geniuses any extra-curricular notions.

He tried again. "The cl—" He swallowed. This itch was . . . "The class will—" He noticed that one head, then another and another, were turning toward the window. He realized that if the class got too interested in what he thought he saw on the window sill, he'd have a panic on his hands. He fumbled for his ruler and rapped twice on the desk. His control was not what it should have been at the moment; he struck far too hard, and the reports were like gunshots. The class turned to him as one; and behind them the thing on the window sill appeared with great distinctness.

It was blue—a truly beautiful blue. It had a small spherical head and an almost identical knob at the other end. There were four stiff, straight legs, a long sinuous body, and two central limbs with a boneless look about them. On the side of the head were four pairs of eyes, of graduated sizes. It teetered there for perhaps ten seconds, and then, without a sound, leapt through the window and was gone.

Mr. Stott, pale and shaking, closed his eyes. His knees trembled and weakened, and a delicate, dewy mustache of perspiration appeared on his upper lip. He clutched at the desk and forced his eyes open; and then, flooding him with relief, pealing into his terror, swinging his control back to him, the bell rang to end the class and the school day.

"Dismissed," he mumbled, and sat down. The class picked up and left, changing itself from a twittering pattern of rows to a rowdy kaleidoscope around the bottleneck doorway. Mr. Stott slumped down in his chair, noticing that the dreadful itch was gone, had been gone since he had made that thunderclap with the ruler.

Now, Mr. Stott was a man of method. Mr. Stott prided himself on his ability to teach his charges to use their powers of observation and all the machinery of logic at their command. Perhaps, then, he had more of both at his command—after he recovered himself—than could be expected of an ordinary man.

He sat and stared at the open window, not seeing the sun-swept lawns outside. And after going over these events a half-dozen times, he fixed on two important facts:

First, that the animal he had seen, or thought he had seen, had six legs.

Second, that the animal was of such nature as to make anyone who had not seen it believe he was out of his mind.

These two thoughts had their corollaries:

First, that every animal he had ever seen which had six legs was an insect, and

Second, that if anything were to be done about this fantastic creature, he had better do it by himself. And whatever action he took must be taken immediately. He imagined the windows being kept shut to keep the thing out—in this heat—and he cowered away from the thought. He imagined the effect of such a monstrosity if it bounded into the midst of a classroom full of children in their early teens, and he recoiled. No; there could be no delay in this matter.

He went to the window and examined the sill. Nothing. There was nothing to be seen outside, either. He stood thoughtfully for a moment, pulling on his lower lip and thinking hard. Then he went downstairs to borrow five pounds of DDT powder from the janitor for an "experiment." He got a wide, flat wooden box and an electric fan, and set them up on a table he pushed close to the window. Then he sat down to wait, in case, just in case the blue beast returned.

When the hurkle kitten fell into the flame, it braced itself for a fall at least as far as the floor of the cabinet. Its shock was tremendous, then, when it found itself so braced and already resting on a surface. It looked around, panting with fright, its invisibility reflex in full operation.

The cabinet was gone. The flame was gone. The laboratory with its windows, lit by the orange Lirhtian sky, its ranks of shining equipment, its hulking, complex machine—all were gone.

The hurkle kitten sprawled in an open area, a sort of lawn. No colors were right; everything seemed half-lit, filmy, out-of-focus. There were trees, but not low and flat and bushy like honest Lirhtian trees, but with straight naked trunks and leaves like a portle's tooth. The different atomospheric gases had colors; clouds of fading, changing faint colors obscured and revealed everything. The kitten twitched its cafmors and ruddled its kump, right there where it stood; for no amount of early training could overcome a shock like this.

It gathered itself together and tried to move; and then it got its second shock. Instead of arching over inchwormwise, it floated into the air and came down three times as far as it had ever jumped in its life.

It cowered on the dreamlike grass, darting glances all about, under, and up. It was lonely and terrified and felt very much put upon. It saw its shadow through the shifting haze, and the sight terrified it even more, for it had no shadow when it was frightened on Lirht. Everything here was all backwards and wrong way up; it got more visible, instead of less, when it was frightened; its legs didn't work right, it couldn't see properly, and there wasn't a single, solitary malapek to be throdded anywhere. It thought it heard some music; happily, that sounded all right inside its round head, though somehow it didn't resonate as well as it had.

It tried, with extreme caution, to move again. This time its trajectory was shorter and more controlled. It tried a small, grounded pace, and was quite successful. Then it bobbed for a moment, seesawing on its flexible middle pair of legs, and, with utter abandon, flung itself skyward. It went up perhaps fifteen feet, turning end over end, and landed with its stiff forefeet in the turf.

It was completely delighted with this sensation. It gathered itself together, gryting with joy, and leapt up again. This time it made more distance than altitude, and bounced two long, happy bounces as it landed.

Its fears were gone in the exploration of this delicious new freedom of motion. The hurkle, as has been said before, is a happy beast. It curvetted and sailed, soared and somersaulted, and at last brought up against a brick wall with stunning and unpleasant results. It was learning, the hard way, a distinction between weight and mass. The effect was slight but painful. It drew back and stared forlornly at the bricks. Just when it was beginning to feel friendly again . . .

It looked upward, and saw what appeared to be an opening in the wall some eight feet above the ground. Overcome by a spirit of high adventure, it sprang upward and came to rest on a window sill—a feat of which it was very proud. It crouched there, preening itself, and looked inside.

It saw a most pleasing vista. More than forty amusingly ugly animals, apparently imprisoned by their lower extremities in individual stalls, bowed and nodded and mumbled. At the far end of the room stood a taller, more slender monster with a naked head—naked compared with those of the trapped ones, which were covered with hair like a mawson's egg. A few moments' study showed the kitten that in reality only one side of the heads was hairy; the tall one turned around and began making tracks in the end wall, and its head proved to be hairy on the other side too.

The hurkle kitten found this vastly entertaining. It began to radiate what was, on Lirht, a purr, or glow. In this fantastic place it was not visible; instead, the trapped animals began to respond with most curious writhings and squirmings and susurrant rubbings of their hides with their claws. This pleased the kitten even more, for it loved to be noticed, and it redoubled the glow. The receptive motions of the animals became almost frantic.

Then the tall one turned around again. It made a curious sound or two. Then it picked up a stick from the platform before it and brought it down with a horrible crash.

The sudden noise frightened the hurkle kitten half out of its wits. It went invisible; but its visibility system was reversed here, and it was suddenly outstandingly evident. It turned and leapt outside, and before it reached the ground, a loud metallic shrilling pursued it. There were gabblings and shufflings from the room which added force to the kitten's consuming terror. It scrambled to a low growth of shrubbery and concealed itself among the leaves.

Very soon, however, its irrepressible good nature returned. It lay relaxed, watching the slight movement of the stems and leaves—some of them may have been flowers—in a slight breeze. A winged creature came humming and dancing about one of the blossoms. The kitten rested on one of its middle legs, shot the other out and caught the creature in flight. The thing promptly jabbed the kitten's foot with a sharp black probe. This the kitten ignored. It ate the thing, and belched. It lay still for a few minutes, savoring the sensation of the bee in its clarfel.

The experiment was suddenly not a success. It ate the bee twice more and then gave it up as a bad job.

It turned its attention again to the window, wondering what those racks of animals might be up to now. It seemed very quiet up there . . . Boldly the kitten came from hiding and launched itself at the window again. It was pleased with itself; it was getting quite proficient at precision leaps in this mad place. Preening itself, it balanced on the window sill and looked inside.

Surprisingly, all the smaller animals were gone. The larger one was huddled behind the shelf at the end of the room. The kitten and the animal watched each other for a long moment. The animal leaned down and stuck something into the wall.

Immediately there was a mechanical humming sound and something on a platform near the window began to revolve. The next thing the kitten knew it was enveloped in a cloud of pungent dust.

It choked and became as visible as it was frightened, which was very. For a long moment it was incapable of motion; gradually, however, it became conscious of a poignant, painfully penctrating scnsation which thrilled it to the core. It gave itself up to the feeling. Wave after wave of agonized ecstasy rolled over it, and it began to dance to the waves. It glowed brilliantly, though the emanation served only to make the animal in the room scratch hysterically.

The hurkle felt strange, transported. It turned and leapt high into the air, out from the building.

Mr. Stott stopped scratching. Disheveled indeed, he went to the window and watched the odd sight of the blue beast, quite invisible now, but coated with dust, so that it was like a bubble in a fog. It bounced across the lawn in huge floating leaps, leaving behind it diminishing patches of white powder in the grass. He smacked his hands, one on the other, and smirking, withdrew to straighten up. He had saved the earth from battle, murder, and bloodshed, forever, but he did not know that. No one ever found out what he had done. So he lived a long and happy life.

And the hurkle kitten?

It bounded off through the long shadows, and vanished in a copse of bushes. There it dug itself a shallow pit, working drowsily, more and more slowly. And at last it sank down and lay motionless, thinking strange thoughts, making strange music, and racked by strange sensations. Soon even its slightest movements ceased, and it stretched out stiffly, motionless . . .

For about two weeks. At the end of that time, the hurkle, no longer a kitten, was possessed of a fine, healthy litter of just under two hundred young. Perhaps it was the DDT, and perhaps it was the new variety of radiation that the hurkle received from the terrestrial sky, but they were all parthenogenetic females, even as you and I.

And the humans? Oh, we *bred* so! And how happy we were!

But the humans had the slidy itch, and the scratchy itch, and the prickly or tingly or titillative paraesthetic formication. And there wasn't a thing they could do about it.

So they left.

Isn't this a lovely place?

NOT FINAL!

BY ISAAC ASIMOV

Jupiter—five times as far from the Sun as Earth—ten times Earth's diameter (over 86,000 miles)—largest of all the solar planets. Unwise to land on it; its gravity, plus the enormous depth and weight of its atmosphere, would make it practically impossible for a spaceship powered by methods now known or imagined by science on Earth to escape from it. Once down, there for good.

Consequently, man will first explore Jupiter's moons (she has eleven), and Ganymede, which is a little larger than our own Moon, will probably be one of the first to be approached. Like our own Moon, it may turn out to be airless and uninhabited; but as to Jupiter itself, no one dare venture so positive a statement. You will get some uncomfortably eerie ideas about the Jovians from this story, though—and the trouble is, none of us ever will know for sure whether such beings exist and what they are like until they discover us!

Nicholas Orloff inserted a monocle in his left eye with all the incorruptible Briticism of a Russian educated at Oxford, and said reproachfully, "But, my dear Mr. Secretary! Half a billion dollars!"

Leo Birnam shrugged his shoulders wearily and allowed his lank body to cramp up still farther in the chair. "The appropriation must go through, Commissioner. The Dominion government here at Ganymede is becoming desperate. So far I've been holding them off, but as secretary of scientific affairs, my powers are small."

"I know, but—" and Orloff spread his hands helplessly.

"I suppose so," agreed Birnam. "The Empire government finds it easier to look the other way. They've done it consistently up to now. I've tried for a year now to have them understand the nature of the danger that hangs over the entire System, but it seems that it can't be done. But I'm appealing to you, Mr. Commissioner. You're new in your post and can approach this Jovian affair with an unjaundiced eye."

Orloff coughed and eyed the tips of his boots. In the three months since he had succeeded Gridley as colonial commissioner he had tabled unread everything relating to "those damned Jovian D.T.'s." That had been according to the established cabinet policy which had labeled the Jovian affair as "deadwood" long before he had entered office.

But now that Ganymede was becoming nasty, he found himself sent out to Jovopolis with instructions to hold the "blasted provincials" down. It was a nasty spot.

Birnam was speaking. "The Dominion government has reached the point where it needs the money so badly, in fact, that if they don't get it, they're going to publicize everything."

Orloff's phelgm broke completely, and he snatched at the monocle as it dropped. "My dear fellow!"

"I know what it would mean. I've advised against it, but they're justified. Once the inside of the Jovian affair is out, once the people know about it, the Empire government won't stay in power a week. And when the Technocrats come in, they'll give us whatever we ask. Public opinion will see to that."

"But you'll also create a panic and hysteria—"

"Surely! That is why we hesitate. But you might call this an ultimatum. We want secrecy, we *need* secrecy; but we need money more."

"I see." Orloff was thinking rapidly, and the conclusions he came to were not pleasant. "In that case, it would be advisable to investigate the case further. If you have the papers concerning the communications with the planet Jupiter—"

"I have them," replied Birnam dryly, "and so has the Empire government at Washington. That won't do, Commissioner. It's the same cud that's been chewed by Earth officials for the last year, and it's gotten us nowhere. I want you to come to Ether Station with me."

The Ganymedan had risen from his chair, and he glowered down upon Orloff from his six and a half feet of height.

Orloff flushed. "Are you ordering me?"

"In a way, yes. I tell you there is no time. If you intend acting, you must act quickly or not at all." Birnam paused, then added, "You don't mind walking, I hope. Power vehicles aren't allowed to approach Ether Station ordinarily, and I can use the walk to explain a few of the facts. It's only two miles off."

"I'll walk," was the brusque reply.

The trip upward to subground level was made in silence, which was broken by Orloff when they stepped into the dimly lit anteroom.

"It's chilly here."

"I know. It's difficult to keep the temperature up to norm this near the surface. But it will be colder outside. Here!"

Birnam had kicked open a closet door and was indicating the garments suspended from the ceiling. "Put them on. You'll need them."

Orloff fingered them doubtfully. "Are they heavy enough?"

Birnam was pouring into his own costume as he spoke. "They're electrically heated. You'll find them plenty warm. That's it! Tuck the trouser legs inside the boots and lace them tight."

He turned then and, with a grunt, brought out a double compressed-gas cylinder from its rack in one corner of the closet. He glanced at the dial reading and then turned the stopcock. There was a thin wheeze of escaping gas, at which Birnam sniffed with satisfaction.

"Do you know how to work one of these?" he asked, as he screwed onto the jet a flexible tube of metal mesh, at the other end of which was a curiously curved object of thick, clear glass.

"What is it?"

"Oxygen nosepiece! What there is of Ganymede's atmosphere is argon and nitrogen, just about half and half. It isn't particularly breathable." He heaved the double cylinder into position and tightened it in its harness on Orloff's back.

Orloff staggered, "It's heavy. I can't walk two miles with this."

"It won't be heavy out there." Birnam nodded carelessly upward and lowered the glass nosepiece over Orloff's head. "Just remember to breathe in through the nose and out through the mouth, and you won't have any trouble. By the way, did you eat recently?"

"I lunched before I came to your place."

Birnam sniffed dubiously. "Well, that's a little awkward." He drew a small metal container from one of his pockets and tossed it to the commissioner. "Put one of those pills in your mouth and keep sucking on it."

Orloff worked clumsily with gloved fingers and finally managed to get a brown spheroid out of the tin and into his mouth. He followed Birnam up a gently sloped ramp. The blind-alley ending of the corridor slid aside smoothly when they reached it, and there was a faint soughing as air slipped out into the thinner atmosphere of Ganymede.

Birnam caught the other's elbow and fairly dragged him out.

"I've turned your air tank on full," he shouted. "Breathe deeply and keep sucking at that pill."

Gravity had flicked to Ganymedan normality as they crossed the threshold, and Orloff, after one horrible moment of apparent levitation, felt his stomach turn a somersault and explode.

He gagged, and fumbled the pill with his tongue in a desperate attempt at self-control. The oxygen-rich mixture from the air cylinders burned his throat, and gradually Ganymede steadied. His stomach shuddered back into place. He tried walking.

"Take it easy, now," came Birnam's soothing voice. "It gets you that way the first few times you change gravity fields quickly. Walk slowly and get the rhythm, or you'll take a tumble. That's right, you're getting it."

The ground seemed resilient. Orloff could feel the pressure of the other's arm holding him down at each step to keep him from springing too high. Steps were longer now—and flatter, as he got the rhythm. Birnam continued speaking, a voice a little muffled from behind the leather flap drawn loosely across mouth and chin.

"Each to his own world," he grinned. "I visited Earth a few years back, with my wife, and had a hell of a time. I couldn't get myself to learn to walk on a planet's surface without a nosepiece. I kept choking—I really did. The sunlight was too bright and the sky was too blue and the grass was too green. And the buildings were right out on the surface. I'll never forget the time they tried to get me to sleep in a room twenty stories up in the air, with the window wide open and the moon shining in.

"I went back on the first spaceship going my way and don't ever intend returning. How are you feeling now?"

"Fine! Splendid!" Now that the first discomfort had gone, Orloff found the low gravity exhilarating. He looked about him. The broken, hilly ground, bathed in a drenching yellow light, was covered with ground-hugging broad-leaved shrubs that showed the orderly arrangement of careful cultivation.

Birnam answered the unspoken question. "There's enough carbon dioxide in the air to keep the plants alive, and they all have the power to fix atmospheric nitrogen. That's what makes agriculture Ganymede's greatest industry. Those plants are worth their weight in gold as fertilizers back on Earth and worth double or triple that as sources for half a hundred alkaloids that can't be gotten anywhere else in the System. And, of course, everyone knows that Ganymedan green-leaf has Terrestrial tobacco beat hollow."

There was the drone of a strato-rocket overhead, shrill in the thin atmosphere, and Orloff looked up.

He stopped—stopped dead—and forgot to breathe!

It was his first glimpse of Jupiter in the sky.

It is one thing to see Jupiter, coldly harsh, against the ebon backdrop of space. At six hundred thousand miles, it is majestic enough. But on Ganymede, barely topping the hills, its outlines softened and ever so faintly hazed by the thin atmosphere, shining mellowly from a purple sky in which only a few fugitive stars dare compete with the Jovian giant—it can be described by no conceivable combination of words.

At first, Orloff absorbed the gibbous disk in silence. It was gigantic, thirty-two times the apparent diameter of the Sun as seen from Earth. Its stripes stood out in faint washes of color against the yellowness beneath, and the Great Red Spot was an oval splotch of orange near the western rim.

And finally Orloff murmured weakly, "It's beautiful!"

Leo Birnam stared, too, but there was no awe in his eyes. There was the mechanical weariness of viewing a sight often seen, and besides that, an expression of sick revulsion. The chin flap hid his twitching smile, but his grasp upon Orloff's arm left bruises through the tough fabric of the surface suit.

He said slowly, "It's the most horrible sight in the System."

Orloff turned reluctant attention to his companion.

"Eh?" Then, disagreeably, "Oh, yes, those mysterious Jovians."

At that, the Ganymedan turned away angrily and broke into swinging, fifteen-foot strides. Orloff followed clumsily after, keeping his balance with difficulty.

"Here, now," he gasped.

But Birnam wasn't listening. He was speaking coldly, bitterly. "You on Earth can afford to ignore Jupiter. You know nothing of it. It's a little pinprick in your sky, a little flyspeck. You don't live here on Ganymede, watching that damned colossus gloating over you. Up and over fifteen hours—hiding God knows what on its surface. Hiding something that's waiting and waiting and *trying to get out*. Like a giant bomb just waiting to explode!"

"Nonsense!" Orloff managed to jerk out. "*Will* you slow down. I can't keep up."

Birnam cut his strides in half and said tensely, "Everyone knows that Jupiter is inhabited, but practically no one ever stops to realize what that means. I tell you that those Jovians, whatever they are, are born to the purple. *They are the natural rulers of the Solar System.*"

"Pure hysteria," muttered Orloff. "The Empire government has been hearing nothing else from your Dominion for a year."

"And you've shrugged it off. Well, listen! Jupiter, discounting the thickness of its colossal atmosphere, is eighty thousand miles in diameter. That means it possesses a surface one hundred times that of Earth, and more than fifty times that of the entire Terrestrial Empire. Its population, its resources, its war potential are in proportion."

"Mere numbers—"

"I know what you mean," Birnam drove on passionately. "Wars are not fought with numbers but with science and with organization. The Jovians have both. In the quarter of a century during which we have communicated with them, we've learned a bit. They have atomic power and they have radio. And in a world of ammonia under great pressure—a world, in other words, in which almost none of the metals can exist *as* metals for any length of time because of the tendency to form soluble ammonia complexes—they have managed to build up a complicated civilization. That means they have had to work through plastics, glasses, silicates, and synthetic building materials of one sort or another. *That* means a chemistry developed just as far as ours is, and I'd put odds on its having developed further."

Orloff waited long before answering. And then, "But how certain are you people about the Jovians' last message? We on Earth are inclined to doubt that the Jovians can possibly be as unreasonably belligerent as they have been described."

The Ganymedan laughed shortly. "They broke off all communication after that last message, didn't they? That doesn't sound friendly on their part, does it? I assure you that we've all but stood on our ears trying to contact them.

"Here, now, don't talk. Let me explain something to you. For twenty-five years here on Ganymede a little group of men have worked their hearts out trying to make sense out of a static-ridden, gravity-distorted set of variable clicks in our radio apparatus, for those clicks were our only connection with living intelligence upon Jupiter. It was a job for a world of scientists, but we never had more than two dozen at the Station at any one time. I was one of them from the very beginning and, as a philologist, did my part in helping construct and interpret the code that developed between ourselves and the Jovians, so that you can see I am speaking from the real inside.

"It was a devil of a heartbreaking job. It was five years before we got past the elementary clicks of arithmetic: three and four are seven; the square root of twenty-five is five; factorial six is seven hundred and twenty. After that, months sometimes passed before we could work out and check by further communication a single new fragment of thought.

"*But*—and this is the point—by the time the Jovians broke off relations, we understood them *thoroughly*. There was no more chance of a mistake in comprehension than there was of Ganymede's suddenly cutting loose from Jupiter. And their last message was a threat and a promise of destruction. Oh, there's no doubt—there's no doubt!"

They were walking through a shallow pass in which the yellow Jupiter light gave way to a clammy darkness.

Orloff was disturbed. He had never had the case presented to him in this fashion before. He said, "But the reason, man. What reason did we give them—"

"No reason! It was simply this: the Jovians had finally discovered from our messages—just where and how I don't know—that *we* were *not* Jovians."

"Well, of course."

"It wasn't 'of course' to them. In their experiences they had never come across intelligences that were not Jovian. Why should they make an exception in favor of those from outer space?"

"You say they were scientists." Orloff's voice had assumed a wary frigidity. "Wouldn't they realize that alien environments would breed alien life? *We* knew it. We never thought the Jovians were Earthmen, though we had never met intelligences other than those of Earth."

They were back in the drenching wash of Jupiter light again, and a spreading region of ice glimmered amberly in a depression to the right.

Birnam answered, "I said they were chemists and physicists—but I never said they were astronomers. Jupiter, my dear Commissioner, has an atmosphere three thousand miles or more thick, and those miles of gas block off everything but the Sun and the four largest of Jupiter's moons. The Jovians know nothing of alien environments."

Orloff considered. "And so they decided we were aliens. What next?"

"If we weren't Jovians, then, in their eyes, we weren't people. It turned out that a non-Jovian was 'vermin' by definition."

Orloff's automatic protest was cut off sharply by Birnam. "In their eyes, I said, vermin we were; and vermin we are. Moreover, we were vermin with the peculiar audacity of having dared to attempt to treat with

Jovians—with *human beings*. Their last message was this, word for word—'Jovians are the masters. There is no room for vermin. We will destroy you immediately.' I doubt if there was any animosity in that message—simply a cold statement of fact. But they meant it."

"But why?"

"Why did man exterminate the housefly?"

"Come sir. You're not seriously presenting an analogy of that nature."

"Why not, since it is certain that the Jovian considers us a sort of housefly—an insufferable type of housefly that dares aspire to intelligence."

Orloff made a last attempt. "But truly, Mr. Secretary, it seems impossible for intelligent life to adopt such an attitude."

"Do you possess much of an acquaintance with any other type of intelligent life than our own?" came with immediate sarcasm. "Do you feel competent to pass on Jovian psychology? Do you know just *how* alien Jovians must be physically? Just think of their world, with its gravity at two and one-half Earth normal; with its ammonia oceans—oceans that you might throw all Earth into without raising a respectable splash; with its three-thousand-mile atmosphere, dragged down by the colossal gravity into densities and pressures in its surface layers that make the sea bottoms of Earth resemble a medium-thick vacuum. I tell you, we've tried to figure out what sort of life could exist under those conditions and we've given up. It's thoroughly incomprehensible. Do you expect their mentality, then, to be any more understandable? Never! Accept it as it is. They intend destroying us. That's all we know and all we need to know."

He lifted a gloved hand as he finished, and one finger pointed. "There's Ether Station just ahead."

Orloff's head swiveled. "Underground?"

"Certainly! All except the Observatory. That's that steel-and-quartz dome to the right—the small one."

They had stopped before two large boulders that flanked an earthy embankment, and from behind either one a nosepieced, suited soldier in Ganymedan orange, with blasters ready, advanced upon the two.

Birnam lifted his face into Jupiter's light, and the soldiers saluted and stepped aside. A short word was barked into the wrist mike of one of them, and the camouflaged opening between the boulders fell into two and Orloff followed the secretary into the yawning airlock.

The Earthman caught one last glimpse of sprawling Jupiter before the closing door cut off the surface altogether.

It was no longer quite so beautiful.

Orloff did not feel quite normal again until he had seated himself in the overstuffed chair in Dr. Edward Prosser's private office. With a sigh of utter relaxation he propped his monocle under his eyebrow.

"Would Dr. Prosser mind if I smoked in here while we're waiting?" he asked.

"Go ahead," replied Birnam carelessly. "My own idea would be to drag Prosser away from whatever he's fooling with just now, but he's a queer chap. We'll get more out of him if we wait until he's ready for us." He withdrew a gnarled stick of greenish tobacco from its case and bit off the edge viciously.

Orloff smiled through the smoke of his own cigarette. "I don't mind waiting. I still have something to say. You see, for the moment, Mr. Secretary, you gave me the jitters, but, after all, granted that the Jovians intend mischief once they get at us, it remains a fact," and here he spaced his words emphatically, "that they can't get at us."

"A bomb without a fuse, hey?"

"Exactly! It's simplicity itself, and not really worth discussing. You will admit, I suppose that under no circumstances can the Jovians get away from Jupiter."

"Under *no* circumstances?" There was a quizzical tinge to Birnam's slow reply. "Shall we analyze that?"

He stared hard at the purple flame of his cigar. "It's an old trite saying that the Jovians can't leave Jupiter. The fact has been highly publicized by the sensation mongers of Earth and Ganymede, and a great deal of sentiment has been driveled about the unfortunate intelligences who are irrevocably surface-bound and must forever stare into the Universe without, watching, watching, wondering, and never attaining.

"But, after all, what holds the Jovians to their planet? Two factors! That's all! The first is the immense gravity field of the planet. Two and a half Earth normal."

Orloff nodded. "Pretty bad!" he agreed.

"And Jupiter's gravitational potential is even worse, for, because of its greater diameter, the intensity of its gravitational field decreases with distance only one-tenth as rapidly as Earth's field does. It's a terrible problem—*but it's been solved."*

"Hey?" Orloff straightened.

"They've got atomic power. Gravity—even Jupiter's—means nothing once you've put unstable atomic nuclei to work for you."

Orloff crushed his cigarette to extinction with a nervous gesture. "But their atmosphere—"

"Yes, that's what's stopping them. They're living at the bottom of a three-thousand-mile-deep ocean of it, where the hydrogen of which it is composed is collapsed by sheer pressure to something approaching the density of *solid* hydrogen. It stays a gas because the temperature of Jupiter is above the critical point of hydrogen, but you just try to figure out the pressure that can make hydrogen *gas* half as heavy as water. You'll be surprised at the number of zeros you'll have to put down.

"No spaceship of metal or of any kind of matter can stand that pressure. No Terrestrial spaceship can land on Jupiter without smashing like an eggshell, and no Jovian spaceship can leave Jupiter without exploding like a soap bubble. That problem has not yet been solved, but it will be some day. Maybe tomorrow, maybe not for a hundred years, or a thousand. We don't know, but when it is solved, the Jovians will be on top of us. And it can be solved in a specific way."

"I don't see how—"

"Force fields! We've got them now, you know."

"Force fields!" Orloff seemed genuinely astonished, and he chewed the word over and over to himself for a few moments. "They're used as meteor shields for ships in the asteroid zone—but I don't see the application to the Jovian problem."

"The ordinary force field," explained Birnam, "is a feeble rarefied zone of energy extending over a hundred miles or more outside the ship. It'll stop meteors, but it's just so much empty ether to an object like a gas molecule. *But* what if you took that same zone of energy and compressed it to a thickness of a tenth of an inch. Molecules would bounce off it like this—*ping-g-g-g-g!* And if you used stronger generators, and compressed the field to a hundredth of an inch, molecules would bounce off even when driven by the unthinkable pressure of Jupiter's atmosphere—and then if you build a ship inside—" He left the sentence dangling.

Orloff was pale. "You're not saying it can be done?"

"I'll bet you anything you like that the Jovians are *trying* to do it. And *we're* trying to do it right here at Ether Station."

The colonial commissioner jerked his chair closer to Birnam and grabbed the Ganymedan's wrist. "Why can't we bombard Jupiter with atomic bombs? Give it a thorough going over, I mean! With her gravity and her surface area, we can't miss."

Birnam smiled faintly. "We've thought of that. But atomite bombs would merely tear holes in the atmosphere. And even if you could penetrate, just divide the surface of Jupiter by the area of damage of a single bomb and find how many years we must bombard Jupiter at the rate of a bomb a minute before we begin to do significant damage. Jupiter's *big!* Don't ever forget that!"

His cigar had gone out, but he did not pause to relight. He continued in a low, tense voice. "No, we can't attack the Jovians as long as they're on Jupiter. We must wait for them to come out—and once they do, they're going to have the edge on us in numbers. A terrific, heartbreaking edge—so we'll just have to have the edge on them in science."

"But," Orloff broke in, and there was a note of

fascinated horror in his voice, "how can we tell in advance what they'll have?"

"We can't. We've got to scrape up everything we can lay our hands on and hope for the best. But there's one thing we *do* know they'll have, and that's force fields. They can't get out without them. And if they have them, we must, too, and that's the problem we're trying to solve here. They will not insure us victory, but without them we will suffer certain defeat. And now you know why we need money—and more than that. We want Earth itself to get to work. It's got to start a drive for scientific armaments and subordinate everything to that. You see?"

Orloff was on his feet. "Birnam, I'm with you—a hundred per cent with you. You can count on me back in Washington."

There was no mistaking his sincerity. Birnam gripped the hand outstretched toward him and wrung it—and at the moment the door flew open and a little pixie of a man hurtled in.

The newcomer spoke in rapid jerks, and exclusively to Birnam. "Where'd you come from? Been trying to get in touch with you. Secretary said you weren't in. Then five minutes later you show up on your own. Can't understand it." He busied himself furiously at his desk.

Birnam grinned. "If you'll take time out, doc, you might say hello to Colonial Commissioner Orloff."

Dr. Edward Prosser turned on his toe like a ballet dancer and looked the Earthman up and down twice. "The new un, hey? We getting any money? We ought to. Been working on a shoestring ever since. At that we might not be needing any. It depends." He was back at the desk.

Orloff seemed a trifle disconcerted, but Birnam winked impressively, and he contented himself with a glassy stare through the monocle.

Prosser pounced upon a black leather booklet in the recesses of a pigionhole, threw himself into his swivel chair, and wheeled about.

"Glad you came, Birnam," he said, leafing through the booklet. "Got something to show you. Commissioner Orloff, too."

"What were you keeping us waiting for?" demanded Birnam. "Where were you?"

"Busy! Busy as a pig! No sleep for three nights." He looked up and his small puckered face fairly flushed with delight. "Everything fell into place of a sudden. Like a jigsaw puzzle. Never saw anything like it. Kept us hopping, I tell you."

"You've gotten the dense force fields you're after?" asked Orloff in sudden exitement.

Prosser seemed annoyed. "No, not that. Something else. Come on." He glared at his watch and jumped out of his seat. "We've got half an hour. Let's go."

An electric-motored flivver waited outside, and Prosser spoke excitedly as he sped the purring vehicle down the ramps into the depths of the Station.

"Theory!" he said. "Theory! Damned important, that. You set a technician on a problem. He'll fool around. Waste lifetimes. Get nowhere. Just putter about at random. A true scientist works with theory. Lets math solve his problems." He overflowed with self-satisfaction.

The flivver stopped on a dime before a huge double door, and Prosser tumbled out, followed by the other two at a more leisurely pace.

"Through here! Through here!" he said. He shoved the door open and led them down the corridor and up a narrow flight of stairs onto a wall-hugging passageway that circled a huge three-level room. Orloff recognized the gleaming quartz-and-steel pipe-sprouting ellipsoid two levels below as an atomic generator.

He adjusted his monocle and watched the scurrying activity below. An earphoned man on a high stood before a control board studded with dials looked up and waved. Prosser waved back and grinned.

Orloff said, "You create your force fields here?"

"That's right! Ever see one?"

"No." The commissioner smiled ruefully. "I don't even know what one *is*, except that it can be used as a meteor shield."

Prosser said, "It's very simple. Elementary matter. All matter is composed of atoms. Atoms are held together by interatomic forces. Take away atoms. Leave interatomic forces behind. *That's* a force field."

Orloff looked blank, and Birnam chuckled deep in his throat and scratched the back of his ear.

"That explanation reminds me of our Ganymedan method of suspending an egg a mile high in the air. It goes like this. You find a mountain just a mile high and put the egg on top. Then, keeping the egg where it is, you take the mountain away. That's all."

The colonial commissioner threw his head back to laugh, and the irascible Dr. Prosser puckered his lips into a pursed symbol of disapproval.

"Come, come. No joke, you know. Force field most important. Got to be ready for the Jovians when they come."

A sudden rasping burr from below sent Prosser back from the railing.

"Get behind screen here," he babbled. "The twenty-millimeter field is going up. Bad radiation."

The burr muted almost into silence, and the three walked out onto the passageway again. There was no apparent change, but Prosser shoved his hand out over the railing and said, "Feel!"

Orloff extended a cautious finger, gasped, and slapped out with the palm of his hand. It was like pushing against very soft sponge rubber or super-resilient steel springs.

Birnam tried, too. "That's better than anything we've done yet, isn't it?" He explained to Orloff, "A twenty-millimeter screen is one that can hold an atmosphere of a pressure of twenty millimeters of mercury against a vacuum without appreciable leakage."

The commissioner nodded. "I see! You'd need a seven-hundred-sixty-millimeter screen to hold Earth's atmosphere, then."

"Yes! That would be a unit atmosphere screen. Well, Prosser, is this what got you excited?"

"This twenty-millimeter screen. Of course not. I can go up to two hundred fifty millimeters using the activated vanadium pentasulphide in the praseodymium breakdown. But it's not necessary. Technician would do it and blow up the place. Scientist checks on theory and goes slow." He winked. "We're hardening the field now. Watch!"

"Shall we get behind the screen?"

"Not necessary now. Radiation bad only at beginning."

The burring waxed again, but not as loudly as before. Prosser shouted to the man at the control board, and a spreading wave of the hand was the only reply.

Then the control man waved a clenched fist and Prosser cried, "We've passed fifty millimeters! Feel the field!"

Orloff extended his hand and poked it curiously. The sponge rubber had hardened! He tried to pinch it between finger and thumb, so perfect was the illusion, but here the "rubber" faded to unresisting air.

Prosser *tch-tched* impatiently. "No resistance at right angles to force. Elementary mechanics that is."

The control man was gesturing again. "Past seventy," explained Prosser. "We're slowing down now. Critical point is 83.42."

He hung over the railing and kicked out with his feet at the other two. "Stay away! Dangerous!"

And then he yelled, "Careful! The generator's bucking!"

The burr had risen to a hoarse maximum and the control man worked frantically at his switches. From within the quartz heart of the central atomic generator the sullen red glow of the bursting atoms had brightened dangerously.

There was a break in the burr, a reverberant roar, and a blast of air that threw Orloff hard against the wall.

Prosser dashed up. There was a cut over his eye. "Hurt? No? Good, good! I was expecting something of the sort. Should have warned you. Let's go down. Where's Birnam?"

The tall Ganymedan picked himself up off the floor and brushed at his clothes. "Here I am. What blew up?"

"Nothing blew up. Something buckled. Come on, down we go." He dabbed at his forehead with a handkerchief and led the way downward.

The control man removed his earphones as he approached, and got off his stool. He looked tired, and his dirt-smeared face was greasy with perspiration.

"The damn thing started going at 82.8, boss. It almost caught me."

"It did, did it?" growled Prosser. "Within limits of error, isn't it? How's the generator? Hey, Stoddard!"

The technician addressed replied from his station at the generator, "Tube Five died. It'll take two days to replace."

Prosser turned in satisfaction and said, "It worked. Went exactly as presumed. Problem solved, gentlemen. Trouble over. Let's get back to my office. I want to eat. And then I want to sleep."

He did not refer to the subject again until once more behind the desk in his office, and then he spoke between huge bites of a liver-and-onion sandwich.

He addressed Birnam. "Remember the work on space strain last June? It flopped, but we kept at it. Finch got a lead last week and I developed it. Everything fell into place. Slick as goose grease. Never saw anything like it."

"Go ahead," said Birnam calmly. He knew Prosser sufficiently well to avoid showing impatience.

"You saw what happened. When a field tops 83.42 millimeters, it becomes unstable. Space won't stand the strain. It buckles and the field blows. *Boom!*"

Birnam's mouth dropped open, and the arms of Orloff's chair creaked under sudden pressure. Silence for a while, and then Birnam said unsteadily, "You mean force fields stronger than that are impossible."

"They're possible. You can create them. But the denser they are, the more unstable they are. If I had turned on the two-hundred-and-fifty-millimeter field, it would have lasted one-tenth of a second. Then, blooie! Would have blown up the Station! *And* myself! Technician would have done it. Scientist is warned by theory. Works carefully, the way I did. No harm done."

Orloff tucked his monocle into his vest pocket and said tremulously, "But if a force field is the same thing as interatomic forces, why is it that steel has such a strong interatomic binding force without bucking space? There's a flaw there."

Prosser eyed him in annoyance. "No flaw. Critical strength depends on number of generators. In steel, each atom is a force-field generator. That means about three hundred billion trillion generators for every ounce of matter. If we could use that many— As it is, one hundred generators would be the practical limit. That only raises the critical point to ninety-seven or thereabouts."

He got to his feet and continued with sudden fervor, "No. Problem's over, I tell you. Absolutely impossible to create a force field capable of holding Earth's atmosphere for more than a hundredth of a second. Jovian atmosphere entirely out of question. Cold figures say that; backed by experiment. *Space won't stand it!*

"Let the Jovians do their damnedest. They can't get out! That's final! That's final! *That's final*!"

Orloff said, "Mr. Secretary, can I send a spacegram anywhere in the Station? I want to tell Earth that I'm returning by the next ship and that the Jovian problem is liquidated—entirely and for good."

Birnam said nothing, but the relief on his face as he shook hands with the colonial commissioner transfigured its gaunt homeliness unbelievably.

And Dr. Prosser repeated, with a birdlike jerk of his head, "That's *final!*"

Hal Tuttle looked up as Captain Everett, of the spaceship *Transparent,* newest ship of the Comet Space Lines, entered his private observation room in the nose of the ship.

The captain said, "A spacegram has just reached me from the home offices at Tucson. We're to pick up Colonial Commissioner Orloff at Jovopolis, Ganymede, and take him back to Earth."

"Good. We haven't sighted any ships?"

"No, no! We're way off the regular space lanes. The first the System will know of us will be the landing of the *Transparent* on Ganymede. It will be the greatest thing in space travel since the first trip to the Moon." His voice softened suddenly. "What's wrong, Hal? This is *your* triumph, after all."

Hal Tuttle looked up and out into the blackness of space. "I suppose it is. Ten years of work, Sam. I lost an arm and an eye in that first explosion, but I don't regret them. It's the reaction that's got me. The problem is solved; my lifework is finished."

"So is every steel-hulled ship in the System."

Tuttle smiled. "Yes. It's hard to realize, isn't it?" He gestured outward. "You see the stars? Part of the time there's nothing between them and us. It gives us a queasy feeling." His voice brooded, "Nine years I worked for nothing. I wasn't a theoretician, and never really knew where I was headed—just tried everything. I tried a little too hard, and space wouldn't stand it. I paid an arm and an eye and started fresh."

Captain Everett balled his fist and pounded the hull—the hull through which the stars shone unobstructed. There was the muffled thud of flies striking an unyielding surface—but no response whatever from the invisible wall.

Tuttle nodded. "It's solid enough, now—though it flicks on and off eight hundred thousand times a second. I got the idea from the stroboscopic lamp. You know them—they flash on and off so rapidly that it gives all the impression of steady illumination.

"And so it is with the hull. It's not on long enough to buckle space. It's not off long enough to allow appreciable leakage of the atmosphere. And the net effect is a strength better than steel."

He paused and added slowly, "And there's no telling how far we can go. Speed up the intermission effect. Have the field flick off and on millions of times per second—billions of times. You can get fields strong enough to hold an atomic explosion. My lifework!"

Captain Everett pounded the other's shoulder. "Snap out of it, man. Think of the landing on Ganymede. The devil! It will be great publicity. Think of Orloff's face, for instance, when he finds he is to be the first passenger in history ever to travel in a spaceship with a forcefield hull. How do you suppose he'll feel?"

Hal Tuttle shrugged. "I imagine he'll be rather pleased."

THE BLIND PILOT

BY CHARLES HENNEBERG

(TRANSLATED BY DAMON KNIGHT)

The shop was low and dark, as if meant for someone who no longer knew day from night. Around it hung a scent of wax and incense, exotic woods, and roses dried in darkness. It was in the cellar of one of the oldest buildings of the old radioactive district, and you had to walk down several steps before you reached a grille of Venerian sandalwood. A cone of Martian crystal lighted the sign:

THE BLIND PILOT

The man who came in this morning, followed by a robot porter with a chest, was a half-crazy old voyager, like many who have gazed on the naked blazing of the stars. He was back from the Aselli—at least, if not there, from the Southern Cross; his face was of wax, ravaged, graven, from lying too long on a keelson at the mercy of the ultraviolets, and in the black jungle of the planets.

The coffer was hewn from a heartwood hard as brass, porous here and there. He had set it down on the floor, and the sides vibrated imperceptibly, as if a great captive bee were struggling inside.

"Look here," he said, giving a rap on the lid, "I wouldn't sell that there for a million credits, but I'm needing to refloat myself, till I get my pay. They tell me you're an honest Yahoo. I'll leave this here in pawn and come back to get in six days. What'll you give me?"

At the back of the shop, a young man raised his head. He was sitting in an old armchair stiff with flowered brocade. He looked like one of those fine Velasquez cavaliers, who had hands of steel, and were not ashamed to be beautiful; but a black bandage covered the upper part of his face.

"I'm no Yahoo," he answered coldly, "and I don't take live animals as pledges."

"Blind! You're blind!" stammered the newcomer.

"You saw my sign."

"Accident?"

"Out in the Pleiades."

"Sorry, shipmate!" said the traveler. But already he was scheming: "How'd you know there was an animal in there?"

"I'm blind—but not deaf."

The whole room was tingling with a crystalline vibration. Suddenly it stopped. The traveler wiped great drops of sweat from his forehead.

"Shipmate," he said, "that ain't really an animal. I'm holding onto that. I don't want to sell it to nobody. And if I don't have any money tonight, it's the jug for me. Understand? No more space voyages, no more loot, no more nothing. I'm an HZ, to be suspended."

"I get it," answered the quiet voice. "How much?" it asked.

The other almost choked. "Will you really give me—?"

"Not a thing, I don't give anything for nothing, and I told you before, I'm not interested in your cricket in a cage. But I can let you have five thousand credits, no more, on your shipping papers. In six days, when you come back to get them, you'll pay me five hundred credits extra. That's all."

"You're *worse* than a Yahoo!"

"No. I'm blind." He added grimly, "My accident was caused by a fool who hadn't insured his rocket. I don't like fools."

"But," said the adventurer, shuffling his feet, "how can you check my papers?"

"My brother's over there. Come on out, Jacky."

A sharp little grin appeared in the shadows. Out between a lunar harmonium in a meteorite, and a dark Terrestrial cloth on which a flayed martyr had bled, came a cripple mounted on a little carriage—legless, with stumps of arms, propelling himself with the aid of two hooks: a malicious little old man of twelve.

"Mutant," said the blind man curtly. "But he makes out, with his prosthetics. Papers in order, Jacky?"

"Sure, North. And dirtier than a dust rag."

"That only means they've seen good use. Give him his five thousand credits."

The blind man pressed a button. A cabinet opened, revealing a sort of dumb-waiter. In the top half there was a little built-in strong box; in the bottom crouched a Foramen chimera, the most bloodthirsty of beasts, half cat, half harpy.

The traveler jumped back.

The cripple rolled himself over to the strong box, grabbed up a bundle of credits and blew on the monster's nose. It purred.

"You see, the money's well guarded here," said North.

"Can I leave my chest with you, anyhow?" asked the traveler humbly.

So the chest remained. Using the dumb-waiter, the cripple sent it up to the small apartment which the two brothers shared in the penthouse of the building.

According to its owner, "the beast which was not really an animal" was in hibernation; it had no need of food. The porous wood allowed enough air to pass. But the box had to be kept in a dark place. "It lives in the great deeps," he had explained; "it can't stand daylight."

The building was really very old, with many elevators and closets. The mutants and cripples of the last war, who lived there because it was cheap, accommodated themselves to it. North dragged the chest into the strong room next to his study.

That evening, the free movie in the building was showing an old stereo film, not even sensorial, about the conquest of the Pleiades, and Jacky announced that he wanted to see it. He asked his brother, "You don't suppose that animal will get cold in there?"

"What are you talking about? It's in hibernation."

"Anyhow," said Jacky spitefully, "we're not getting paid to keep it in fuel."

The movie lasted till midnight, and when Jacky came back, there was a full moon. The boy testified later that he had been a little overexcited. A white glimmer flooded the upper landing, and he saw that the window of the "garret," as they called his brother's study, was masked with a black cloth. Jacky supposed North had taken this extra precaution on account of the animal; he pushed himself forward with his hooks and knocked on the door, but no one answered, and there was no key in the lock.

He told himself then that maybe North had gone down six stories to the bar in the building, and he decided to wait. He sat on the landing; the night was mild, and he would not have traded the air at that height for any amount of conditioned and filtered atmosphere. The silver star floated overhead in the black sky. Jacky mused that "it means something after all, that shining going on just the same for *x* years—that moon that's seen so many old kings, and poets, and lovers' stories. The cats that yowl at night must feel it; and the dogs too." In the lower-class buildings, there were only robot-dogs. Jacky longed for a real dog—after all, he was only twelve. But mutants couldn't own living animals.

And then . . .

(On the magnetic tape where Jacky's deposition was taken down, it seemed that at that moment the boy began to choke. The recording was interrupted, and the next reel began: "Thanks for the coffee. It was good and bitter.")

He had heard an indefinable sound, very faint . . . just the sound of the sea-tide in a bed of shells. It grew, and grew. . . . At the same time (though he couldn't say how) there were images. A pearl-colored sky, and green crystal waves, with crests of sparkling silver. Jacky felt no surprise; he had just left the stereo theater. Perhaps someone in the building opposite had turned on a sensorial camera—and the vibrations, the waves, were striking their landing by accident.

But the melody swelled, and the boy sank under the green waves. The sea stank of seaweed and fish. . . . Carried along by the currents, the little cripple felt light and free. Banks of rustling diatoms parted for him; a blue phosphorescence haloed the medusas and starfish, and pearly blue anemones formed a forest. Grazed by a transparent jellyfish, Jacky felt a nettle-like burning. The shadow of a hammerhead shark went by, and scattered a twinkling cloud of smelt. Farther down, the shadow grew denser, more opaque and mysterious—caverns gaped in a coral reef. The tentacle of an octopus lashed the water, and the cripple shuddered.

He found himself thrown back against the hull of a ship, half buried in the sand. A little black-and-gold siren, garlanded with barnacles, smiled under the prow; and he fell, transported, against a breach that spilled out a pirate treasure, coffers full of barbaric jewels. Heaps of bones were whitening at the bottom of the hold, and a skull smiled with empty sockets. This must be an amateur film, Jacky thought: a little too realistic. He freed himself, pushed away as hard as he could with his hooks, rose to the surface at last—and almost cried out.

The sky above him was not that of Earth. North had told him how that other dark ocean looked—the sub-ether. The stars were naked and dazzling. Reefs, that were burning meteors, sprang up out of nowhere. And the planets seemed to whirl near enough to touch—one was ruby, another orange, still another a tranquil blue; Saturn danced in its airy ring.

Jacky thrust his hooks out before him to push away those torches. In so doing, he slipped and rolled across the landing. The door opened a second later—he hadn't had time to fall three steps, but this time he wasn't diving alone: beside him, in the hideously reddened water, whirled and danced the body of a disjointed puppet, with gullied features in a face of wax.

Jacky raised his head. North stood on the sill, terrible, pale as a statue of old ivory; the black bandage cut his face in two. He called, "Who's there? Answer me, or I'll call the militia!"

His voice was loud and angry. North, who always spoke so softly to Jacky . . .

"It's me—Jack," said the boy, trembling. "I was coming back, and I missed a step . . ."

("I told a lie," said Jacky later, to the militiamen who were questioning him. And he stared into their eyes with a look of open defiance. "That's right, sure, I told a lie. Because I knew he'd kill me.")

The next morning there was no blood and no corpse on the landing. Only a smell of seaweed . . .

Jacky was filling the coffee cups, in the back of the shop, while the television news broadcast was on. Toward the end, the announcer reported that the body of a drowned man had been taken from the harbor. The dead man's face appeared on the tiny screen, at the moment North came into the shop.

"Hey, look at that!" called the cripple. "Your five thousand credits are done for."

"What's that?" asked his brother, picking up his china cup and his buttered bread with delicate accuracy.

"The character with the pet. They've just fished him out of the channel. Guess what, they don't know who he is: somebody swiped his wallet."

"A dead loss," said the older. "You're certain he's the one?"

"He's still on the screen. He isn't a pretty sight."

An indefinable expression passed over North's mobile features. "You'd think he was relieved," Jacky told himself. Aloud, he asked, "What do we do with the animal?"

"Does it bother you?" asked North, a little too negligently.

"Me, old man?" said the cripple in a clownish tone, imitating a famous fat actor. "As long as there's no wrinkles in my belly! Where did he come from?"

"He talked about the Aselli," said North, reaching with a magician's deftness for another slice of bread. "And a lot of other things, too. What are you up to this morning? Got any work to do?"

"Not much! The Stimpson order to send out. A crate of lunar bells coming in. I ought to go to the Re-education Center, too."

"Okay. Can you bring me back a copy of the weekly news disc?"

"Sure."

But Jacky didn't go to the Re-education Center that morning, nor to his customers. With his carriage perched on the slidewalk, he rode to Astronautics Headquarters, a building among others, and had some difficulty getting upstairs in the elevator, amid the students' jibes. Some of them asked, "You want to do the broad jump in a rocket?" And others, "He thinks these are the good old days, when everybody was hunting for round-bottoms to send to the Moon!" It was not really spiteful, and Jacky was used to it.

He felt a touch of nostalgia, not for himself but for North—he knew North would never come here again. The walls were covered with celestial charts, microfilm shelves rose from one floor to the next, and in all the glass cases there were models of spaceship engines, from the multi-stage rockets and sputniks all the way up to the great ships that synthesized their own fissionables. Jacky arrived all out of breath in front of the robot card-sorter, and handed it his card.

"The Aselli," spat the robot. "Asellus Borealis? Asellus Australis? Gamma Cancri or Delta Cancri?"

"Nothing else out there?"

"Yes, Al-Phard, longitude twenty-six degrees nineteen minutes. Alpha Hydrae."

"Hydra, that's an aquatic monster? Is it a water planet? Read me the card."

"There is little to tell," crackled the robot. "The planet is almost unexplored, its surface being composed of oceans."

"Fauna? Flora?"

"Without evidence to the contrary, those of oceans in general."

"Intelligent life?"

The robot made a face with its revolving spheres. "Without evidence to the contrary, none. Nor any human beings. Nothing but sea lions and manatees."

"Manatees? What are they?" asked Jacky, suddenly apprehensive.

"Herbivorous sirenian mammals which live on Earth, along the shores of Africa and America. Manatees sometimes grow as long as three meters, and frequent the estuaries of rivers."

"But—'sirenians'?"

"A genus of mammals, related to the cetaceans, and comprising the dugongs, manatees, and so on."

Jacky's eyebrows went up and he cried, "I thought it came from 'siren'!"

"So it does," said the robot laconically. "Fabulous monsters, half woman, half bird or fish. With their sweet singing, they lured voyagers onto the reefs—"

"Where did this happen?"

"On Earth, where else?" said the robot, offended. "Between the isle of Capri and the coast of Italy. Young man, you don't know quite what you mean to ask."

But Jacky knew.

On his return, as he expected, he found the shop closed and a note tacked to the door: "The pilot is out." Jacky hunted in his pockets for the key, slipped inside. All was calm and ordinary, except for the smell which ruled now like the mistress of the house, the smell that you breathe on the beaches, in little coves, in summer: seaweed, shells, fish, perhaps a little tar. Jacky set the table, set to work in the kitchenette and prepared a nice little snack, lobster salad and ravioli. Secretive and spiteful, imprisoned among the yellowing antiques of the shop, the young cripple really loved them all. When everything was ready—fresh flowers in the vases, the ravioli hot, ice cubes in the glasss—Jacky rang three times, according to custom. No one answered. Everything was a pretext for a secret language between the two mutilated brothers, who adored each other; the first stroke of the bell meant: "The meal is ready, his lordship may come down," the second: "I'm hungry," and the third: "I'm hungry, hungry!" The fourth had almost the sense of: "Have you had an accident?"

Jacky hesitated a moment, then pressed the button. The silence was deep among the crystallized plants and the gems of seven planets. Did this mean that North was really away? The cripple hoisted himself into the dumb-waiter and rode up to the penthouse.

On the upper landing, the scent had changed; it had flowered now into unknown spices, and it would have taken a more expert observer than Jacky to recognize the aromatics of the fabulous past: nard, aloes, and benzoin, the bitter thyme of Shelba's Belkis, the myrrh and olibanum of Cleopatra.

In the midst of all this, the music was real, almost palpable, like a pillar of light, and Jacky asked himself how it could be that the others, on the floors below, didn't hear it.

That morning, North Ellis had closed the door of the dark room behind him, turned the key, and shot the bolt. His blind man's hands, strong and slender, executed these movements with machine-like precision, but he was panting a little, and in spite of old habit, had almost missed the landing. He was so pressed . . . but he had to foresee everything. Jacky . . . Resting his back against the door, North gave a moment's thought to the idea of sending Jacky to Europe. Their aunt, their mother's sister, lived somewhere in a little village with a musical name. He felt responsible for Jacky.

He swept away these preoccupations like dead leaves, and walked toward the dark corner where the chest lay under a black cloth. His fingers crept over the porous wood which scented his palms.

"You're there," he said in a cold, harsh voice. "You've been waiting for me, you!"

The being that crouched at the heart of the shadows did not immediately answer, but the concentric waves of the music swelled out. And the man who had tumbled to earth with broken wings, awaited neither by his mother, dead of leukemia, nor by a Russian girl who had laughed, turning her primrose face beside a white neck . . . the blind pilot felt himself neither deprived nor unhappy.

"You're beautiful, aren't you? You're very beautiful! Your voice . . ."

"What else would you like to know?" responded the waves, growing stronger. "You are sightless, I faceless. I told you, yesterday when you opened the strong room: I am all that streams and sings. The glittering cascades, the torrents of ice that break on the columbines, the reflections of the multiple moons on the oceans . . . And I am the ocean. Let yourself float on my wave. Come . . ."

"You made me kill that man, yesterday."

"What is a man? I speak to you of tumbling abysses, dark and luminous by turns, of the crucibles where new life is forged, and you answer me with the death of a spaceman! Anyhow, he deserved it: he captured me, imprisoned me, and he had come back to separate us!"

"Separate us . . ." said North. "Do you think that's possible?"

"No—if you follow me."

The central melody grew piercing. It was like a spire, or a bridge over a limitless space. And the unconscious part of the human soul darted out to encounter that harmony. The wheeling abyss opened, it was peopled with trembling nebulae, with diamonds and roses of fire . . .

North toppled into it.

. . . It was strange to recognize, in this *n*th dimension, the crowds of stars he had encountered in real voyages—the glacial scintillation of Polaris, the scattered pearls of

Orion's Belt. North marveled to find himself again in this night, weightless and free, without spacesuit or rocket. Jets of photons bore him on immense wings. The garret, the mutants' building, the Earth? He laughed at them. The Boreal Dragon twisted its spirals in a spray of stars. He crossed in one bound an abyss streaming with fire—Berenice's Hair—and cut himself on the blue sapphire of Vega in the Lyre. He was not climbing alone: the living music wound him in its rings.

"Do you think to know the Infinite?" said the voice enfolded in the harmonies. "Poor Earthlings, who claim to have discovered everything! Because you've built heavy machines that break all equilibrium, that burst into flame and fall, and martyr your vulnerable human flesh? Come, I'll show you what we can see, we obscure and immobile ones, in the abysses, since what is on high is also down below. . . ."

The star-spirals and the harmonies surged up. In the depths of his night, North gazed upon those things which the pilots, constrained by their limited periscopic screens, never saw: oceans of rubies, furnaces of emeralds, dark stars, constellations coiled like luminous dragons. Meteorites were a rain of motionless streaks. Novas came to meet him; they exploded and shattered in sidereal tornadoes, the giants and dwarfs fell again in incandescent cascades. Space-time was nothing but a flaming chalice.

"Higher! Faster!" sang the voice.

All that passed beyond vertigo and the tipsiness of the flesh. North felt himself tumbled, dissolved in the astral foam, he was nothing but an atom in the infinite.

"Higher! Faster!"

Was it at that moment, among the dusty arcs, far down at the bottom of the abyss, at the heart of his being, that he felt that icy breath, that sensation of horror? It was more than unclean. It was as if he had leaped over the abysses and the centuries, passed beyond all human limits—and ended at this. At nothingness, the void. He was down at the bottom of a well, in utter darkness, and his mouth was full of blood. Rhythmic blows were shaking that closed universe. Trying to raise himself, he felt under his hands the porous, wrinkled wood. A childish voice was crying, "North! Oh! North! Don't you hear me? Let me in, let me in!"

North came back to himself, numbed, weak as if he had bled to death. For a little, he thought himself in the wrecked starship, out in the Pleiades. He hoisted himself up on his elbows and crawled toward the door. He had strength enough left to draw the bolt, turn the key, and then he fainted on the sill.

("It was those trips, you know . . .") Jacky looked up at the Spacial Militiamen who were taking thier turn opposite him. They were not hardhearted; they had given him a sandwich and a big quilt. But how much could they understand? "I never knew when North started getting unhappy. Me, I never went on a trip farther away than the coast. Ever since he's been blind, he always seemed to be so calm! I thought he was like me. When I was around him, I felt good, I never wanted to go anywhere. Sometimes, to try and be the same as him, I'd put a bandage around my eyes, and try to see everything in sounds instead of colors. Sure, the switchboard operator, and the night watchman—not the robot, the other one—they said this was no life for two boys. But North was blind and I was crippled. Who would have wanted us?"

. . . The next day was a day of trouble; North pulled an old spacesuit out of a pile of scrap iron and began to polish the plates, whistling. He explained to Jacky that he was going to put it at the entrance of the shop. Toward noon, Jacky took a phone message for North: he was told that the board of directors of a famous sanatorium hesitated to accept a boarder mutated to that extent. He accepted their excuses and hung up, silently.

So that was what it was all about: North wanted to get rid of him. He was crazy—it was as if he had gone blind all over again! During a miserable lunch, the idea came to him to put the building's telephone line out of commission; that way, the outer world would leave them alone. But first he wanted to call up Dr. Evers, their family doctor, and the telephone did not respond. Jacky understood that North had got ahead of him.

After that, he made himself small, rolled his carriage behind some crates, and installed himself on a shelf of the bookcase. It was his favorite hiding place. There were still in the shop some volumes bound in blond leather, almost golden, which smelled of incense or cigars, with yellowing pages and the curious printing of the twentieth century. They had quaint pictures, not even animated. Without looking, he stumbled upon the marvelous story of the navigator who sailed the wine-dark sea. The sail was purple, and the hull of sandalwood. Off the mythological coasts, a divine singing arose, inviting the sailors to more distant flights. The reefs were fringed with pearls; the white moon rose high above the fabulous mountains. Ulysses stopped up their ears with wax and tied himself to the mast. But he himself heard the songs of the sirens. . . .

"North," the boy asked later, forgetting all caution, "is there such a thing as sirens?"

"What?" asked the blind man, with a start.

"I mean, the sailors in the olden days, they said—"

"Crud," said North. "Those guys went out of their heads, sailing across the oceans. Just think, it took them longer between Crete, a little island, and Ithaca than it takes us to get to Jupiter. They went short of food, and their ships were walnut shells. And on top of everything else, for months on end they'd see nobody except a few shipmates, as chapped and hairy as they were. Well, they'd start to go off their rockers, and the first woman pirate was Circe or Calypso to them, and the first cetacean they met was an ocean princess."

"A manatee," said Jacky.

"That's right, a manatee. Have you ever seen one?"

"No."

"Sure, that's right, I don't think there is one in the Zoo. Maybe in the exotic specimens. Take down the fourth book from the left, on the 'Nat. Sciences' shelf. Page seven hundred ninety-two. Got it?"

Jacky found it. It was a big beast with a round head and

mustaches, and a thick oily skin. The female was giving suck to a little tar-baby. They all had serious expressions. Jacky was overcome with mad laughter.

"Ridiculous, isn't it?" North asked in an unrecognizable dived into the water on account of that! I think they must dived into the water, on account of that! I think they must have been sick."

But that evening, he offered Jacky a ticket to the planetarium and a trip to the amusement park. Jacky refused politely; he was content to stay on his shelf. Again he plunged into the volume bound in blond leather, discovering for the first time that life has always been mysterious and that destiny puts on many masks. The isles with the fabulous names flickered past to the rhythm of strophes; the heroes sailed for the conquest of the Golden Fleece, or perhaps they led a pale well-beloved out of Hades. Some burned their wings in the sun and fell . . .

North walked around cat-footed, closing the shutters, arranging the planetary knickknacks. He disappeared so quietly that Jacky was not aware of it, and it was only when the boy wanted to ask him for some information about sailing ships that his absence became a concrete fact. Suddenly afraid, Jacky slipped to the floor, and discovered that his carriage had also disappeared. He crawled then, with the aid of his hooks, among the scattered pieces of iron, and it was then that he stumbled over a horrible viscous thing: the wet billfold of the dead spaceman. The five thousand credits were still inside.

After that, his fear had no limit, and Jacky crawled instinctively toward the door, which he found shut; then to the dumb-waiter, where he heard the Foramen chimera, caged, mew pleasantly. "It won't work, old lady," he breathed at it. "They've locked us both up together." He licked a little blood out of the corners of his mouth, and thought hard. He would have to be quick. To be sure, he could hammer on the door, but the street was deserted at night, the normals were all getting ready to watch their telesets, or some other kind of screen—and there was no use knocking on the walls; the shop was surrounded by empty cellars. And the telephone was dead.

Jacky then did what any imprisoned boy of his age would have done (but from him, it demanded a superhuman effort): he clambered up the curtains, managed to open the window with his hook, and jumped out. He was hurt, falling on the pavement.

. . . "That damn' kid!" thought North as he opened the door of the garret. "Sirens!"

His hands were trembling. A wave of aromatics, already familiar, came into his night and surrounded him: he had breathed them on other worlds. He understood what was required of him, and he let himself go, abandoned himself to the furious maelstrom of sounds and smells, to the tide of singing and perfumes. His useless, mutilated body lay somewhere out of the way, on a shelf.

"Look at me," said the music. "I am in you, and you are me. They tried in vain to keep you on Earth, with chains of falsehood. You are no longer of Earth, since we live one life together. Yesterday I showed you the abysses I know. Now you show me the stars you have visited: memory by memory, I shall take them. In that way, perhaps, shall we not find the world that calls us? Come. I shall choose a planet, like a pearl."

He saw them again, all of them.

Alpha Spicae, in the constellation of the Virgin, is a frozen globe, whose atmosphere is so rich in water vapor that a rocket sticks in the ground like a needle of frost. Under a distant green sun, this world scintillates like a million-faceted diamond, and its icecap spreads toward the equator. On the ground, you are snared in a net of rainbows and green snow, a snow that smells like benzoin (all the pilots know that stellar illusion). On Alpha Spicae, in a few hours, a lost explorer goes mad.

North was irresistibly drawn away, and shortly recognized the magnetic planet of the Ditch in Cygnus. That one, too, he had learned to avoid on his voyages: it was followed in its orbit by the thousands of sidereal corpses it had captured. The bravest pilots followed it in their coffins of sparkling ice; for that sphere, no larger than the Moon, is composed of pure golden ore.

They passed like a waterspout across a lake of incandescent crystal—Altair. Another trap lay in wait for them in the constellation Orion, where the gigantic diamond of Betelgeuse flashed: a phantasmagoria of deceptive images, a spiderweb of lightnings. The orb which cowered behind these mirages had no name, only a nickname: Sundew. Space pilots avoided it like the Pit.

"Higher!" sang the voice, made up now of thousands of etheric currents, millions of astral vibrations. "Farther!"

But here, North struggled. He knew now where she was drawing him, and what incandescent hell he would meet on that path, because he had already experienced it. He knew of a peculiar planet with silvery-violet skies, out in the mysterious constellation of Cancer. It was the most beautiful he had ever glimpsed, the only one he had loved like a woman, because its oceans reminded him of a pair of eyes. Ten dancing moons crowned that Alpha Hydrae, which the ancient nomads called Al-Phard. It was a deep watery world, with frothing waves: an odor of sea-salt, of seaweed, of ambergris drifted over its surface. A perpetual ultrasonic music jumbled all attempts at communication, and baffled the starships. The oxygen content of Alpha Hydrae's atmosphere was so high that it intoxicated living beings, and burned them up. The rockets which succeeded in escaping the attraction of Al-Phard carried back crews of the blissful dead.

It was in trying to escape its grip that an uncontrolled machine, with North aboard, had once headed toward the Pleiades and crashed on an asteroid.

Heavy blows shook the temples of the solitary navigator. The enormous sun of Pollux leaped out of space, exploded, fell to ruin in the darkness, with Procyon and the Goat; the whole Milky Way trembled and vibrated. The human soul lost in that torrent of energy, the soul that struggled, despaired, foundered, was only an infinitesimal atom, a sound—or the echo of a sound, in the harmony of the spheres.

"This is it," said Jacky, wiping his bloody mouth.

"Honest, this is it, inspector. There's the window I jumped out of . . ."

There it was, with its smashed glass, and Jacky did not mention how painful the fall had been. His forearms slashed, he had hung suspended by his hooks. On the pavement, he had lost consciousness. Coming to, later, under a fine drizzle of rain, he had, he said, "crawled and crawled." Few of the passing autos had even slowed down for that crushed human caterpillar. "Oh, Marilyn, did you see that funny little round-bottom?"—"It must be one of those mutant cripples, don't stop, Galla . . ."—"Space! Are they still contagious?" Jacky bit his lips.

Finally, a truck had stopped. Robots—a crew of robots from the highway commission—had picked him up. He began to cry, seeing himself already thrown onto the junk heap. By chance, the driver was human; he heard, and took him to the militia post.

"I don't hear anything," said the inspector after a moment of silence.

"The others in the block didn't hear anything either!" breathed Jacky. "I think he must be very unhappy, or else drunk. . . . Are there ultrasonics, maybe? Look, the dogs are restless."

Certainly, the handsome Great Danes of the Special Service were acting strangely: they were padding around in circles and whining.

"A quarrel between monsters," thought Inspector Morel. "Just my luck: a mutant stump of a kid, a space pilot with the D.T.'s, and a siren! They'll laugh in my face down at headquarters!"

But, as Jacky cried and beat on the door, he gave the order to break it in. The boy crawled toward the dumbwaiter; one of the militiamen almost fired on the chimera, which leaped from its cabinet, purring.

"That's nothing, it's only a big cat from Foramen!" Jacky wailed. "Come on, please come on, I'm going up the shaft."

"I was never in such a madhouse before," thought the inspector. There were things in every corner—robots or idols, with three heads or seven hands. There were talking shells. One of the men shouted, feeling a mobile creeper twine itself in his hair. They ought to forbid the import of these parlor tricks into an honest Terrestrial port. Not surprising that the lad upstairs should have gone off his nut, the inspector told himself.

When the militia reached the topmost landing of the building, Jacky was stretched out in front of the closed door, banging it desperately with his fists. Whether on account of ultrasonics or not, the men were pale. The enormous harmony which filled the garret was here perceptible, palpable.

Morel called, but no one answered.

"He's dead?" asked Jacky. "Isn't he?"

They sensed a living, evil presence inside.

Morel disposed his men in pairs, one on either side of the door. A ferret-faced little locksmith slipped up and began to work on the bolt. When he was finished, the militiamen were supposed to break the door down quickly and rush inside, while Morel covered them, with heat gun in hand. But it was black inside the garret; someone would have to carry a powerful flashlight and play it back and forth.

"Me," said Jacky. He was white as a sheet, trembling all over. "If my brother's dead, Inspector, you should let me go in. Anyhow, what risk would I take? You'll be right behind me. And I promise not to let go of the flashlight, no matter what."

The inspector looked at the legless child. "You might get yourself shot," he said. "You never know what weapons these extra-terrestrials are going to use. Or what they're thinking, or what they want. That thing . . . maybe it sings the way we breathe."

"I know," said Jacky. He neglected to add, "That's why I asked to carry the flashlight. So as to get to it first."

The inspector handed him the flashlight. He seized it firmly with one of his hooks. And the first sharp ray, like a sword, cut through the keyhole into the attic.

They all felt the crushing tension let go. Released, with frothing tongues, the dogs lay down on the floor. It was as if a tight cord had suddenly snapped. And abruptly, behind the closed door, something broke with a stunning crash. Something fell with a dull sound to the floor.

At the same instant, there was a great crash, and the landing was flooded with an intolerable smell of burned flesh. Down in the street, passers-by screamed and ran like ants. The building was burning. An object falling in flames had buried itself in the roof. . . .

The militiamen broke down the door, and Morel stumbled over a horrible mass of flesh, calcined, crushed, which no longer bore any resemblance to North. A man who had fallen from a starship, across the stellar void, might have looked like that. A man who had leaped into vacuum without a spacesuit . . . a half-disintegrated manikin. North Ellis, the blind pilot, had suffered his last shipwreck.

Overcome by nausea, the militiamen backed away. Jacky himself had not moved from the landing. He clung to the flashlight, and the powerful beam of light implacably searched, swept the dark cave. The symphony which only his ears had heard plainly grew fainter, then lost itself in a tempest of discordant sounds. The invisible being gave one last sharp wail (in the street, all the windows broke and the lights went out).

Then there was silence.

Jacky sat and licked his bloody lips. Inside, in the garret, the militiamen were pulling down the black drapes, breaking furniture. One of them shouted, "There's nothing here!"

Jacky dropped the flashlight, raised himself on his stumps. "Look in the chest! In the strong room, to the side—"

"Nothing in here. Nothing in the chest."

"Wait a minute," said the youngest of the militiamen, "there it is—on the floor."

When they dragged her out, her round head bobbed, and Jacky recognized the thick glossy skin and the flippers. She had died, probably, at the first touch of the light, but her corpse was still pulsing in a heavy rhythm. An ultrasonic machine? No. Two red slits wept bloody tears. . . . The sirens of Alpha Hydrae cannot bear the light.

THE SILLY SEASON

BY C. M. KORNBLUTH

It was a hot summer afternoon in the Omaha bureau of the World Wireless Press Service, and the control bureau in New York kept nagging me for copy. But since it was a hot summer afternoon, there was no copy. A wrap-up of local baseball had cleared about an hour ago, and that was that. Nothing but baseball happens in the summer. During the dog days, politicians are in the Maine woods fishing and boozing, burglars are too tired to burgle, and wives think it over and decide not to decapitate their husbands.

I pawed through some press releases. One sloppy stencil-duplicated sheet began: "Did you know that the lemonade way to summer comfort and health has been endorsed by leading physiotherapists from Maine to California? The Federated Lemon-Growers association revealed today that a survey of 2,500 physiotherapists in 57 cities of more than 25,000 population disclosed that 87 per cent of them drink lemonade at least once a day between June and September, and that another 72 per cent not only drink the cooling and healthful beverage but actually prescribe it . . ."

Another note tapped out on the news circuit printer from New York: "960M-HW KICKER? ND SNST-NY."

That was New York saying they needed a bright and sparkling little news item immediately—"soonest." I went to the east-bound printer and punched out: "96NY-UPCMNG FU MINS-OM."

The lemonade handout was hopeless; I dug into the stack again. The State University summer course was inviting the governor to attend its summer conference on aims and approaches in adult secondary education. The Agricultural College wanted me to warn farmers that white-skinned hogs should be kept from the direct rays of the summer sun. The manager of a fifth-rate local pug sent a write-up of his boy and a couple of working press passes to his next bout in the Omaha Arena. The Schwartz and White Bandage Company contributed a glossy eight-by-ten of a blonde in a bathing suit improvised from two S & W Redi-Dressings.

Accompanying text: "Pert starlet Miff McCoy is ready for any seaside emergency. That's not only a darling swim suit she has on—it's two standard all-purpose Redi-Dressing bandages made by the Schwartz and White Bandage Company of Omaha. If a broken rib results from too-strenous beach athletics, Miff's dress can supply the dressing." Yeah. The rest of the stack wasn't even that good. I dumped them all in the circular file, and began to rack my brains in spite of the heat.

I'd have to fake one, I decided. Unfortunately, there had been no big running silly-season story so far this summer—no flying saucers, or monsters in the Florida Everglades, or chloroform bandits terrifying the city. If there had, I could have hopped on and faked a "with." As it was, I'd have to fake a "lead," which is harder and riskier.

The flying saucers? I couldn't revive them; they'd been forgotten for years, except by newsmen. The giant turtle of Lake Huron had been quiet for years too. If I started a chloroform bandit scare, every old maid in the state would back me up by swearing she heard the bandit trying to break in and smelled chloroform—but the cops wouldn't like it. Strange messages from space received at the state university's radar lab? That might do it. I put a sheet of copy paper in the typewriter and sat, glaring at it and hating the silly season.

There was a slight reprieve—the Western Union tie-line printer by the desk dinged at me, and its sickly-yellow bulb lit up. I tapped out, "WW GA PLS," and the machine began to eject yellow, gummed tape which told me this:

> WU CO62-DPR COLLECT—FT HICKS ARK AUG 22 105P—WORLD-WIRELESS OMAHA—TOWN MARSHAL PINKNEY CRAWLES DIED MYSTERIOUS CIRCUMSTANCES FISHTRIPPING OZARK HAMLET RUSH CITY TODAY. RUSHERS PHONED HICKSERS "BURNED DEATH SHINING DOMES APPEARED YESTERWEEK." JEEPING BODY HICKSWARD. QUERIED RUSH CONSTABLE P. C. ALLENBY LEARNING "SEVEN GLASSY DOME EACH HOUSESIZE CLEARING MILE SOUTH TOWN. RUSHERS UNTOUCHED, UNAPPROACHED. CRAWLES WARNED BUT TOUCHED AND DIED BURNS." NOTE DESK—RUSH FONECALL 1.85 SHALL I FOLLOW UP?—BENSON—FISHTRIPPING RUSHERS HICKSERS YESTERWEEK JEEPING HICKSWARD HOUSESIZE, 1.85 428PCLR . . .

It was just what the doctor ordered. I typed an acknowledgment for the message and pounded out a story, fast. I punched it and started the tape waggling through the eastbound transmitter before New York could send any more irked notes. The news circuit printer from New York clucked and began relaying my story immediately:

WW72 (KICKER)

FORT HICKS, ARKANSAS, AUG 22—(WW)—MYSTERIOUS DEATH TODAY STRUCK DOWN A LAW ENFORCEMENT OFFICER IN A TINY OZARK MOUNTAIN HAMLET. MARSHAL PINKNEY CRAWLES OF FORT HICKS, ARKANSAS, DIED OF BURNS WHILE ON A FISHING TRIP TO THE LITTLE VILLAGE OF RUSH CITY. TERRIFIED NATIVES OF RUSH CITY BLAMED THE TRAGEDY ON WHAT THEY CALLED "SHINING DOMES." THEY SAID THE SO-CALLED DOMES APPEARED IN A CLEARING LAST WEEK ONE MILE SOUTH OF TOWN. THERE ARE SEVEN OF THE MYSTERIOUS OBJECTS—EACH ONE THE SIZE OF A HOUSE. THE INHABITANTS OF RUSH CITY DID NOT DARE APPROACH THEM. THEY WARNED THE VISITING MARSHAL CRAWLES—BUT HE DID NOT HEED THEIR WARNING. RUSH CITY'S CONSTABLE P. C. ALLENBY WAS A WITNESS TO THE TRAGEDY. SAID HE: "THERE ISN'T MUCH TO TELL. MARSHAL CRAWLES JUST WALKED UP TO ONE OF THE DOMES AND PUT HIS HAND ON IT. THERE WAS A BIG FLASH, AND WHEN I COULD SEE AGAIN, HE WAS BURNED TO DEATH." CONSTABLE ALLENBY IS RETURNING THE BODY OF MARSHAL CRAWLES TO FORT HICKS.

602P220M

That, I thought, should hold them for a while. I remembered Benson's "note desk" and put through a long-distance call to Fort Hicks, person to person. The Omaha operator asked for Fort Hicks information, but there wasn't any. The Fort Hicks operator asked whom she wanted. Omaha finally admitted that we wanted to talk to Mr. Edwin C. Benson. Fort Hicks figured out loud and then decided that Ed was probably at the police station, and I got Benson. He had a pleasant voice, not particularly backwoods Arkansas. I gave him some of the old oil about a fine dispatch and a good, conscientious job, and so on.

He took it with plenty of dry reserve, which was odd. Our rural stringers always ate that kind of stuff up. Where, I asked, was he from?

"Fort Hicks," he told me, "but I've moved around. I did the courthouse beat in Little Rock"—I nearly laughed out loud at that, but the laugh died as he went on—"rewrite for the A.P. in New Orleans, got to be bureau chief there but I didn't like wire-service work. Got an opening on the Chicago *Trib* desk. That didn't last—they sent me to head up their Washington bureau. There I switched to the New York *Times*. They made me a war correspondent and I got hurt—back to Fort Hicks. I do some magazine writing now. Did you want a follow-up on the Rush City story?"

"Sure," I told him weakly. "Give it a real ride—use your own judgment. Do you think it's a fake?"

"I saw Pink's body a little while ago at the undertaker's parlor, and I had a talk with Allenby, from Rush City. Pink got burned, all right, and Allenby didn't make his story up. Maybe somebody else did—he's pretty dumb—but as far as I can tell, this is the real thing. I'll keep the copy coming. Don't forget about that dollar eighty-five phone call, will you?"

I told him I wouldn't, and hung up. Mr. Edwin C. Benson had handed me quite a jolt. I wondered how badly he had been hurt that he had been forced to abandon a brilliant news career and bury himself in the Ozarks.

Then there came a call from God, the board chairman of World Wireless. He was fishing in Canada, as all good board chairmen do during the silly season, but he had caught a news broadcast which used my Rush City story. He had a mobile phone in his trailer, and it was but the work of a moment to ring Omaha and louse up my carefully planned vacation schedules and rotations of night shifts. He wanted me to go down to Rush City and cover the story personally. I said yes and began trying to round up the rest of the staff. My night editor was sobered up by his wife and delivered to the bureau in fair shape. A telegrapher on vacation was reached at his summer resort and talked into checking out. I got a taxi company on the phone and told them to have a cross-country cab on the roof in an hour. I specified their best driver, and told them to give him maps of Arkansas.

Meanwhile, two "with domes" dispatches arrived from Benson and got moved on the wire. I monitored a couple of newscasts; the second one carried a story by another wire service on the domes—a pickup of our stuff, but they'd have their own men on the scene fast enough. I filled in the night editor, and went up to the roof for the cab.

The driver took off in the teeth of a gathering thunderstorm. We had to rise above it, and by the time we could get down to the sight-pilotage altitude, we were lost. We circled most of the night until the driver picked up a beacon he had on his charts at about 3:30 A.M. We landed at Fort Hicks as day was breaking, not on speaking terms.

The Fort Hicks field clerk told me where Benson lived, and I walked there. It was a white frame house. A quiet, middle-aged woman let me in. She was his widowed sister, Mrs. McHenry. She got me some coffee and told me she had been up all night waiting for Edwin to come back from Rush City. He had started out about 8:00 P.M., and it was only a two-hour trip by car. She was worried. I tried to pump her about her brother, but she'd only say that he was the bright one of the family. She didn't want to talk about his work as war correspondent. She did show me some of his magazine stuff—boy-and-girl stories in national weeklies. He seemed to sell one every couple of months.

We had arrived at a conversational stalemate when her brother walked in, and I discovered why his news career had been interrupted. He was blind. Aside from a long, puckered brown scar that ran from his left temple back over his ear and onto the nape of his neck, he was a pleasant-looking fellow in his mid-forties.

"Who is it, Vera?" he asked.

"It's Mr. Williams, the gentleman who called you from Omaha today—I mean yesterday."

"How do you do, Williams. Don't get up," he added, hearing, I suppose, the chair squeak as I leaned forward to rise.

"You were so *long*, Edwin," his sister said with relief and reproach.

"That young jackass Howie—my chauffeur for the night"—he added an aside to me—"got lost going there and coming back. But I did spend more time than I'd planned at Rush City." He sat down, facing me. "Williams, there is some difference of opinion about the shining domes. The Rush City people say that they exist, and I say they don't."

His sister brought him a cup of coffee.

"What happened, exactly?" I asked.

"That Allenby took me and a few other hardy citizens to see them. They told me just what they looked liked. Seven hemispheres in a big clearing, glassy, looming up like houses, reflecting the gleam of the headlights. But they weren't there. Not to me, and not to any blind man. I know when I'm standing in front of a house or anything else that big. I can feel a little tension on the skin of my face. It works unconsciously, but the mechanism is thoroughly understood.

"The blind get—because they have to—an aural picture of the world. We hear a little hiss of air that means we're at the corner of a building; we hear and feel big, turbulent air currents that mean we're coming to a busy street. Some of the boys can thread their way through an obstacle course and never touch a single obstruction. I'm not that good, maybe because I haven't been blind as long as they have, but by hell, I know when there are seven objects the size of houses in front of me, and there just were no such things in the clearing at Rush City."

"Well"—I shrugged—"there goes a fine piece of silly-season journalism. What kind of a gag are the Rush City people trying to pull, and why?"

"No kind of gag. My driver saw the domes too—and don't forget the late marshal. Pink not only saw them but touched them. All I know is that people see them and I don't. If they exist, they have a kind of existence like nothing else I've ever met."

"I'll go up there myself," I decided.

"Best thing," said Benson. "I don't know what to make of it. You can take our car." He gave me directions and I gave him a schedule of deadlines. We wanted the coroner's verdict, due today, an eyewitness story—his driver would do for that—some background stuff on the area, and a few statements from local officials.

I took his car and got to Rush City in two hours. It was an unpainted collection of dog-trot homes, set down in the big pine forest that covers all that rolling Ozark country. There was a general store that had the place's only phone. I suspected it had been kept busy by the wire services and a few enterprising newspapers. A state trooper in a flashy uniform was lounging against a fly-specked tobacco counter when I got there.

"I'm Sam Williams, from World Wireless," I said. "You come to have a look at the domes?"

"World Wireless broke that story, didn't they?" he asked me, with a look I couldn't figure out.

"We did. Our Fort Hicks stringer wired it to us."

The phone rang, and the trooper answered it. It seemed to have been a call he had placed with the governor's office.

"No, sir," he said over the phone. "No, sir. They're all sticking to the story, but I didn't see anything. I mean, they don't see them any more, but they say they were there, and now they aren't any more." A couple more "No, sirs" and he hung up.

"When did that happen?" I asked.

"About a half hour ago. I just came from there on my bike to report."

The phone rang again, and I grabbed it. It was Benson, asking for me. I told him to phone a flash and bulletin to Omaha on the disappearance and then took off to find Constable Allenby. He was a stage reuben with a nickelplated badge and a six-shooter. He cheerfully climbed into the car and guided me to the clearing.

There was a definite little path worn between Rush City and the clearing by now, but there was a disappointment at the end of it. The clearing was empty. A few small boys sticking carefully to its fringes told wildly contradictory stories about the disappearance of the domes, and I jotted down some kind of dispatch out of the most spectacular versions. I remember it involved flashes of blue fire and a smell like sulphur candles. That was all there was to it.

I drove Allenby back. By then a mobile unit from a TV network had arrived. I said hello, waited for an A.P. man to finish a dispatch on the phone, and then dictated my lead direct to Omaha. The hamlet was beginning to fill up with newsmen from the wire services, the big papers, the radio and TV nets and the newsreels. Much good they'd get out of it. The story was over—I thought. I had some coffee at the general store's two-table restaurant corner and drove back to Fort Hicks.

Benson was tirelessly interviewing by phone and firing off copy to Omaha. I told him he could begin to ease off, thanked him for his fine work, paid him for his gas, said good-by and picked up my taxi at the field. Quite a bill for waiting had been run up.

I listened to the radio as we were flying back to Omaha, and wasn't at all surprised. After baseball, the shining domes were top news. Shinging domes had been seen in twelve states. Some vibrated with a strange sound. They came in all colors and sizes. One had strange writing on it. One was transparent, and there were big green men and women inside. I caught a women's midmorning quiz show, and the M.C. kept gagging about the domes. One crack I remember was a switch on the "pointed-head" joke. He made it "dome-shaped head," and the ladies in the audience laughed until they nearly burst.

We stopped in Little Rock for gas, and I picked up a couple of afternoon papers. The domes got banner heads on both of them. One carried the World Wireless lead and had slapped in the bulletin on the disappearance of the domes. The other paper wasn't a World Wireless client, but between its other services and "special correspondents"—phone calls to the general store at Rush City—it had kept practically abreast of us. Both papers had shining-dome cartoons on their editorial pages, hastily drawn and slapped in. One paper, anti-Administration, showed the President cautiously reaching out a finger to touch the dome of the Capitol, which was rendered as a shining dome and labeled: "Shining Dome of Congressional Immunity to Executive Dictatorship." A little man labeled "Mr. and Mrs. Plain, Self-Respecting Citizens of the United States of America" was in one corner of the cartoon saying: "CAREFUL, MR. PRESIDENT! REMEMBER WHAT HAPPENED TO PINKNEY CRAWLES!!"

The other paper, pro-Administration, showed a shining dome that had the President's face. A band of fat little men in Prince Albert coats, string ties, and broad-brimmed hats labeled "Congressional Smear Artist and Hatchet-men" were creeping up on the dome with the President's face, their hands reached out as if to strangle. Above the cartoon a cut line said: "WHO'S GOING TO GET HURT?"

We landed at Omaha, and I checked into the office. Things were clicking right along. The clients were happily gobbling up our dome copy and sending wires asking for more. I dug into the morgue for the "Flying Disk" folder, and the "Huron Turtle" and the "Bayou Vampire" and a few others even further back. I spread out the old clippings and tried to shuffle and arrange them into some kind of underlying sense. I picked up the latest dispatch to come out of the tie-line printer from Western Union. It was from our man in Owosso, Michigan, and told how Mrs. Lettie Overholtzer, age sixty-one, saw a shining dome in her own kitchen at midnight. It grew like a soap bubble until it was as big as her refrigerator, and then disappeared.

I went over to the desk man and told him: "Let's have a downhold on stuff like Lettie Overholtzer. We can move a sprinkling of it, but I don't want to run this into the ground. Those things might turn up again, and then we wouldn't have any room left to play around with them. We'll have everybody's credulity used up."

He looked mildly surprised. "You mean," he asked, "there really *was* something there?"

"I don't know. Maybe. I didn't see anything myself, and the only man down there I trust can't make up his mind. Anyhow, hold it down as far as the clients let us."

I went home to get some sleep. When I went back to

work, I found the clients hadn't let us work the downhold after all. Nobody at the other wire services seemed to believe seriously that there had been anything out of the ordinary at Rush City, so they merrily pumped out solemn stories like the Lettie Overholtzer item, and wirefoto maps of locations where domes were reported, and tabulations of number of domes reported.

We had to string along. Our Washington bureau badgered the Pentagon and the A.E.C. into issuing statements, and there was a race between a navy and an air force investigating mission to see who could get to Rush City first. After they got there there was a race to see who could get the first report out. The Air Force won that contest. Before the week was out, "Domies" had appeared. they were hats for juveniles—shining-dome skull-caps molded from a transparent plastic. We had to ride with it. I'd started the mania, but it was out of hand and a long time dying down.

The World Series, the best in years, finally killed off the domes. By an unspoken agreement among the services, we simply stopped running stories every time a hysterical woman thought she saw a dome or wanted to get her name in the paper. And of course when there was no longer publicity to be had for the asking, people stopped seeing domes. There was no percentage in it. Brooklyn won the series, international tension climbed as the thermometer dropped, burglars began burgling again, and a bulky folder labeled "Domes, Shining," went into our morgue. The shining domes were history, and earnest graduate students in psychology would shortly begin to bother us with requests to borrow that folder.

The only thing that had come of it, I thought, was that we had somehow got through another summer without too much idle wire time, and that Ed Benson and I had struck up a casual correspondence.

A newsman's strange and weary year wore on. Baseball gave way to football. An off-year election kept us on the run. Christmas loomed ahead, with its feature stories and its kickers about Santa Claus, Indiana. Christmas passed, and we began to clear jolly stories about New Year hang-overs, and tabulate the great stories of the year. New Year's Day, a ghastly rat-race of covering 10 bowl games. Record snowfalls in the Great Plains and Rockies. Spring floods in Ohio and the Columbia River Valley. Twenty-one tasty Lenten menus, and Holy Week around the world. Baseball again, daylight-saving time, Mother's Day, Derby Day, the Preakness, and the Belmont Stakes.

It was about then that a disturbing letter arrived from Benson. I was concerned not about its subject matter but because I thought no sane man would write such a thing. It seemed to me that Benson was slipping his trolley. All he said was that he expected a repeat performance of the domes, or of something like the domes. He said "they" probably found the tryout a smashing success and would continue according to plan. I replied cautiously, which amused him.

He wrote back: "I wouldn't put myself out on a limb like this if I had anything to lose by it, but you know my station in life. It was just an intelligent guess, based on a study of power politics and Aesop's fables. And if it does happen, you'll find it a trifle harder to put me over, won't you?"

I guessed he was kidding me, but I wasn't certain. When people begin to talk about "them" and what "they" are doing, it's a bad sign. But, guess or not, something pretty much like domes did turn up in late July, during a crushing heat wave.

This time it was big black spheres rolling across the countryside. The spheres were seen by a Baptist congregation in central Kansas which had met in a prairie to pray for rain. About eighty Baptists took their Bible oaths that they saw large black spheres some ten feet high rolling along the prairie. They had passed within five yards of one man. The rest had run from them as soon as they could take in the fact that they really were there.

World Wireless didn't break that story, but we got on it fast enough as soon as we were tipped. Being now the recognized silly-season authority in the W. W. Central Division, I took off for Kansas.

It was much the way it had been in Arkansas. The

Baptists really thought they had seen the things—with one exception. The exception was an old gentleman with a patriarchal beard. He had been the one man who hadn't run, the man the objects passed nearest to. He was blind. He told me with a great deal of heat that he would have known all about it, blind or not, if any large spheres had rolled within five yards of him—or twenty-five, for that matter.

Old Mr. Emerson didn't go into the matter of air currents and turbulence, as Benson had. With him, it was all well below the surface. He took the position that the Lord had removed his sight, and in return had given him another sense which would do for emergency use.

"You just try me out, son!" he piped angrily. "You come stand over here, wait awhile and put your hand up in front of my face. I'll tell you when you do it, no matter how quiet you are!" He did it, too, three times, and then took me out into the main street of his little prairie town. There were several wagons drawn up before the grain elevator, and he put on a show for me by threading his way around and between them without touching once.

That—and Benson—seemed to prove that whatever the things were, they had some connection with the domes. I filed a thoughtful dispatch on the blind-man angle, and got back to Omaha to find that it had been cleared through our desk but killed in New York before relay.

We tried to give the black spheres the usual ride, but it didn't last as long. The political cartoonists tired of it sooner, and fewer old maids saw them. People got to jeering at them as newspaper hysteria, and a couple of highbrow magazines ran articles on "the irresponsible press." Only the radio comedians tried to milk the new mania as usual, but they were disconcerted to find their ratings falling. A network edict went out to kill all sphere gags. People were getting sick of them.

"It makes sense," Benson wrote to me. "An occasional exercise of the sense of wonder is refreshing, but it can't last forever. That plus the ingrained American cynicism toward all sources of public information has worked against the black spheres being greeted with the same naïve delight with which the domes were received. Nevertheless, I predict—and I'll thank you to remember that my predictions have been right so far 100 percent of the time—that next summer will see another mystery comparable to the domes and the black things. And I also predict that the new phenomenon will be imperceptible to any blind person in the immediate vicinity, if there should be any."

If, of course, he was wrong this time, it would only cut his average down to 50 per cent. I managed to wait out the year—the same interminable round I felt I could do in my sleep. Staffers got ulcers and resigned, staffers got tired and were fired, libel suits were filed and settled, one of our desk men got a Nieman Fellowship and went to Harvard, one of our telegraphers got his working hand mashed in a car door and jumped from a bridge but lived with a broken back.

In mid-August, when the weather bureau had been correctly predicting "fair and warmer" for sixteen straight days, it turned up. It wasn't anything on whose nature a blind man could provide a negative check, but it had what I had come to think of as "their" trademark.

A summer seminar was meeting outdoors, because of the frightful heat, at our own State University. Twelve trained schoolteachers testified that a series of perfectly circular pits opened up in the grass before them, one directly under the education professor teaching the seminar. They testified further that the professor, with an astonished look and a heart-rending cry, plummeted down into that perfectly circular pit. They testified further that the pits remained there for some thirty seconds and then suddenly were there no longer. The scorched summer grass was back where it had been, the pits were gone and so was the professor.

I interviewed every one of them. They weren't yokels, but intelligent men and women, all with masters' degrees, working toward their doctorates during the summers. They agreed closely on their stories, as I would expect trained and capable persons to do.

The police, however, did not expect agreement, being used to dealing with the lower I.Q. brackets. They arrested the twelve on some technical charge—"obstructing peace officers in the performance of their duties," I believe—and were going to beat the living hell out of them when an attorney arrived with twelve writs of habeas corpus. The cops' unvoiced suspicion was that the teachers had conspired to murder their professor, but nobody ever tried to explain why they'd do a thing like that.

The cops' reaction was typical of the way the public took it. Newspapers—which had reveled wildly in the shining domes story and less so in the black spheres story—were cautious. Some went overboard and gave the black pits a ride, in the old style, but they didn't pick up any sales that way. People declared that the press was insulting their intelligence, and also that they were bored with marvels.

The few papers who had played up the pits were soundly spanked in very dignified editorials printed by other sheets which played down the pits.

At World Wireless we sent out a memo to all stringers: "File no more enterpriser dispatches on black-pit story. Mail queries should be sent to regional desk if a new angle breaks in your territory." We got about ten mail queries, mostly from journalism students acting as string men, and we turned them all down. All the older hands got the pitch, and didn't bother to file it to us when the town drunk or the village old maid loudly reported that she saw a pit open up on High Street across from the drugstore. They knew it was probably untrue, and that, furthermore, nobody cared.

I wrote Benson about all this, and humbly asked him what his prediction for next summer was. He replied, obviously having the time of his life, that there would be at least one more summer phenomenon like the last three, and possibly two more—but none after that.

It's so easy now to reconstruct, with out bitterly earned knowledge!

Any youngster could whisper now of Benson: "Why, the damned fool! Couldn't anybody with the brains of a louse see that they wouldn't keep it up for two years?" One did whisper that to me the other day, when I told this story to him. And I whispered back that, far from being a damned fool, Benson was the one person on the face of the Earth, as far as I knew, who had bridged with logic the widely separated phenomena with which this reminiscence deals.

Another year passed. I gained three pounds, drank too much, rowed incessantly with my staff and got a tidy raise. A telegrapher took a swing at me midway through the office Christmas party and I fired him. My wife and kids didn't arrive in April when I expected them. I phoned Florida, and she gave me some excuse or other about missing the plane. After a few more missed planes and a few more phone calls, she got around to telling me that she didn't *want* to come back. That was okay with me. In my own intuitive way I knew that the upcoming season was more important than who stayed married to whom.

In July a dispatch arrived by wire while a new man was working the night desk. It was from Hood River, Oregon. Our stringer there reported that more than one hundred "green capsules" about fifty yards long had appeared in and around an apple orchard. The new desk man was not so new that he did not recall the downhold policy on silly-season items. He killed it, but left it on the spoke for my amused inspection in the morning. I suppose exactly the same thing happened in every wire service newsroom in the region. I rolled in at 10:30 and riffled through the stuff on the spike. When I saw the "green capsules" dispatch I tried to phone Portland, but couldn't get a connection. Then the phone buzzed and a correspondent of ours in Seattle began to yell at me, but the line went dead.

I shrugged and phoned Benson, in Fort Hicks. He was at the police station and asked me: "Is this it?"

"It is," I told him. I read him the telegram from Hood River and told him about the line trouble in Seattle.

"So," he said wonderingly, "I called the turn, didn't I?"

"Called what turn?"

"On the invaders. I don't know who they are—but it's the story of the boy who cried wolf. Only this time the wolves realized——" Then the phone went dead.

But he was right.

The people of the world were the sheep.

We newsmen—radio, TV, press and wire services—were the boy, who should have been ready to sound the alarm.

But the cunning wolves had tricked us into sounding the alarm so many times that the villagers were weary, and would not come when there was real peril.

The wolves who were then burning their way through the Ozarks, utterly without opposition—the wolves were the Martians under whose yoke and lash we now endure our miserable existences.

GOLDFISH BOWL

BY ROBERT A. HEINLEIN

On the horizon lay the immobile cloud which capped the incredible waterspouts known as the Pillars of Hawaii.

Captain Blake lowered his binoculars. "There they stand, gentlemen."

In addition to the naval personnel of the watch, the bridge of the hydrographic survey ship U. S. S. *Mahan* held two civilians; the captain's words were addressed to them. The elder and smaller of the pair peered intently through a spyglass he had borrowed from the quartermaster. "I can't make them out," he complained.

"Here—try my glasses, doctor," Blake suggested, passing over his binoculars. He turned to the officer of the deck and added, "Have the forward range finder manned, if you please, Mr. Mott." Lieutenant Mott caught the eye of the bos'n's mate of the watch, listening from a discreet distance, and jerked a thumb upward. The petty officer stepped to the microphone, piped a shrill stand-by, and the metallic voice of the loudspeaker filled the ship, drowning out the next words of the captain:

"Raaaaange *I!* Maaaaaaaan and cast loose!"

"I asked," the captain repeated, "if that was any better."

"I think I see them," Jacobson Graves acknowledged. "Two dark vertical stripes, from the cloud to the horizon."

"That's it."

The other civilian, Bill Eisenberg, had taken the telescope when Graves had surrendered it for the binoculars. "I got 'em, too," he announced. "There's nothing wrong with this 'scope, Doc. But they don't look as big as I had expected," he admitted.

"They are still beyond the horizon," Blake explained. "You see only the upper segments. But they stand just under eleven thousand feet from water line to cloud—if they are still running true to form."

Graves looked up quickly. "Why the mental reservation? Haven't they been?"

Captain Blake shrugged. "Sure. Right on the nose. But they ought not to be there at all—four months ago they did not exist. How do I know what they will be doing today—or tomorrow?"

Graves nodded. "I see your point—and agree with it. Can we estimate their height from the distance?"

"I'll see." Blake stuck his head into the charthouse. "Any reading, Archie?"

"Just a second, captain." The navigator stuck his face against a voice tube and called out, "Range!"

A muffled voice replied, "Range I—no reading."

"Something greater than twenty miles," Blake told Graves cheerfully. "You'll have to wait, doctor."

Lieutenant Mott directed the quartermaster to make three bells; the captain left the bridge, leaving word that he was to be informed when the ship approached the critical limit of three miles from the Pillars. Somewhat reluctantly,

Graves and Eisenberg followed him down; they had barely time enough to dress before dining with the captain.

Captain Blake's manners were old-fashioned; he did not permit the conversation to turn to shop talk until the dinner had reached the coffee and cigars stage. "Well, gentlemen," he began, as he lit up, "just what is it you propose to do?"

"Didn't the navy department tell you?" Graves asked with a quick look.

"Not much. I have had one letter, directing me to place my ship and command at your disposal for research concerning the Pillars, and a dispatch two days ago telling me to take you aboard this morning. No details."

Graves looked nervously at Eisenberg, then back to the captain. He cleared his throat. "Uh—we propose, captain, to go up the Kanaka column and down the Wahini."

Blake gave him a sharp look, started to speak, reconsidered, and started again. "Doctor—you'll forgive me, I hope; I don't mean to be rude—but that sounds utterly crazy. A fancy way to commit suicide."

"It may be a little dangerous—"

"Hummph!"

"—but we have the means to accomplish it, if, as we believe to be true, the Kanaka column supplies the water which becomes the Wahini column on the return trip." He outlined the method. He and Eisenberg totaled between them nearly twenty-five years of bathysphere experience, eight for Eisenberg, seventeen for himself. They had brought aboard the *Mahan*, at present in an uncouth crate on the fantail, a modified bathysphere. Externally it was a bathysphere with its anchor weights removed; internally it much more nearly resembled some of the complicated barrels in which foolhardy exhibitionists have essayed the spectacular, useless trip over Niagara Falls. It would supply air, stuffy but breatheable, for forty-eight hours; it held water and concentrated food for at least that period; there were even rude but adequate sanitary arrangements.

But its principal feature was an anti-shock harness, a glorified corset, a strait jacket, in which a man could hang suspended clear of the walls by means of a network of Gideon cord and steel springs. In it, a man might reasonably hope to survive most violent pummeling. He could perhaps be shot from a cannon, bounced down a hillside, subjected to the sadistic mercy of a baggage smasher, and still survive with bones intact and viscera unruptured.

Blake poked a finger at a line sketch with which Graves had illustrated his description. "You actually intend to try to ascend the Pillars in that?"

Eisenberg replied. "Not him, captain. Me."

Graves reddened. "My damned doctor—"

"*And* your colleagues," Eisenberg added. "It's this way, captain: There's nothing wrong with Doc's nerve, but he has a leaky heart, a pair of submarine ears, and a set of not-so-good arteries. So the Institute has delegated me to kinda watch over him."

"Now look here," Graves protested, "Bill, you're not going to be stuffy about this. I'm an old man; I'll never have another such chance."

"No go," Eisenberg denied. "Captain, I wish to inform you that the Institute vested title of record to that gear we brought aboard in me, just to keep the old war horse from doing anything foolish."

"That's your pidgin," Blake answered testily. "My instructions are to facilitate Dr. Graves' research. Assuming that one or the other of you wish to commit suicide in that steel coffin, how do you propose to enter the Kanaka Pillar?"

"Why, that's your job, captain. You put the sphere into the up column and pick it up again when it comes down the down column."

Blake pursed his lips, then slowly shook his head. "I can't do that."

"Huh? Why not?"

"I will not take my ship closer than three miles to the Pillars. The *Mahan* is a sound ship, but she is not built for speed. She can't make more than twelve knots. Some place inside that circle the surface current which feeds the Kanaka column will exceed twelve knots. I don't care to find out where, by losing my ship.

"There have been an unprecedented number of unreported fishing vessels out of the islands lately. I don't care to have the *Mahan* listed."

"You think they went up the column?"

"I do."

"But, look, captain," suggested Bill Eisenberg, "you wouldn't have to risk the ship. You could launch the sphere from a power boat."

Blake shook his head. "Out of the question," he said grimly. "Even if the ship's boats were built for the job, which they aren't, I will not risk naval personnel. This isn't war."

"I wonder," said Graves softly.

"What's that?"

Eisenberg chuckled. "Doc has a romantic notion that all the odd phenomena turned up in the past few years can be hooked together into one smooth theory with a single, sinister cause—everything from the Pillars to LaGrange's fireballs."

"LaGrange's fireballs? How could there be any connection there? They are simply static electricity, allee samee heat lightning. I know; I've seen 'em."

The scientists were at once attentive, Graves' pique and Eisenberg's amusement alike buried in truth-tropism. "You did? When? Where?"

"Golf course at Hilo. Last March. I was—"

"*That* case! That was one of the disappearance cases!"

"Yes, of course. I'm trying to tell you. I was standing in a sand trap near the thirteenth green, when I happened to look up—" A clear, balmy island day. No clouds, barometer normal, light breeze. Nothing to suggest atmospheric disturbance, no maxima of sunspots, no static on the radio. Without warning a half dozen, or more, giant fireballs—ball "lightning" on an unprecedented scale —floated across the golf course in a sort of skirmish line, a line described by some observers as mathematically even—an assertion denied by others.

A woman player, a tourist from the mainland, screamed and began to run. The flanking ball nearest her left its place in line and danced after her. No one seemed sure that the ball touched her—Blake could not say, although he had watched it happen—but when the ball had passed on, there she lay on the grass, dead.

A local medico of somewhat flamboyant reputation insisted that he found evidence in the cadaver of both coagulation and electrolysis, but the jury that sat on the case followed the coroner's advice in calling it heart failure, a verdict heartily approved by the local chamber of commerce and tourist bureau.

The man who disappeared did not try to run; his fate came to meet him. He was a caddy, a Japanese-Portygee-Kanaka mixed breed, with no known relatives, a fact which should have made it easy to leave his name out of the news reports had not a reporter smelled it out. "He was standing on the green, not more than twenty-five yards away from me," Blake recounted, "when the fireballs approached. One passed on each side of me. My skin itched, and my hair stood up. I could smell ozone. I stood still—"

"That saved you," observed Graves.

"Nuts," said Eisenberg. "Standing in the dry sand of the trap was what saved him."

"Bill, you're a fool," Grabves said wearily. "These fireball things perform with intelligent awareness."

Blake checked his account. "Why do you assume that, doctor?"

"Never mind, for the moment, please. Go on with your story."

"Hm-m-m. Well, they passed on by me. The caddy fellow was directly in the course of one of them. I don't believe he saw it—back toward it, you see. It reached him, enveloped him, passed on—but the boy was gone."

Graves nodded. "That checks with the accounts I have seen. Odd that I did not recall your name from the reports."

"I stayed in the background," Blake said shortly. "Don't like reporters."

"Hm-m-m. Anything to add to the reports that did come out? Any errors in them?"

"None that I can recall. Did the reports mention the bag

of golf clubs he was carrying?"

"I think not."

"They were found on the beach, six miles away."

Eisenberg sat up. "That's news," he said. "Tell me: Was there anything to suggest how far they had fallen? Were they smashed or broken?"

Blake shook his head. "They weren't even scratched, nor was the beach sand disturbed. But they were—ice-cold."

Graves waited for him to go on; when the captain did not do so he inquired, "What do you make of it?"

"Me? I make nothing of it."

"How do you explain it?"

"I don't. Unclassified electrical phenomena. However, if you want a rough guess, I'll give you one. This fireball is a static field of high potential. It inglobes the caddy and charges him, whereupon he bounces away like a pith ball—electrocuted, incidentally. When the charge dissipates, he falls into the sea."

"So? There was a case like it in Kansas, rather too far from the sea."

"The body might simply never have been found."

"They never are. But even so—how do you account for the clubs being deposited so gently? And why were they cold?"

"Dammit, man, *I* don't know! I'm no theoretician; I'm a maritime engineer by profession, an empiricist by disposition. Suppose you tell me."

"All right—but bear in mind that my hypothesis is merely tentative, a basis for investigation. I see in these several phenomena, the Pillars, the giant fireballs, a number of other assorted phenomena which should never have happened, but did—including the curious case of a small mountain peak south of Boulder, Colorado, which had its tip leveled off 'spontaneously'—I see in these things evidence of intelligent direction, a single conscious cause." He shrugged. "Call it the 'X' factor. I'm looking for X."

Eisenberg assumed a look of mock sympathy. "Poor old Doc," he sighed. "Sprung a leak at last."

The other two ignored the crack. Blake inquired, "You are primarily an ichthyologist, aren't you?"

"Yes."

"How did you get started along this line?"

"I don't know. Curiosity, I suppose. My boisterous young friend here would tell you that ichthyology is derived from 'icky.' "

Blake turned to Eisenberg. "But aren't *you* an ichthyologist?"

"Hell, no! I'm an oceanographer specializing in ecology."

"He's quibbling," observed Graves. "Tell Captain Blake about Cleo and Pat."

Eisenberg looked embarrassed. "They're damned nice pets," he said defensively.

Blake looked puzzled; Graves explained. "He kids me, but *his* secret shame is a pair of goldfish. Goldfish! You'll find 'em in the washbasin in his stateroom this minute."

"Scientific interest?" Blake inquired with a dead pan.

"Oh, no! He thinks they are devoted to him."

"They're damned nice pets," Eisenberg insisted. "They don't bark, they don't scratch, they don't make messes. And Cleo does so have expression!"

In spite of his initial resistance to their plans Blake cooperated actively in trying to find a dodge whereby the proposed experiment could be performed without endangering naval personnel or matériel. He liked these two; he understood their curious mixture of selfless recklessness and extreme caution; it matched his own—it was professionalism, as distinguished from economic motivation.

He offered the services of his master diver, an elderly commissioned warrant officer, and his technical crew in checking their gear. "You know," he added, "there is some reason to believe that your bathysphere could make the round trip, aside from the proposition that what goes up must come down. You know of the *VJ-14*?"

"Was that the naval plane lost in the early investigation?"

"Yes." He buzzed for his orderly. "Have my writer bring up the jacket on the *VJ-14*," he directed.

Attempts to reconnoiter the strange "permanent" cloud and its incredible waterspouts had been made by air soon after its discovery. Little was learned. A plane would penetrate the cloud. Its ignition would fail; out it would glide, unharmed, whereupon the engines would fire again. Back into the cloud—engine failure. The vertical reach of the cloud was greater than the ceiling of any plane.

"The *VJ-14*," Blake stated, referring occasionally to the file jacket which had been fetched, "made an air reconnaissance of the Pillars themselves on 12 May, attended by the U. S. S. *Pelican*. Besides the pilot and radioman she carried a cinematographer and a chief aerographer. Mm-m-m—only the last two entries seem to be pertinent: 'Changing course. Will fly between the Pillars—*14*,' and '0913—Ship does not respond to controls—*14*.' Telescopic observation from the *Pelican* shows that she made a tight upward spiral around the Kanaka Pillar, about one and a half turns, and was sucked into the column itself. Nothing was seen to fall.

"Incidentally the pilot, Lieutenant—m-m-m yes—Mattson—Lieutenant Mattson was exonerated posthumously by the court of inquiry. Oh, yes, here's the point pertinent to our question: From the log of the *Pelican*: '1709—Picked up wreckage identified as part of *VJ-14*. See additional sheet for itemized description.' We needn't bother with that. Point is, they picked it up four miles from the base of the Wahini Pillar on the side away from the Kanaka. The inference is obvious and your scheme might work. Not that you'd live through it."

"I'll chance it," Eisenberg stated.

"Mm-m-m—yes. But I was going to suggest we send up a dead load, say a crate of eggs packed into a hogshead." The buzzer from the bridge sounded; Captain Blake raised his voice toward the brass funnel of a voice tube in the overhead. "Yes?"

"Eight o'clock, captain. Eight o'clock lights and galley fires out; prisoners secured."

"Thank you, sir." Blake stood up. "We can get together on the details in the morning."

A fifty-foot motor launch bobbed listlessly astern the *Mahan*. A nine-inch coir line joined it to its mother ship; bound to it at fathom intervals was a telephone line ending in a pair of headphones worn by a signalman seated in the stern sheets of the launch. A pair of flags and a spyglass lay on the thwart beside him; his blouse had crawled up, exposing part of the lurid cover of a copy of *Dynamic Tales*, smuggled as a precaution against boredom.

Already in the boat were the coxswain, the engineman, the boat officer, Graves and Eisenberg. With them, forward in the boat, was a breaker of water rations, two fifty-gallon drums of gasoline—and a hogshead. It contained not only a carefully packed crate of eggs but also a jury-rigged smoke-signal device, armed three ways—delayed action set for eight, nine and ten hours; radio relay triggered from the ship; and simple salt-water penetration to complete an electrical circuit. The torpedo gunner in charge of diving hoped that one of them might work and thereby aid in locating the hogshead. He was busy trying to devise more nearly foolproof gear for the bathysphere.

The boat officer signaled ready to the bridge. A megaphoned bellow responded, "Pay her out handsomely!" The boat drifted slowly away from the ship and directly toward the Kanaka Pillar, three miles away.

The Kanaka Pillar loomed above them, still nearly a mile away but loweringly impressive nevertheless. The place where it disappeared in cloud seemed almost overhead, falling toward them. Its five-hundred-foot-thick trunk gleamed purplish-black, more like polished steel than water.

"Try your engine again, coxswain."

"Aye, aye, sir!" The engine coughed, took hold; the engineman eased in the clutch, the screw bit in, and the boat surged forward, taking the strain off the towline. "Slack line, sir."

"Stop your engine." The boat officer turned to his passengers. "What's the trouble, Mr. Eisenberg? Cold feet?"

"No, dammit—seasick. I *hate* a small boat."

"Oh, that's too bad. I'll see if we haven't got a pickle in that chow up forward."

"Thanks, but pickles don't help me. Never mind, I can stand it."

The boat officer shrugged, turned and let his eye travel up the dizzy length of the column. He whistled, something which he had done every time he had looked at it. Eisenberg, made nervous by his nausea, was beginning to find it cause for homicide. "*Whew!* You really intend to try to go up that thing, Mr. Eisenberg?"

"I do!"

The boat officer looked startled at the tone, laughed uneasily, and added, "Well, you'll be worse than seasick, if you ask me."

Nobody had. Graves knew his friend's temperament; he made conversation for the next few minutes.

"Try your engine, coxswain." The petty officer acknowledged, and reported back quickly:

"Starter doesn't work, sir."

"Help the engineman get a line of the flywheel. I'll take the tiller."

The two men cranked the engine over easily, but got no answering cough. "Prime it!" Still no results.

The boat officer abandoned the useless tiller and jumped down into the engine space to lend his muscle to heaving on the cranking line. Over his shoulder he ordered the signalman to notify the ship.

"Launch 3, calling bridge. Launch 3, calling bridge. Bridge—reply! Testing—testing." The signalman slipped a phone off one ear. "Phone's dead, sir."

"Get busy with your flags. Tell 'em to haul us in!" The officer wiped sweat from his face and straightened up. He glanced nervously at the current *slap-slapping* against the boat's side.

Graves touched his arm. "How about the barrel?"

"Put it over the side if you like. I'm busy. Can't you raise them, Sears?"

"I'm trying, sir."

"Come on, Bill," Graves said to Eisenberg. The two of them slipped forward in the boat, threading their way past the engine on the side away from the three men sweating over the flywheel. Graves cut the hogshead loose from its lashings, then the two attempted to get a purchase on the awkward, unhandy object. It and its light load weighed less than two hundred pounds, but it was hard to manage, especially on the uncertain footing of heaving floorboards.

They wrestled it outboard somehow, with one smashed finger for Eisenberg, a badly banged shin for Graves. It splashed heavily, drenching them with sticky salt water, and bobbed astern, carried rapidly toward the Kanaka Pillar by the current which fed it.

"Ship answers, sir!"

"Good! Tell them to haul us in—*carefully*." The boat officer jumped out of the engine space and ran forward, where he checked again the secureness with which the towline was fastened.

Graves tapped him on the shoulder. "Can't we stay here until we see the barrel enter the column?"

"No! Right now you had better pray that that line holds, instead of worrying about the barrel—or we go up the column, too. Sears, has the ship acknowledged?"

"Just now, sir."

"Why a coir line, Mr. Parker?" Eisenberg inquired, his nausea forgotten in the excitement. "I'd rather depend on steel, or even good stout Manila."

"Because coir floats, and the others don't," the officer answered snappishly. "Two miles of line would drag us to the bottom. *Sears!* Tell them to ease the strain. We're shipping water."

"Aye, aye, sir!"

The hogshead took less than four minutes to reach the column, enter it, a fact which Graves ascertained by borrowing the signalman's glass to follow it on the last leg of its trip—which action won him a dirty look from the nervous boat officer. Some minutes later, when the boat was about five hundred yards farther from the Pillar than it had been at nearest approach, the telephone came suddenly to life. The starter of the engine was tested immediately; the engine roared into action.

The trip back was made with engine running to take the

strain off the towline—at half speed and with some maneuvering, in order to avoid fouling the screw with the slack bight of the line.

The smoke signal worked—one circuit or another. The plume of smoke was sighted two miles south of the Wahini Pillar, elapsed time from the moment the vessel had entered the Kanaka column just over eight hours.

Bill Eisenberg climbed into the saddle of the exerciser in which he was to receive antibends treatment—thirty minutes of hard work to stir up his circulation while breathing an atmosphere of helium and oxygen, at the end of which time the nitrogen normally dissolved in his blood stream would be largely replaced by helium. The exerciser itself was simply on old bicycle mounted on a stationary platform. Blake looked it over. "You needn't have bothered to bring this," he remarked. "We've a better one aboard. Standard practice for diving operations these days."

"We didn't know that," Graves answered. "Anyhow, this one will do. All set, Bill?"

"I guess so." He glanced over his shoulder to where the steel bulk of the bathysphere lay, uncrated, checked and equipped, ready to be swung outboard by the boat crane. "Got the gasket-sealing compound?"

"Sure. The Iron Maiden is all right. The gunner and I will seal you in. Here's your mask."

Eisenberg accepted the inhaling mask, started to strap it on, checked himself. Graves noticed the look on his face. "What's the trouble, son?"

"Doc . . . uh—"

"Yes?"

"I say—you'll look out for Cleo and Pat, won't you?"

"Why sure. But they won't need anything in the length of time you'll be gone."

"Um-m-m, no, I suppose not. But you'll look out for 'em?"

"Sure."

"O.K.." Eisenberg slipped the inhaler over his face, waved his hand to the gunner waiting by the gas bottles.

The gunner eased open the cut-off valves, the gas lines hissed, and Eisenberg began to pedal like a six-day racer.

With thirty minutes to kill, Blake invited Graves to go forward with him for a smoke and a stroll on the fo'c's'le. They had completed about twenty turns when Blake paused by the wildcat, took his cigar from his mouth and remarked, "Do you know, I believe he has a good chance of completing the trip."

"So? I'm glad to hear that."

"Yes, I do, really. The success of the trial with the dead load convinced me. And whether the smoke gear works or not, if that globe comes back down the Wahini Pillar, *I'll find it.*"

"I know you will. It was a good idea of yours, to paint it yellow."

"Help us to spot it, all right. I don't think he'll learn anything, however. He won't see a thing through those ports but blue water, from the time he enters the column to the time we pick him up."

"Perhaps so."

"What else *could* he see?"

"I don't know. Whatever it is that *made* those Pillars, perhaps."

Blake dumped the ashes from his cigar carefully over the rail before replying. "Doctor, I don't understand you. To my mind, those Pillars are a natural, even though strange, phenomenon."

"And to me it's equally obvious that they are not 'natural.' They exhibit intelligent interference with the ordinary processes of nature as clearly as if they had a sign saying so hung on them."

"I don't see how you can say that. Obviously, they are not man-made."

"No."

"Then who did make them—if they were made?"

"I don't know."

Blake started to speak, shrugged, and held his tongue. They resumed their stroll. Graves turned aside to chuck his cigarette overboard, glancing outboard as he did so.

He stopped, stared, then called out: "Captain Blake!"

"Eh?" The captain turned and looked where Graves pointed. "Great God! Fireballs!"

"That's what I thought."

"They're some distance away," Blake observed, more to himself than to Graves. He turned decisively. "Bridge!" he shouted. "Bridge! Bridge ahoy!"

"Bridge, aye, aye!"

"Mr. Weems—pass the word: 'All hands, below decks.' Dog down all ports. Close all hatches. And close up the bridge itself! Sound the general alarm."

"Aye, aye, sir!"

"Move!" Turning to Graves, he added, "Come inside." Graves followed him; the captain stopped to dog down the door by which they entered, himself. Blake pounded up the inner ladders to the bridge, Graves in his train. The ship was filled with whine of the bos'n pipe, the raucous voice of the loud-speaker, the clomp of hurrying feet, and the monotonous, menacing *cling-cling-cling!* of the general alarm.

The watch on the bridge were still struggling with the last of the heavy glass shutters of the bridge when the captain burst into their midst. "I'll take it, Mr. Weems," he snapped. In one continous motion he moved from one side of the bridge to the other, letting his eye sweep the port side aft, the fo'c's'le, the starboard side aft, and finally rest on the fireballs—distinctly nearer and heading straight for the ship. He cursed. "Your friend did not get the news," he said to Graves. He grasped the crank which could open or close the after starboard shutter of the bridge.

Graves looked past his shoulder, saw what he meant—the afterdeck was empty, save for one lonely figure pedaling away on a stationary bicycle. The LaGrange fireballs were closing in.

The shutter stuck, jammed tight, would not open. Blake stopped trying, swung quickly to the loud-speaker control panel, and cut in the whole board without bothering to select the proper circuit. "Eisenberg! *Get below!*"

Eisenberg must have heard his name called, for he turned his head and looked over his shoulder—Graves saw distinctly—just as the fireball reached him. It passed on, and the saddle of the exerciser was empty.

The exerciser was undamaged, they found, when they were able to examine it. The rubber hose to the inhaler mask had been cut smoothly. There was no blood, no marks. Bill Eisenberg was simply gone.

"I'm going up."

"You are in no physical shape to do so, doctor."

"You are in no way responsible, Captain Blake."

"I know that. You may go if you like—after we have searched for your friend's body."

"Search be damned! I'm going up to *look* for him."

"Huh? Eh? How's that?"

"If you are right, he's dead, and there is no point in searching for his body. If I'm right, there is just an outside chance of finding him—up there!" He pointed toward the cloud cap of the Pillars.

Blake looked him over slowly, then turned to the master diver. "Mr. Hargreave, find an inhaler mask for Dr. Graves."

They gave him thirty minutes of conditioning against the caisson disease while Blake looked on with expressionless silence. The ship's company, bluejackets and officers alike, stood back and kept quiet; they walked on eggs when the Old Man had that look.

Exercise completed, the diver crew dressed Graves rapidly and strapped him into the bathysphere with dispatch, in order not to expose him too long to the nitrogen in the air. Just before the escape port was dogged down Graves spoke up. "Captain Blake."

"Yes, doctor?"

"Bill's goldfish—will you look out for them?"

"Certainly, doctor."

"Thanks."

"Not at all. Are you ready?"

"Ready."

Blake stepped forward, stuck an arm through the port of the sphere and shook hands with Graves. "Good luck." He withdrew his arm. "Seal it up."

They lowered it over the side; two motor launches nosed

it half a mile in the direction of the Kanaka Pillar where the current was strong enough to carry it along. There they left it and bucked the current back to the ship, were hoisted in.

Blake followed it with his glasses from the bridge. It drifted slowly at first, then with increased speed as it approached the base of the column. It whipped into rapid motion the last few hundred yards; Blake saw a flash of yellow just above the water line, then nothing more.

Eight hours—no plume of smoke. Nine hours, ten hours, nothing. After twenty-four hours of steady patrol in the vicinity of the Wahini Pillar, Blake radioed the Bureau.

Four days of vigilance—Blake knew that the bathysphere's passenger must be dead; whether by suffocation, drowning, implosion, or other means was not important. He so reported and received orders to proceed on duty assigned. The ship's company was called to quarters; Captain Blake read the service for the dead aloud in a harsh voice, dropped over the side some rather wilted hibiscus blooms—all that his steward could produce at the time—and went to the bridge to set his course for Pearl Harbor.

On the way to the bridge he stopped for a moment at his cabin and called his steward: "You'll find some goldfish in the stateroom occupied by Mr. Eisenberg. Find an appropriate container and place them in my cabin."

"Yes, suh, cap'n."

When Bill Eisenberg came to his senses he was in a Place.

Sorry, but no other description is suitable; it lacked features. Oh, not entirely, of course—it was not dark where he was, nor was it in a state of vacuum, nor was it cold, nor was it too small for comfort. But it did lack features to such a remarkable extent that he had difficulty in estimating the size of the place. Consider—stereo vision, by which we estimate the size of things *directly*, does not work beyond twenty feet or so. At greater distances we depend on previous knowledge of the true size of familiar objects, usually making our estimates subconsciously—a man *so high* is about *that far* away, and vice versa.

But the Place contained no familiar objects. The ceiling was a considerable distance over his head, too far to touch by jumping. The floor curved up to join the ceiling and thus prevented further lateral progress of more than a dozen paces or so. He would become aware of the obstacle by losing his balance. (He had no reference lines by which to judge the vertical; furthermore, his sense of innate balance was affected by the mistreatment his inner ears had undergone through years of diving. It was easier to sit than to walk, nor was there any reason to walk, after the first futile attempt at exploration.)

When he first woke up he stretched and opened his eyes, looked around. The lack of detail confused him. It was as if he were on the inside of a giant eggshell, illuminated from without by a soft, mellow, slightly amber light. The formless vagueness bothered him; he closed his eyes, shook his head, and opened them again—no better.

He was beginning to remember his last experience before losing consciousness—the fireball swooping down, his frenzied, useless attempt to duck, the "Hold your hats, boys!" thought that flashed through his mind in the long-drawn-out split second before contact. His orderly mind began to look for explanations. Knocked cold, he thought, and my optic nerve paralyzed. Wonder if I'm blind for good?

Anyhow, they ought not to leave him alone like this in his present helpless condition. "Doc!" he shouted. "Doc Graves!"

No answer, no echo—he became aware that there was no sound, save for his own voice, none of the random little sounds that fill completely the normal "dead" silence. This place was as silent as the inside of a sack of flour. Were his ears shot, too?

No, he had heard his own voice. At that moment he realized that he was looking at his own hands. Why, there was nothing wrong with his eyes—he could see them plainly!

And the rest of himself, too. He was naked.

It might have been several hours later, it might have been moments, when he reached the conclusion that he was dead. It was the only hypothesis which seemed to cover the facts. A dogmatic agnostic by faith, he had expected no survival after death; he had expected to go out like a light, with a sudden termination of consciousness. However, he had been subjected to a charge of static electricity more than sufficient to kill a man; when he regained awareness, he found himself without all the usual experience which makes up living. Therefore—he was dead. Q. E. D.

To be sure, he seemed to have a body, but he was acquainted with the subjective-objective paradox. He still had memory; the strongest pattern in one's memory is body awareness. This was not his body, but his detailed sensation memory of it. So he reasoned. Probably, he thought, his dream-body would slough away as his memory of the object-body faded.

There was nothing to do, nothing to experience, nothing to distract his mind. He fell asleep at last, thinking that, if this were death, it was damned dull!

He awoke refreshed, but quite hungry and extremely thirsty. The matter of dead, or not-dead, no longer concerned him; he was interested in neither theology nor metaphysics. He was hungry.

Furthermore, he experienced on awakening a phenomenon which destroyed most of the basis for his intellectual belief in his own death—it had never reached the stage of emotional conviction. Present there with him in the Place he found material objects other than himself, objects which could be seen and touched.

And eaten.

Which last was not immediately evident, for they did not look like food. There were two sorts. The first was an amorphous lump of nothing in particular, slightly greasy to the touch, and not appetizing. The second sort was a group of objects of uniform and delightful appearance. They were spheres, a couple of dozen; each one seemed to Bill Eisenberg to be a duplicate of a crystal ball he had once purchased—true Brazilian rock crystal the perfect beauty of which he had not been able to resist; he had bought it and smuggled it home to gloat over in private.

The little spheres were like that in appearance. He

touched one. It was smooth as crystal and had the same chaste coolness, but it was soft as jelly. It quivered like jelly, causing the lights within it to dance delightfully, before resuming its perfect roundness.

Pleasant as they were, they did not look like food, whereas the cheesy, soapy lump might be. He broke off a small piece, sniffed it, and tasted it tentatively. It was sour, nauseating, unpleasant. He spat it out, made a wry face, and wished heartily that he could brush his teeth. If that was food, he would have to be much hungrier—

He turned his attention back to the delightful little spheres of crystal-like jelly. He balanced them in his palms, savoring their soft, smooth touch. In the heart of each he saw his own reflection, imaged in miniature, made elfin and graceful. He became aware almost for the first time of the serene beauty of the human figure, almost any human figure, when viewed as a composition and not as a mass of colloidal detail.

But thirst became more pressing than narcissist admiration. It occurred to him that the smooth, cool spheres, if held in the mouth, might promote salivation, as pebbles will. He tried it; the sphere he selected struck against his lower teeth as he placed it in his mouth, and his lips and chin were suddenly wet, while drops trickled down his chest. The spheres were water, nothing but water, no cellophane skin, no container of any sort. Water had been delivered to him, neatly packaged, by some esoteric trick of surface tension.

He tried another, handling it more carefully to insure that it was not pricked by his teeth until he had it in his mouth. It worked; his mouth was filled with cool, pure water—too quickly; he choked. But he had caught on to the trick; he drank four of the spheres.

His thirst satisfied, he became interested in the strange trick whereby water became its own container. The spheres were tough; he could not squeeze them into breaking down, nor did smashing them hard against the floor disturb their precarious balance. They bounced like golf balls and came up for more. He managed to pinch the surface of one between thumb and fingernail. It broke down at once, and the water trickled between his fingers—water alone, no skin nor foreign substance. It seemed that a cut alone could disturb the balance of tensions; even wetting had no effect, for he could hold one carefully in his mouth, remove it, and dry it off on his own skin.

He decided that, since his supply was limited, and no more water was in prospect, it would be wise to conserve what he had and experiment no further.

The relief of thirst increased the demands of hunger. He turned his attention again to the other substance and found that he could force himself to chew and swallow. It might not be food, it might even be poison, but it filled his stomach and stayed the pangs. He even felt well fed, once he had cleared out the taste with another sphere of water.

After eating he rearranged his thoughts. He was not dead, or, if he were, the difference between living and being dead was imperceptible, verbal. O. K., he was alive. But he was shut up alone. Somebody knew where he was and was aware of him, for he had been supplied with food and drink—mysteriously but cleverly. Ergo—he was a prisoner, a word which implies a warden.

Whose prisoner? He had been struck by a LaGrange fireball and had awakened in his cell. It looked, he was forced to admit, as if Doc Graves had been right; the fireballs were intelligently controlled. Furthermore, the person or persons behind them had novel ideas as to how to care for prisoners as well as strange ways of capturing them.

Eisenberg was a brave man, as brave as the ordinary run of the race from which he sprang—a race as foolhardy as Pegingese dogs. He had the high degree of courage so common in the human race, a race capable of conceiving death, yet able to face its probability daily, on the highway, on the obstetrics table, on the battlefield, in the air, in the subway—and to face lightheartedly the certainty of death in the end.

Eisenberg was apprehensive, but not panic-stricken. His situation was decidedly interesting; he was no longer bored. If he were a prisoner, it seemed likely that his captor would come to investigate him presently, perhaps to question him, perhaps to attempt to use him in some fashion. The fact that he had been saved and not killed implied some sort of plans for his future. Very well, he would concentrate on meeting whatever exigency might come with a calm and resourceful mind. In the meantime, there was nothing he could do toward freeing himself; he had satisfied himself of that. This was a prison which would baffle Houdini—smooth continuous walls, no way to get a purchase.

He had thought once that he had a clue to escape; the cell had sanitary arrangements of some sort, for that which his body rejected went elsewhere. But he got no further with that lead; the cage was self-cleaning—and that was that. He could not tell how it was done. It baffled him.

Presently he slept again.

When he awoke, one element only was changed—the food and water had been replenished. The "day" passed without incident, save for his own busy and fruitless thoughts.

And the next "day." And the next.

He determined to stay awake long enough to find out how food and water were placed in his cell. He made a colossal effort to do so, using drastic measures to stimulate his body into consciousness. He bit his lips, he bit his tongue. He nipped the lobes of his ears violently with his nails. He concentrated on difficult mental feats.

Presently he dozed off; when he awoke, the food and water had been replenished.

The waking periods were followed by sleep, renewed hunger and thirst, the satisfying of same, and more sleep. It was after the sixth or seventh sleep that he decided that some sort of a calendar was necessary to his mental health. He had no means of measuring time except by his sleeps; he arbitrarily designated them as days. He had no means of keeping records, save his own body. He made that do. A thumbnail shred, torn off, made a rough tatooing needle. Continued scratching of the same area on his thigh produced a red welt which persisted for a day or two, and could be renewed. Seven welts made a week. The progression of such welts along ten fingers and ten toes gave him the means to measure twenty weeks—which was a much longer period than he anticipated any need to measure.

He had tallied the second set of seven thigh welts on the ring finger of his left hand when the next event occurred to disturb his solitude. When he awoke from the sleep following said tally, he became suddenly and overwhelmingly aware that he was not alone!

There was a human figure sleeping beside him. When he had convinced himself that he was truly wide awake—his dreams were thoroughly populated—he grasped the figure by the shoulder and shook it. "Doc!" he yelled. "Doc! Wake up!"

Graves opened his eyes, focused them, sat up, and put out his hand. "Hi, Bill," he remarked. "I'm damned glad to see you."

"Doc!" He pounded the older man on the back. "Doc! For Criminy sake! You don't know how glad *I* am to see *you*."

"I can guess."

"Look, Doc—where have you been? How did you get here? Did the fireballs snag you, too?"

"One thing at a time, son. Let's have breakfast." There was a double ration of food and water on the "floor" near them. Graves picked up a sphere, nicked it expertly, and drank it without losing a drop. Eisenberg watched him knowingly.

"You've been here for some time."

"That's right."

"Did the fireballs get you the same time they got me?"

"No." He reached for the food. "I came up the Kanaka Pillar."

"What!"

"That's right. Matter of fact, I was looking for you."

"The hell you say!"

"But I do say. It looks as if my wild hypothesis was right; the Pillars and the fireballs are different manifestations of the same cause—X!"

It seemed almost possible to hear the wheels whir in Eisenberg's head. "But, Doc . . . look here, Doc, that means your whole hypothesis was correct. Somebody *did* the whole thing. Somebody has us locked up here now."

"That's right." He munched slowly. He seemed tired, older and thinner than the way Eisenberg remembered him. "Evidence of intelligent control. Always was. No other explanation."

"But *who*?"

"Ah!"

"Some foreign power? Are we up against something utterly new in the way of an attack?"

"Hummph! Do you think the Japs, for instance, would bother to serve us water like *this*?" He held up one of the dainty little spheres.

"Who, then?"

"I wouldn't know. Call'em Martians—that's a convenient way to think of them."

"Why Martians?"

"No reason. I said that was a convenient way to think of them."

"Convenient how?"

"Convenient because it keeps you from thinking of them as human beings—which they obviously aren't. Nor animals. Something very intelligent, but not animals, because they are smarter than we are. Martians."

"But . . . but— Wait a minute. Why do you assume that your X people aren't human? Why not humans who have a lot of stuff on the ball that we don't have? New scientific advances?"

"That's a fair question," Graves answered, picking his teeth with a forefinger. "I'll give you a fair answer. Because in the present state of world peace and good feeling we know pretty near where all the best minds are and what they are doing. Advances like these couldn't be hidden and would be a long time in developing. X indicates evidence of half a dozen different lines of development that are clearly beyond our ken and which would require years of work by dozens of researchers, to say the very least. *Ipso facto*, nonhuman science.

"Of course," he continued, "if you want to postulate a mad scientist and a secret laboratory, I can't argue with you. But I'm not writing Sunday supplements."

Bill Eisenberg kept very quiet for some time, while he considered what Graves said in the light of his own experience. "You're right, Doc," he finally admitted. "Shucks—you're usually right when we have an argument. It has to be Martians. Oh, I don't mean inhabitants of Mars; I mean some form of intelligent life from outside this planet."

"Maybe."

"But you just said so!"

"No, I said it was a convenient way to look at it."

"But it has to be, by elimination."

"Elimination is a tricky line of reasoning."

"What else could it be?"

"Mm-m-m. I'm not prepared to say just what I do think—yet. But there are stronger reasons than we have mentioned for concluding that we are up against nonhumans. Psychological reasons."

"What sort?"

"X doesn't treat prisoners in any fashion that arises out of human behavior patterns. Think it over."

They had a lot to talk about; much more than X, even though X was a subject they were bound to return to. Graves gave Bill a simple bald account of how he happened to go up the Pillar—an account which Bill found very moving for what was left out, rather than told. He felt suddenly very humble and unworthy as he looked at his elderly, frail friend. "Doc, you don't look well."

"I'll do."

"That trip up the Pillar was hard on you. You shouldn't have tried it."

Graves shrugged. "I made out all right." But he had not, and Bill could see that he had not. The old man was "poorly."

They slept and they ate and they talked and they slept again. The routine that Eisenberg had grown used to alone continued, save with company. But Graves grew no stronger.

"Doc, it's up to us to do something about it."

"About what?"

"The whole situation. This thing that has happened to us is an intolerable menace to the whole human race. We don't know what may have happened down below—"

"Why do you say 'down below'?"

"Why, you came up the Pillar."

"Yes, true—but I don't know when or how I was taken out of the bathysphere, nor where they may have taken me. But go ahead. Let's have your idea."

"Well, but—O. K.—we don't know what may have happened to the rest of the human race. The fireballs may be picking them off one at a time, with no chance to fight back and no way of guessing what has been going on. We have some idea of the answer. It's up to us to escape and warn them. There may be some way of fighting back. It's our duty; the whole future of the human race may depend on it."

Graves was silent so long after Bill had finished his tocsin that Bill began to feel embarrassed, a bit foolish. But when he finally spoke it was to agree. "I think you are right, Bill. I think it quite possible that you are right. Not necessarily, but distinctly possible. And that possibility does place an obligation on us to all mankind. I've known it. I knew it before we got into this mess, but I did not have enough data to justify shouting, 'Wolf!'

"The question is," he went on, "how can we give such a warning—now?"

"We've got to escape!"

"Ah!"

"There *must* be some way."

"Can you suggest one?"

"Maybe. We haven't been able to find any way in or out of this place, but there must be a way—has to be; we were brought in. Furthermore, our rations are put inside every day—somehow. I tried once to stay awake long enough to see how it was done, but I fell asleep—"

"So did I."

"Uh-huh. I'm not surprised. But there are two of us now; we could take turns, watch on and watch off, until something happened."

Graves nodded. "It's worth trying."

Since they had no way of measuring the watches, each kept the vigil until sleepiness became intolerable, then awakened the other. But nothing happened. Their food ran out, was not replaced. They conserved their water balls with care, were finally reduced to one, which was not drunk because each insisted on being noble about it—the other must drink it! But still no manifestation of any sort from their unseen captors.

After an unmeasured and unestimated length of time—but certainly long, almost intolerably long—at a time when Eisenberg was in a light, troubled sleep, he was suddenly awakened by a touch and the sound of his name. He sat up, blinking, disoriented. "Who? What? Wha'sa matter?"

"I must have dozed off," Graves said miserably. "I'm sorry, Bill." Eisenberg looked where Graves pointed. Their food and water had been renewed.

Eisenberg did not suggest a renewal of the experiment. In the first place, it seemed evident that their keepers did not intend for them to learn the combination to their cell and were quite intelligent enough to outmaneuver their necessarily feeble attempts. In the second place, Graves was an obviously sick man; Eisenberg did not have the heart to suggest another long, grueling, half-starved vigil.

But, lacking knowledge of the combination, it appeared impossible to break jail. A naked man is a particularly helpless creature; lacking materials wherewith to fashion tools, he can do little. Eisenberg would have swapped his chances for eternal bliss for a diamond drill, an acetylene torch, or even a rusty, secondhand chisel. Without tools of some sort it was impressed on him that he stood about as much chance of breaking out of his cage as his goldfish, Cleo and Patra, had of chewing their way out of a glass bowl.

"Doc."

"Yes, son."

"We've tackled this the wrong way. We know that X is

intelligent; instead of trying to escape, we should be trying to establish communication."

"How?"

"I don't know. But there must be *some* way."

But if there was, he could never conjure it up. Even if he assumed that his captors could see and hear him, how was he to convey intelligence to them by word or gesture? Was it theoretically possible for any nonhuman being, no matter how intelligent, to find a pattern of meaning in human speech symbols, if he encountered them without context, without background, without pictures, with *pointing*? It is certainly true that the human race, working under much more favorable circumstances, has failed almost utterly to learn the languages of the other races of animals.

What should he do to attract their attention, stimulate their interest? Recite the "Gettysburg Address"? Or the multiplication table? Or, if he used gestures, would deaf-and-dumb language mean any more, or any less, to his captors than the sailor's hornpipe?

"Doc."

"What is it, Bill?" Graves was sinking; he rarely initiated a conversation these "days."

"Why are we here? I've had it in the back of my mind that *eventually* they would take us out and do something with us. Try to question us, maybe. But it doesn't look like they meant to."

"No, it doesn't."

"Then why are we here? Why do they take care of us?"

Graves paused quite a long time before answering: "I think that they are expecting us to reproduce."

"What!"

Graves shrugged.

"But that's ridiculous."

"Surely. But would they know it?"

"But they are intelligent."

Graves chuckled, the first time he had done so in many sleeps. "Do you know Roland Young's little verse about the flea:

'A funny creature is the Flea
You cannot tell the She from He.
But *He* can tell—and so can *She*.'

"After all, the visible differences between men and women are quite superficial and almost negligible—except to men and women!"

Eisenberg found the suggestion repugnant, almost revolting; he struggled against it. "But look, Doc—even a little study would show them the human race is divided up into sexes. After all, we aren't the first specimens they've studied."

"Maybe they don't study us."

"Huh?"

"Maybe we are just—pets."

Pets! Bill Eisenberg's morale had stood up well in the face of danger and uncertainty. This attack on it was more subtle. Pets! He had thought of Graves and himself as prisoners of war, or, possibly, objects of scientific research. But pets!

"I know how you feel," Graves went on, watching his face. "It's . . . it's *humiliating* from an anthropocentric viewpoint. But I think it may be true. I may as well tell you my own private theory as to the possible nature of X, and the relation of X to the human race. I haven't up to now, as it is almost sheer conjecture, based on very little data. But it does cover the known facts.

"I conceive of the X creatures as being just barely aware of the existence of men, unconcerned by them, and almost completely uninterested in them."

"But they hunt us!"

"Maybe. Or maybe they just pick us up occasionally by accident. A lot of men have dreamed about an impingement of nonhuman intelligences on the human race. Almost without exception the dream has taken one of two forms, invasion and war, or exploration and mutual social intercourse. Both concepts postulate that nonhumans are enough like us either to fight with us or talk to us—treat us as equals, one way or the other.

"I don't believe that X is sufficiently interested in human beings to want to enslave them, or even exterminate them. They may not even study us, even when we come under their notice. They may lack the scientific spirit in the sense of having a monkeylike curiosity about everything that moves. For that matter, how thoroughly do *we* study other life forms? Did you ever ask your goldfish for their views on goldfish poetry or politics? Does a termite think that a woman's place is in the home? Do beavers prefer blondes or brunettes?"

"You are joking."

"No, I'm not. Maybe the life forms I mentioned don't have such involved ideas. My point is: if they did, or do, we'd never guess it. I don't think X conceives of the human race as intelligent."

Bill chewed this for a while, then added: "Where do you think they came from, Doc? Mars, maybe? Or clear out of the Solar System?"

"Not necessarily. Not even probably. It's my guess that they came from the same place we did—*from up out of the slime of this planet.*"

"Really, Doc—"

"I mean it. And don't give me that funny look. I may be sick, but I'm not balmy. *Creation took eight days!*"

"Huh?"

"I'm using biblical language. 'And God blessed them, and God said unto them, Be fruitful and multiply, and replenish the earth, and subdue it: and have dominion over the fish of the sea, and over the fowl of the air, and over every living thing that moveth upon the earth.' And so it came to pass. But nobody mentioned the stratosphere."

"Doc—are you sure you feel all right?"

"Dammit—quit trying to psychoanalyze me! I'll drop the allegory. What I mean is: We aren't the latest nor the highest stage in evolution. First the oceans were populated. The lungfish to amphibian, and so on up, until the continents were populated, and, in time, man ruled the surface of the earth—or thought he did. But did evolution stop there? I think not. Consider—from a fish's point of view air is a hard vacuum. From our point of view the upper reaches of the atmosphere, sixty, seventy, maybe a hundred thousand feet up, seem like a vacuum and unfit to sustain life. But it's not vacuum. It's thin, yes, but there is matter there and radiant energy. Why not life, intelligent life, highly evolved as it would have to be—but evolved from the same ancestry as ourselves and fish? We wouldn't see it happen; man hasn't been aware, in a scientific sense, that long. When our granddaddies were swinging in the trees, it had already happened."

Eisenberg took a deep breath. "Just wait a minute, Doc. I'm not disputing the theoretical possibility of your thesis, but it seems to me it is out on direct evidence alone. We've never seen them, had no direct evidence of them. At least, not until lately. And we *should* have seen them."

"Not necessarily. Do ants see men? I doubt it."

"Yes—but, consarn it, a man has better eyes than an ant."

"Better eyes for what? For his own needs. Suppose the X creatures are too high up, or too tenuous, or too fast-moving for us to notice them. Even a thing as big and as solid and as slow as an airplane can go up high enough to pass out of sight, even on a clear day. If X is tenuous and even semi-transparent, we never *would* see them—not even as occultations of stars, or shadows against the moon—though as a matter of fact there have been some very strange stories of just that sort of thing."

Eisenberg got up and stomped up and down. "Do you mean to suggest," he demanded, "that creatures so insubstantial they can float in a soft vacuum built the Pillars?"

"Why not? Try explaining how a half-finished, naked embryo like *homo sapiens* built the Empire State Building."

Bill shook his head. "I don't get it."

"You don't try. Where do you think *this* came from?" Graves held up one of the miraculous little water spheres. "My guess is that life on this planet is split three ways, with almost no intercourse between the three. Ocean culture, land culture, and another—call it stratoculture. Maybe a fourth, down under the crust—but we don't know. We know a little about life under the sea, because we are curious. But how much do they know of us? Do a few dozen bathysphere descents constitute an invasion? A fish that sees our bathysphere might go home and take to his bed with a sick headache, but he wouldn't talk about it, and he wouldn't be believed if he did. If a lot of fish see us and swear out affidavits, along comes a fish-psychologist and explains it as mass hallucination.

"No, it takes something at least as large and solid and permanent as the Pillars to have any effect on orthodox conceptions. Casual visitations have no real effect."

Eisenberg let his thoughts simmer for some time before commenting further. When he did, it was half to himself. "I don't believe it. I won't believe it!"

"Believe what?"

"Your theory. Look, Doc—if you are right, don't you see what it means? We're helpless, we're outclassed."

"I don't think they will bother much with human beings. They haven't, up till now."

"But that isn't it. Don't you see? We've had some dignity as a race. We've striven and accomplished things. Even when we failed, we had the tragic satisfaction of knowing that we were, nevertheless, superior and more able than the other animals. We've had faith in the race—we would accomplish great things yet. But if we are just one of the lower animals ourselves, what does our great work amount to? Me, I couldn't go on pretending to be a 'scientist' if I thought I was just a fish, mucking around in the bottom of a pool. My work wouldn't *signify* anything."

"Maybe it doesn't."

"No, maybe it doesn't." Eisenberg got up and paced the constricted area of their prison. "Maybe not. But I won't surrender to it. I *won't*! Maybe you're right. Maybe you're wrong. It doesn't seem to matter very much *where* the X people came from. One way or the other, they are a threat to our own kind. Doc, we've got to get out of here and warn them!"

"How?"

Graves was comatose a large part of the time before he died. Bill maintained an almost continuous watch over him, catching only occasional cat naps. There was little he could do for his friend, even though he did watch over him, but the spirit behind it was comfort to them both.

But he was dozing when Graves called his name. He woke at once, though the sound was a bare whisper. "Yes, Doc?"

"I can't talk much more, son. Thanks for taking care of me."

"Shucks, Doc."

"Don't forget what you're here for. Some day you'll get a break. Be ready for it and don't muff it. People have to be warned."

"I'll do it, Doc. I swear it."

"Good boy." And then, almost inaudibly, "G'night, son."

Eisenberg watched over the body until it was quite cold and had begun to stiffen. Then, exhausted by his long vigil and emotionally drained, he collapsed into a deep sleep. When he woke up the body was gone.

It was hard to maintain his morale, after Graves was gone. It was all very well to resolve to warn the rest of mankind at the first possible chance, but there was the endless monotony to contend with. He had not even the relief from boredom afforded the condemned prisoner—the checking off of limited days. Even his "calendar" was nothing but a counting of his sleeps.

He was not quite sane much of the time, and it was the twice-tragic insanity of intelligence, aware of its own instability. He cycled between periods of elation and periods of extreme depression, in which he would have destroyed himself, had he the means.

During the periods of elation he made great plans for fighting against the X creatures—after he escaped. He was not sure how or when, but, momentarily, he was sure. He would lead the crusade himself; Diesel-motored planes could withstand the dead zone of the Pillars and the cloud; heavy artillery could destroy the dynamic balance of the

Pillars. They would harry them and hunt them down; the globe would once again be the kingdom of man, to whom it belonged.

During the bitter periods of relapse he would realize clearly that the puny engineering of mankind, Diesel engines or no, would be of no force against the powers and knowledge of the creatures who built the Pillars, who kidnaped himself and Graves in such a casual and mysterious fashion. They were outclassed. Could codfish plan a sortie against the city of Boston? Would it matter if the chattering monkeys in Guatemala passed a resolution to destroy the British navy?

They were outclassed. The human race had reached its highest point—the point at which it began to be aware that it was not the highest race, and the knowledge was death to it, one way or the other—the mere knowledge alone, even as the knowledge was now destroying him, Bill Eisenberg, himself. Eisenberg—*homo piscis.* Poor fish!

His overstrained mind conceived a means by which he might possibly warn his fellow beings. He could not escape as long as his surroundings remained unchanged. That was established and he accepted it; he no longer paced his cage. But certain things *did* leave his cage: left-over food, refuse—and Graves' body. If he died, his own body would be removed, he felt sure. Some, at least, of the things which had gone up the Pillars had come down again—he knew that. Was it not likely that the X creatures disposed of any heavy mass for which they had no further use by dumping it down the Wahini Pillar? He convinced himself that it was so.

Very well, his body would be returned to the surface, eventually. How could he use it to give a message to his fellow men, if it were found? He had no writing materials, nothing but his own body.

But the same make-do means which served him as a calendar gave him a way to write a message. He could make welts on his skin with a shred of thumbnail. If the same spot were irritated over and over again, not permitted to heal, scar tissue would form. By such means he was able to create permanent tattooing.

The letters had to be large; he was limited in space to the fore part of his body; involved argument was impossible. He was limited to a fairly simple warning. If he had been quite right in his mind, perhaps he would have been able to devise a more cleverly worded warning—but then he was not.

In time, he had covered his chest and belly with cicatrix tatooing worthy of a bushman chief. He was thin by then and of an unhealthy color; the welts stood out plainly.

His body was found floating in the Pacific, by Portuguese who could not read the message, but who turned it in to the harbor police of Honolulu. They, in turn, photographed the body, fingerprinted it, and disposed of it. The fingerprints were checked in Washington, and William Eisenberg, scientist, fellow of many distinguished societies, and high type of *homo sapiens*, was officially dead for the second time, with a new mystery attached to his name.

The cumbersome course of official correspondence unwound itself and the record of his reappearance reached the desk of Captain Blake, at a port in the South Atlantic. Photographs of the body were attached to the record, along with a short official letter telling the captain that, in view of his connection with the case, it was being provided for his information and recommendation.

Captain Blake looked at the photographs for the dozenth time. The message told in scar tissue was plain enough: "BEWARE—CREATION TOOK EIGHT DAYS." But what did it mean?

Of one thing he was sure—Eisenberg had not had those scars on his body when he disappeared from the *Mahan*.

The man had lived for a considerable period after he was grabbed up by the fireball—that was certain. And he had learned something. What? The reference to the first chapter of Genesis did not escape him; it was not such as to be useful.

He turned to his desk and resumed making a draft in painful longhand of his report to the bureau. "—the message in scar tissue adds to the mystery, rather than clarifying it. I am now forced to the opinion that the Pillars and the LaGrange fireballs are connected in some way. The patrol around the Pillars should not be relaxed. If new opportunities or methods for investigating the nature of the Pillars should develop, they should be pursued thoroughly. I regret to say that I have nothing of the sort to suggest—"

He got up from his desk and walked to a small aquarium supported by gimbals from the inboard bulkhead, and stirred up the two goldfish therein with a forefinger. Noticing the level of the water, he turned to the pantry door. "Johnson, you've filled this bowl too full again. Pat's trying to jump out again!"

"I'll fix it, captain." The steward came out of the pantry with a small pan. ("Don't know why the Old Man keeps these tarnation fish. He ain't interested in 'em—*that's* certain.") Aloud he added: "That Pat fish don't want to stay in there, captain. Always trying to jump out. And he don't *like* me, captain."

"What's that?" Captain Blake's thoughts had already left the fish; he was worrying over the mystery again.

"I say that fish don't *like* me, captain. Tries to bite my finger every time I clean out the bowl."

"Don't be silly, Johnson."

IN VALUE DECEIVED

BY H. B. FYFE

What is valuable? That will depend on the nature of the planetary civilization of which one is a part. In this story we see through the eyes of a strange but highly intelligent life-form a picture of how two utterly dissimilar civilizations are forced by their own needs to establish completely different sets of values for various commodities, techniques, and inventions. One man's meat is another man's sawdust; in the world of the Galaxy you never can be sure what will be valueless and what will turn out to be worth more than fine jewels. . .

Rylat was quite disappointed at the barrenness of the planet. At that, it was the only one circling the small white star in Sector Twelve that had offered any hope at all.

"Things are as bleak as at home on Olittra," he thought to Akyro. "Nothing growing but a few creepers and moss. No wonder, with the dim light."

He shifted his four eyestalks so as to examine the shallow hills shown on the telescreen. From above the surface, no life had been discernible. They had made the landing only on the strength of Akyro's detection of radiation. That might have meant habitation, which seldom appeared without some form of agriculture.

"It could have been artificial," Akyro had thought in mild hope, raising his tapering, dull-blue body to the flat tips of his eight walking legs.

Seeing the surface at close range, however, he now lost his enthusiasm.

"You look it over," he thought to Rylat. "I'm hungry."

He opened a locker and removed a chunk of synthetic food and a plastic tube of liquid. He manipulated the grayish chunk between two of his tiny eating legs, using the other pair to squirt a drink into his mouth at intervals.

"How can you enjoy that awful stuff?" demanded Rylat in some annoyance. "And how will you like it if we go outside and you get sick in your vacuum suit?"

"One must replenish his energy," replied Akyro contentedly.

Rylat thought a red flame.

"You are nearly as broad as long already," he added.

Before he could invent further caustic ideas, Akyro dropped his food to the plastic deck and waddled hastily to the bank of detector instruments. They were his specialty, upon which he always had at least one eye trained.

"Something?" inquired Rylat.

"Approaching radiation," Akyro answered. "A ship, perhaps."

He worked over his dials, then gave Rylat coordinates for his telescreen. His guess proved correct; it was a spaceship. Not one from Olittra, certainly, to judge by the elongated lines. It cruised close above the surface.

"Only one," announced Akyro. "Shall we signal it down?"

"No harm," Rylat agreed.

He crept over to the piloting bench and pushed certain levers. A series of flares shot up into the thinner part of the planet's shallow atmosphere, there to explode into a standard greeting in Galactic Code.

The other ship leaped straight away from the surface, at considerable acceleration. Then, as the flares were recognized for a peaceful message, it headed more slowly toward the grounded ship. Rylat gestured approvingly.

"If they can maneuver like that, they must be quite advanced. Perhaps they know the location of uninhabited planets where we can obtain plant life for our sterile lands."

Akyro, intent upon translating the answering flares from the other vessel, made no comment. He analyzed the pattern of radiation to check his visual perception—not all beings in the known Galaxy saw the same images from the same stimuli.

"Send them our home identification," he told Rylat. "They say they come from a star in Sector . . . Fourteen, I think. Yes, here it is in the list—Sol, Class G, nine major planets, one dominant race inhabiting three planets, members Sector Fourteen Confederation, rating 'civilized.' "

"What are they doing over here in Twelve?"

"Let us not be impolite," reproved Akyro. "They may be wondering the same about us."

Rylat thought a bad taste at him, but halfheartedly, for he recognized the justice of the reproof.

"Well, I shall invite them down to meet us," he thought back. "See about unpacking a shelter assembly, in case they come out wearing something clumsy."

Sometime later, they watched the port of the other ship open, after a landing that met with Rylat's approval. Since they had set up the shelter on the dimly lit, sandy soil a few lengths from their ship, and did not know how well the visitors could see, he lit a portable light-tube to show the location.

Two of the strangers presently bounded across the irregular ground. They had four large limbs apiece, two of which were sufficient for locomotion. Rylat considered their vacuum suits and personal equipment well made but unnecessarily prettified. He saw no working parts, which suggested added weight to conceal them.

"Notice how easily they run," he observed to Akyro. "They must come from a fairly large, solid planet."

When the Solarians arrived, Rylat invited them by gestures to enter the temporary shelter. Akyro had a heat converter operating, producing as a waste product an atmosphere breathable by the Olittrans. The latter opened the head ends of their suits.

The larger Solarian resorted to the Galactic Gesture Code to express appreciation of the shelter. His vacuum suit was topped by a globular fixture, partly transparent, behind which Rylat could see what must be the creature's face.

There were various rudimentary features, but no small limbs about the mouth. Rylat could not imagine how the Solarian fed himself. The single pair of eyes were further limited by being set immovably in the head.

Yet, Rylat reflected, these beings had obviously overcome such handicaps. Their equipment was, if anything, superior to his own. He decided they must be quite intelligent.

"What does he want to know?" inquired Akyro, as his companion replied to the Solarian's next gestures.

"He was surprised that we set up the shelter in so short a time, and wanted to know what the heat converter is."

"Maybe it is new to them," suggested Akyro.

"I doubt it, for they seemed to lose interest when I explained the principle and how one can produce any element at all as waste."

"Have they identified themselves?"

Rylat went through a series of formal gestures with one

of his forelegs. The Solarian answered in kind.

"The one with the reddish fur on top is called 'Clothmaker,' or perhaps 'Weaver' would be closer. The other is named 'Strong-foreleg' as nearly as I can translate."

He proceeded to exchange general information with the Solarian. The smaller one, meanwhile, inspected the shelter curiously. He showed interest in the system for supporting the dome with the pressure of the enclosed atmosphere, and made rough gestures to Akyro to indicate admiration for the simple but effective entrance chamber. He did not pay any further attention to the heat converter, apparently taking it for granted after the first explanation.

From the conversation between Rylat and the Weaver, it developed that the Solarians were also a form of oxygen-breathing life, but that they required much denser air than their hosts. Rylat reported that they acted rather like traders. When he told the Weaver that he and Akyro were merely on an exploring expedition, the Solarian amended his business offer to a suggestion that they exchange souvenirs.

"Perhaps they could tell us of some planet such as we seek," Akyro thought to Rylat.

"I judge it unwise for us to seem overcurious. They might demand some fantastic reward if we reveal the necessity of our finding new plant stocks."

"But that would hardly be ethical," protested Akyro.

Rylat thought a stupid, newly hatched cub, and told Akyro that he was always too trusting with alien beings. "Time enough," he suggested, "to worry about ethics when we are acquainted. Besides," he added, "the Weaver has invited us to see their ship. We should learn what they are like."

They left the shelter one by one. The Solarians, being considerably larger, squeezed gingerly through the exit. Then they led the way to their own ship, moderating their pace politely to accommodate the Olittrans.

The Solarian ship fulfilled the promise of the equipment of its crew. Good workmanship was the rule in the section into which they were guided. Rylat was surprised at the luxury that permitted a division of the living and piloting quarters.

"But then," he reflected, "they are traders and doubtless can afford to waste materials on such refinements."

"What does he think?" inquired Akyro as the Weaver made a series of code gestures to Rylat.

"He invites us to inspect samples of their cargo. I fear he still believes us willing to trade something."

Out of politeness, they permitted the red-topped Solarian to lead them to another compartment. Here he displayed various wares. The Olittrans noted that the Solarian objects ran mostly to gadgets and precision instruments, while things they had obtained by trading were in many cases minerals. The Weaver displayed with strange pride some large chunks of white carbon crystals and small quantities of some of the heavier elements. Those which radiated were kept in shielded containers.

Rylat did not blame him for that. He himself had once incurred a severe rash on his thick hide when he had left too much uranium—a waste product from a heat converter—lying around outside his shelter. The Solarians, without their vacuum suits, looked unpleasantly thin-skinned. He could actually see outlines of a circulatory system right through the Weaver's hide.

"There is little here to attract us," he thought to Akyro.

"True," the other agreed. "Their workmanship is very fine, but our own instruments are adequate. As for the minerals, we could make up any quantity of those in a short time."

"I shall not tell them exactly that," decided Rylat.

"Why not?"

"Oh . . . it would hardly be polite."

He indicated to the Weaver that it was time for them to return to their own ship, at least temporarily, to check its mechanisms and to replenish the tanks of their vacuum suits.

As they passed forward through the living quarters, Rylat glanced with one eye at a flat-topped piece of furniture upon which the other Solarian was setting out food and drink. This included, he noted half unconsciously, a portion of an obviously synthetic substance, but also a number of what looked like vegetables. In fact, one platter held a heap of untreated white stalks with green leaves.

The idea came to Rylat that these must be raw and fresh plants, grown recently; and he turned another eye upon them.

Grown recently!

The realization smote him with almost physical force. His eyestalks retracted halfway before he could control himself, and his walking legs involuntarily bowed in the vestige of a crouch.

Akyro noticed this evidence of excitement, a holdover from primitive times when the best physical defense of their remote ancestors had been to flatten themselves to the ground and rely upon their thick, armorlike hides.

"What is the trouble?" he asked.

"Look at the food!"

Akyro looked, and *his* eyestalks twitched.

"A fresh plant! Quickly—ask them where they got it!"

Rylat controlled himself with an effort. The red-thatched Weaver had turned his head at the Olittrans' hesitation, and was training both eyes curiously upon them.

"Pay no attention to it," Rylat ordered his companion. "And come along! He notices our actions."

"For your love of posterity!" Akyro insisted. "Ask him where he got it! *Ask him!*"

"Later," Rylat thought to him, moving toward the exit port between that compartment and the piloting chamber forward.

Akyro bounced irritably on his walking legs and stared back at the foodstuffs with three of his eyes.

"Do not be a fool!" he urged. "Do you realize what it may mean to us? Since the blight struck Olittra, and with the population what it is? We were not sent to pick up pretty crystals, you know!"

"You need not be sarcastic," retorted Rylat. "I know our mission as well as you, but I have also heard about these races proficient in trading. I know what I am doing."

"Are you sure?"

"Of course! Now stop acting mentally deficient and follow!"

Akyro thought a bottomless swamp of sticky ooze—but quietly, to himself—and followed the others to the exit.

The little Solarian politely donned a vacuum suit to see them safely through the outer valve. Rylat gestured that they would return before long, and led the way across the sand.

Back in their own vessel, after a routine check and a brief rest period, Akyro put a record of the Galactic Gesture Code on the visiplayer for a thorough review. Consequently, he was able to catch some inkling of the conversation when next they called at the Solarian ship.

He was still sufficiently uncertain of the motions to make any communications himself, but he understood the Weaver's greeting and opening remarks.

The Solarians, it developed, had stopped at this star only in search of barter. They were as disappointed with it, in their way, as were the Olittrans.

"We, also, were passing and stopped out of curiosity," Rylat signaled. "But we are merely explorers."

"Traders such as we," waved the Weaver, "often must be their own explorers."

"That is interesting," Rylat told him. "Perhaps you would describe for me how a trading expedition operates."

Akyro was annoyed.

"Why make yourself a simpleton?" he asked Rylat.

His companion briefly thought a set of eyestalks tied in a knot, and continued his gesture talk. The Solarian explained that it was not always necessary to obtain something more valuable than what one gave for it.

"Sometimes," he indicated, "the mere act of transporting an object to a different planetary system increases its value enormously. It may be rare or peculiarly useful there."

"It seems to me close to cheating," thought Akyro, but his thought was ignored.

"Well, of course, I would not understand these matters," Rylat informed the Solarian.

The Weaver gaped at him a moment with small blue

eyes, then turned to Strong-foreleg. The two Solarians exchanged a series of oral vibrations which apparently served for communication with them. After a little discussion, the Weaver turned his red-furred head again to Rylat.

"Perhaps, for luck or amusement or what you will, we might make some token exchange. It would provide us with souvenirs of this meeting."

Rylat expressed willingness. There followed rather floundering attempts on both sides to suggest something desirable to the opposite parties.

The Solarians regretfully declined any of the Olittran instruments that Rylat thought he could spare, apologizing that their own were satisfactory. Nor did Rylat profess any interest in the Solarians' knick-knacks, picked up on half a dozen worlds lately visited.

"But we have some very good maps of Sector Eleven," he offered in his turn.

The Weaver thanked him, but the Solarians did not plan to travel in that direction. In the end, he suggested that they visit his cargo compartments again.

"Ask him about the plants!" Akyro urged.

"How can I?" Rylat thought back. "What have we to offer for such information? They will surely want something!"

"Well, if you refuse to ask him, I shall stay here and watch to see if his friend brings out any more of them."

"As you please," answered Rylat, and followed the Weaver from the compartment.

They walked along a metal-decked corridor to the same storeroom of samples that Rylat had seen earlier. He found nothing new that interested him, and was careful to make this fact diplomatically clear to the Solarian.

During the process, he felt Akyro calling him, and so he indicated as soon as possible a desire to rejoin the others.

"They grow them themselves!" his friend greeted him as he entered the living quarters with the Weaver.

"Explain that!" demanded Rylat, noting that the

Solarians were also seizing the opportunity to communicate privately.

"The *plants!*" Akyro thought to him. "They have tanks on the ship where they grow them in water with chemicals and artificial radiation. I have seen them!"

"How?"

"I stood here looking bored until Strong-foreleg showed me through some of the compartments."

"Did you let him see what interested you?" Rylat paused to think a hollow bubble of clear plastic. "Of course you did, or they would not be vibrating their mouths at each other. Really, Akyro!"

The Weaver turned to Rylat and inquired if he might not be interested in seeing the hydroponic tanks. Rylat agreed without outward enthusiasm. He hoped that the Solarian would not know how to interpret the slight shrinking of his eyestalks.

They all walked into the compartment mentioned, and Rylat's walking legs nearly buckled.

All about the bulkheads of the compartment, and in rows down the center, were large, transparent tanks with plants in various stages of growth. Most were some shade of green in the parts that Rylat guessed normally grew above the ground.

He allowed himself, for a brief moment, to picture Olittra's blighted agricultural areas repopulated with such plant life. The food problem he would solve if he could only get some seeds or cuttings! He was *so* tired of synthetic foods—

"They are very pretty," he signaled. "They remind me of the gorgeous foliage of my home planet."

"Rylat!" came Akyro's horrified thought. "How can you deliver such an untruth? It is not ethical!"

"It is not an untruth. *Any* vegetable matter at present makes me remember Olittra. Besides, how could he know our vegetation was mostly purple?"

He had to request that the Weaver repeat his last gestures.

"I said, we would be very glad to let you have a few. They are quite nourishing."

"Oh, we seldom eat such," replied Rylat. "Still, they would be pleasant decoration in our bare and functional ship."

The Solarians exchanged stares that made him wonder if perhaps they, too, had a form of telepathy. Then the Weaver reached into the nearest tank of dark-green specimens.

"Perhaps—" Rylat began; and then, as the Weaver looked up, "But never mind. It is not necessary—"

Akyro's walking legs folded completely. He crouched on the deck, heedless of the Solarians' astonished glances, and thought a violent volcanic eruption. Rylat caught the whole image distinctly. It included himself at the zenith of the upjetting burst of flames.

"I was about to suggest," he signaled the waiting Weaver imperturbably, "that perhaps you could spare us a complete tank, since you have so many. Growing new plants would be an amusing hobby to us in the loneliness of space."

The Weaver signified that he would be only too pleased. He insisted upon including a supply of chemicals and a special light-tube. He and Rylat examined the latter, and the Olittran assured him that he could arrange to feed the proper power into it. The Olittrans carried enough water to supply the tank.

Both Solarians donned vacuum suits to assist with the transportation of the tank, which they thoughtfully enclosed in an insulated cylinder. Rylat was qualified to bear only a token share of the burden across the sand outside. Akyro trailed the group unsteadily, eyestalks still a bit retracted.

The Solarians helped get the cylinder inside the Olittran vessel but declined to be shown around.

"Probably feel a bit clumsy because of their size and those bulky suits," Rylat thought to Akyro.

To the Solarians, he expressed appreciation and asked if they had not hit upon some gift he could make in return.

"It is nothing!" waved the Weaver. "Do you intend to leave soon?"

"Rylat!" pleaded Akyro. "Tell him *yes*, and quickly! If they take time to reflect, they will surely realize the value of what they are giving us!"

"Patience! I, too, deeply desire to mount a starbeam."

He signaled to the Solarian that they did intend to leave almost immediately. The Weaver expressed regret.

"But tell me what we can do," insisted Rylat, fearful lest cause arise to make him surrender his booty.

"We had considered inspecting the planet's surface and its mineral content," the Weaver informed him.

"An interesting hobby," replied Rylat doubtfully.

By the looks they exchanged, the two Solarians were as puzzled at *that* as he was at their project. Who cared what minerals could be dug up? One could convert them any time.

"Our object," the Weaver tried again, "was to make ourselves comfortable on the surface and take a holiday from the confines of the ship."

"Ah!" answered Rylat, comprehending at last. "Why, if you wish to use our shelter, you are more than welcome."

The Weaver accepted with thanks, but wondered about the Olittrans' departure.

"It will not matter," Rylat assured him. "We can pick up the shelter the next time we pass this way."

"Rylat! *Give* it to him! Let us leave this place with some dispatch," pleaded Akyro.

"In fact," continued Rylat, "I recall that we have another, so you might as well keep the one outside. I will get you a set of instructions for the entrance valve and the heat converter. You will be able to understand the diagrams, at least."

He did so, and after many exchanges of courtesies, the Solarians departed.

Akyro wasted no time in securing the tank of plants in the hold. As soon as the Solarians were safely in their own ship, Rylat took off.

He spiraled away from the planet and set a tentative course for the limit between Sectors Twelve and Eleven.

"About my remark on returning to pick up that shelter," he teased Akyro, "you did not believe I would really risk facing them again? After cheating them like that?"

Akyro did not reply. Rylat turned an eye toward him and saw that he was watching his dials intently.

"What is it?" he asked, vaguely uneasy.

"Moving radiation of the same pattern. It must be the Solarians, leaving the planet."

"How fast?" demanded Rylat, wondering if he dared step up the acceleration even more.

"About as fast as we, perhaps a bit more."

Rylat's eyestalks cringed. He hastily estimated the emergency power available to him.

"Enough to catch us?" he inquired anxiously.

"Oh, no," Akyro told him calmly. "They are heading in the opposite direction."

"*What?*"

"No doubt of it. As fast as they can, apparently."

Rylat rose from the piloting bench and joined the other at the bank of instruments.

"I do not understand it," he thought to Akyro. "They claimed they intended to stay. And we certainly left nothing to make them hurry home."

"Perhaps the mechanism of the entrance valve?"

"No . . . they had better on their ship. And they showed no special interest in the heat converter. I doubt they would want to play at transmuting elements."

"Who would want a heat converter for that? They, too, must have better ways."

"Exactly. So what could be on their consciences?"

They pondered until Rylat returned to the piloting bench and curiously focused the image of the Solarian vessel on the telescreen.

"Let us admire their folly," Akyro suggested, "but not to the extent of lingering."

"No . . . and yet, I wonder why—"

He watched the other ship move out of focus.

"Look at them go!" he thought to Akyro. Anyone would suspect that *they*—not we—had practically committed theft!"

THE WAVERIES

BY FREDRIC BROWN

Definitions from the school-abridged Webster-Hamlin Dictionary 1998 edition:

> wavery (WA-ver-i) n. a vader—*slang*
> vader (VA-der) n. inorgan of the class Radio
>
> inorgan (in-OR-gan) n. noncorporeal ens, vader
>
> radio (RA-di-ō) n. 1. class of inorgans 2. etheric frequency between light and electricity 3. (obsolete) method of communication used up to 1977

The opening guns of invasion were not at all loud, although they were heard by millions of people. George Bailey was one of the millions. I choose George Bailey because he was the only one who came within a googol of light-years of guessing what they were.

George Bailey was drunk and under the circumstances one can't blame him for being so. He was listening to radio advertisements of the most nauseous kind. Not because he wanted to listen to them, I hardly need say, but because he'd been told to listen to them by his boss, J. R. McGee of the MID network.

George Bailey wrote advertising for the radio. The only thing he hated worse than advertising was radio. And here on his own time he was listening to fulsome and disgusting commercials on a rival network.

"Bailey," J. R. McGee had said, "you should be more familiar with what others are doing. Particularly, you should be informed about those of our own accounts who use several networks. I strongly suggest . . ."

One doesn't quarrel with an employer's strong suggestions and keep a five hundred dollar a week job.

But one can drink whisky sours while listening. George Bailey did.

Also, between commercials, he was playing gin rummy with Maisie Hetterman, a cute little redheaded typist from the studio. It was Maisie's apartment and Maisie's radio (George himself, on principle, owned neither a radio nor a TV set) but George had brought the liquor.

"—only the very finest tobaccos," said the radio, "go *dit-dit-dit* nation's favorite cigarette—"

George glanced at the radio. "Marconi," he said.

He meant Morse, naturally, but the whisky sours had muddled him a bit so his first guess was more nearly right than anyone else's. It *was* Marconi, in a way. In a very peculiar way.

"Marconi?" asked Maisie.

George, who hated to talk against a radio, leaned over and switched it off.

"I meant Morse," he said. "Morse, as in Boy Scouts or the Signal Corps. I used to be a Boy Scout once."

"You've sure changed," Maisie said.

Georbe sighed. "Somebody's going to catch hell, broadcasting code on that wave length."

"What did it mean?"

"Mean? Oh, you mean what did it mean. Uh—S, the letter S. *Dit-dit-dit* is S. SOS is *did-dit-dit dah-dah-dah dit-dit-dit.*"

"O is *dah-dah-dah?*"

George grinned. "Say that again, Maisie. I like it. And I think you are *dah-dah-dah* too."

"George, maybe it's really an SOS message. Turn it back on."

George turned it back on. The tobacco ad was still going. "—gentlemen of the most *dit-dit-dit* -ing taste prefer the finer taste of *dit-dit-dit* arettes. In the new package that keeps them *dit-dit-dit* and ultra fresh—"

"It's not SOS. It's just S's."

"Like a teakettle or—say, George, maybe it's just some advertising gag."

George shook his head. "Not when it can blank out the name of the product. Just a minute till I—"

He reached over and turned the dial of the radio a bit to the right and then a bit to the left, and an incredulous look came into his face. He turned the dial to the extreme left, as far as it would go. There wasn't any station there, not even the hum of a carrier wave. But:

"*Dit-dit-dit,*" said the radio, "*dit-dit-dit.*"

He turned the dial to the extreme right. "*Dit-dit-dit.*"

George switched it off and stared at Maisie without seeing her, which was hard to do.

"Something wrong, George?"

"I hope so," said George Bailey. "I certainly hope so."

He started to reach for another drink and changed his mind. He had a sudden hunch that something big was happening and he wanted to sober up to appreciate it.

He didn't have the faintest idea *how* big it was.

"George, what do you mean?"

"I don't know what I mean. But Maisie, let's take a run down the studio, huh? There ought to be some excitement."

April 5, 1977; that was the night the waveries came.

It had started like an ordinary evening. It wasn't one, now.

George and Maisie waited for a cab but none came so they took the subway instead. Oh yes, the subways were still running in those days. It took them within a block of the MID Network Building.

The building was a madhouse. George, grinning, strolled through the lobby with Maisie on his arm, took the elevator to the fifth floor and for no reason at all gave the elevator boy a dollar. He'd never before in his life tipped an elevator operator.

The boy thanked him. "Better stay away from the big shots, Mr. Bailey," he said. "They're ready to chew the ears off anybody who even looks at 'em."

"Wonderful," said George.

From the elevator he headed straight for the office of J. R. McGee himself.

There were strident voices behind the glass door. George reached for the knob and Maisie tried to stop him. "But George," she whispered, "you'll be fired!"

"There comes a time," said George. "Stand back away from the door, honey."

Gently but firmly he moved her to a safe position.

"But George, what are you—?"

"Watch," he said.

The frantic voices stopped as he opened the door a foot. All eyes turned toward him as he stuck his head around the corner of the doorway into the room.

"*Dit-dit-dit,*" he said. "*Dit-dit-dit.*"

He ducked back and to the side just in time to escape the flying glass as a paperweight and an inkwell came through the pane of the door.

He grabbed Maisie and ran for the stairs.

"Now we get a drink," he told her.

The bar across the street from the network building was

crowded but it was a strangely silent crowd. In deference to the fact that most of its customers were radio people it didn't have a TV set but there was a big cabinet radio and most of the people were bunched around it.

"*Dit,*" said the radio. "*Dit-dah-d'dah-dit-dahditdah dit—*"

"Isn't it beautiful?" George whispered to Maisie.

Somebody fiddled with the dial. Somebody asked, "What band is that?" and somebody said, "Police." Somebody said, "Try the foreign band," and somebody did. "This ought to be Buenos Aires," somebody said. "*Dit-d'dah-dit—*" said the radio.

Somebody ran fingers through his hair and said, "Shut that damn thing off." Somebody else turned it back on.

George grinned and led the way to a back booth where he'd spotted Pete Mulvaney sitting alone with a bottle in front of him. He and Maisie sat across from Pete.

"Hello," he said gravely.

"Hell," said Pete, who was head of the technical research staff of MID.

"A beautiful night, Mulvaney," George said. "Did you see the moon riding the fleecy clouds like a golden galleon tossed upon silver-crested whitecaps in a stormy—"

"Shut up," said Pete. "I'm thinking."

"Whisky sours," George told the waiter. He turned back to the man across the table. "Think out loud, so we can hear. But first, how did you escape the booby hatch across the street?"

"I'm bounced, fired, discharged."

"Shake hands. And then explain. Did you say *dit-dit-dit* to them?"

Pete looked at him with sudden admiration. "Did you?"

"I've a witness. What *did* you do?"

"Told 'em what I thought it was and they think I'm crazy."

"Are you?"

"Yes."

"Good," said George. "Then we want to hear—" He snapped his fingers. "What about TV?"

"Same thing. Same sound on audio and the pictures

flicker and dim with every dot or dash. Just a blur by now."

"Wonderful. And now tell me what's wrong. I don't care what it is, as long as it's nothing trivial, but I want to know."

"I think it's space. Space is warped."

"Good old space," George Bailey said.

"George," said Maisie, "please shut up. I want to hear this."

"Space," said Pete, "is also finite." He poured himself another drink. "You go far enough in any direction and get back where you started. Like an ant crawling around an apple."

"Make it an orange," George said.

"All right, an orange. Now suppose the first radio waves ever sent out have just made the round trip. In seventy-six years."

"Seventy-six years? But I thought radio waves traveled at the same speed as light. If that's right, then in seventy-six years they could go only seventy-six light-years, and *that* can't be around the universe because there are galaxies known to be millions or maybe billions of light-years away. I don't remember the figures, Pete, but our own galaxy alone is a hell of a lot bigger than seventy-six light-years."

Pete Mulvaney sighed. "That's why I say space must be warped. There's a short cut somewhere."

"*That* short a short cut? Couldn't be."

"But George, listen to that stuff that's coming in. Can you read code?"

"Not any more. Not that fast, anyway."

"Well, I can," Pete said. "That's early American ham. Lingo and all. That's the kind of stuff the air was full of before regular broadcasting. It's the lingo, the abbreviations, the barnyard to attic chitchat of amateurs with keys, with Marconi coherers or Fessenden barreters—and you can listen for a violin solo pretty soon now. I'll tell you what it'll be."

"What?"

"Handel's *Largo*. The first phonograph record ever broadcast. Sent out by Fessenden from Brant Rock in

1906. You'll hear his CQ-CQ any minute now. Bet you a drink."

"Okay, but what was the *dit-dit-dit* that started this?"

Mulvaney grinned. "Marconi, George. What was the most powerful signal ever broadcast and by whom and when?"

"Marconi? *Dit-dit-dit*? Seventy-six years ago?"

"Head of the class. The first transatlantic signal on December 12, 1901. For three hours Marconi's big station at Poldhu, with two-hundred-foot masts, sent out an intermittent S, *dit-dit-dit*, while Marconi and two assistants at St. Johns in Newfoundland got a kite-born aerial four hundred feet in the air and finally got the signal. Across the Atlantic, George, with sparks jumping from the big Leyden jars at Poldhu and 20,000-volt juice jumping off the tremendous aerials—"

"Wait a minute, Pete, you're off the beam. If that was in 1901 and the first broadcast was about 1906 it'll be five years before the Fessenden stuff gets here on the same route. Even if there's a seventy-six light-year short cut across space and even if those signals didn't get so weak en route that we couldn't hear them—it's crazy."

"I told you it was," Pete said gloomily. "Why, those signals after traveling that far would be so infinitesimal that for practical purposes they wouldn't exist. Furthermore they're all over the band on everything from microwave on up and equally strong on each. And, as you point out, we've already come almost five years in two hours, which isn't possible. I told you it was crazy."

"But—"

"Ssshh. Listen," said Pete.

A blurred, but unmistakably human voice was coming from the radio, mingling with the cracklings of code. And then music, faint and scratchy, but unmistakably a violin. Playing Handel's *Largo*.

Only suddenly it climbed in pitch as though modulating from key to key until it became so horribly shrill that it hurt the ear. And kept on going past the high limit of audibility until they could hear it no more.

Somebody said, "Shut that God damn thing off." Somebody did, and this time nobody turned it back on.

Pete said, "I didn't really believe it myself. And there's another thing against it, George. Those signals affect TV too, and radio waves are the wrong length to do that."

He shook his head slowly. "There must be some other explanation, George. The more I think about it now the more I think I'm wrong."

He was right: he was wrong.

"Preposterous," said Mr. Ogilvie. He took off his glasses, frowned fiercely, and put them back on again. He looked through them at the several sheets of copy paper in his hand and tossed them contemptuously to the top of his desk. They slid to rest against the triangular name plate that read:

B. R. Ogilvie
Editor-in-Chief

"Preposterous," he said again.

Casey Blair, his best reporter, blew a smoke ring and poked his index finger through it. "Why?" he asked.

"Because—why, it's *utterly* preposterous."

Casey Blair said, "It is now three o'clock in the morning. The interference has gone on for five hours and not a single program is getting through on either TV or radio. Every major broadcasting and telecasting station in the world has gone off the air.

"For two reasons. One, they were just wasting current. Two, the communications bureaus of their respective governments requested them to get off to aid their campaigns with the direction finders. For five hours now, since the start of the interference, they've been working with everything they've got. And what have they found out?"

"It's preposterous!" said the editor.

"Perfectly, but it's true. Greenwich at 11 P.M. New York time; I'm translating all these times into New York time—got a bearing in about the direction of Miami. It shifted northward until at two o'clock the direction was approximately that of Richmond, Virginia. San Francisco at eleven got a bearing in about the direction of Denver; three hours later it shifted southward toward Tucson. Southern hemisphere: bearings from Capetown, South Africa, shifted from direction of Buenos Aires to that of Montevideo, a thousand miles north.

"New York at eleven had weak indications toward Madrid; but by two o'clock they could get no bearings at all." He blew another smoke ring. "Maybe because the loop antennae they use turn only on a horizontal plane?"

"Absurd."

Casey said, "I like 'presposterous' better. Mr. Ogilvie. Preposterous it is, but it's not absurd. I'm scared stiff. Those lines—and all other bearings I've heard about—run in the *same direction* if you take them as straight lines running as tangents off the Earth instead of curving them around the surface. I did it with a little globe and a star map. They converge on the constellation Leo."

He leaned forward and tapped a forefinger on the top page of the story he'd just turned in. "Stations that are directly under Leo in the sky get no bearings at all. Stations on what would be the perimeter of Earth relative to that point get the strongest bearings. Listen, have an astronomer check those figures if you want before you run the story, but get it done damn quick—unless you want to read about it in the other newspapers first."

"But the heaviside layer, Casey—isn't that supposed to stop all radio waves and bounce them back."

"Sure, it does. But maybe it leaks. Or maybe signals can get through it from the outside even though they can't get out from the inside. It isn't a solid wall."

"But—"

"I know, it's preposterous. But there it is. And there's only an hour before press time. You'd better send this story through fast and have it set up while you're having somebody check my facts and directions. Besides, there's something else you'll want to check."

"What?"

"I didn't have the data for checking the positions of the

planets. Leo's on the ecliptic; a planet could be in line between here and there. Mars, maybe."

Mr. Ogilvie's eyes brightened, then clouded again. He said, "We'll be the laughingstock of the world, Blair, if you're wrong."

"And if I'm right?"

The editor picked up the phone and snapped an order.

April 6th headline of the New York *Morning Messenger*, final (6 A.M.) edition:

RADIO INTERFERENCE
COMES FROM SPACE,
ORIGINATES IN LEO

May Be Attempt at Communication by Beings
Outside Solar

System

All television and radio broadcasting was suspended.

Radio and television stocks opened several points off the previous day and then dropped sharply until noon when a moderate buying rally brought them a few points back.

Public reaction was mixed; people who had no radios rushed out to buy them and there was a boom, especially in portable and table-top receivers. On the other hand, no TV sets were sold at all. With telecasting suspended there were no pictures on their screens, even blurred ones. Their audio circuits, when turned on, brought in the same jumble as radio receivers. Which, as Pete Mulvaney had pointed out to George Bailey, was impossible; radio waves cannot activate the audio circuits of TV sets. But these did, if they *were* radio waves.

In radio sets they seemed to be radio waves, but horribly hashed. No one could listen to them very long. Oh, there were flashes—times when, for several consecutive seconds, one could recognize the voice of Will Rogers or Geraldine Farrar or catch flashes of the Dempsey-Carpentier fight or the Pearl Harbor excitement. (Remember Pearl Harbor?) But things even remotely worth hearing were rare. Mostly it was a meaningless mixture of soap opera, advertising and off-key snatches of what had once been music. It was utterly indiscriminate, and utterly unbearable for any length of time.

But curiosity is a powerful motive. There *was* a brief boom in radio sets for a few days.

There were other booms, less explicable, less capable of analysis. Reminiscent of the Welles Martian scare of 1938 was a sudden upswing in the sale of shotguns and sidearms. Bibles sold as fast as books on astronomy—and book on astronomy sold like hotcakes. One section of the country showed a sudden interest in lightning rods; builders were flooded with orders for immediate installation.

For some reason which has never been clearly ascertained there was a run on fishhooks in Mobile, Alabama; every hardware and sporting goods store sold out of them within hours.

The public libraries and bookstores had a run on books on astrology and books on Mars. Yes, on Mars—despite the fact that Mars was at that moment on the other side of the sun and that every newspaper article on the subject stressed the fact that *no* planet was between Earth and the constellation Leo.

Something strange was happening—and no news of developments available except through the newspapers. People waited in mobs outside newspaper buildings for each new edition to appear. Circulation managers went quietly mad.

People also gathered in curious little knots around the silent broadcasting studios and stations, talking in hushed voices as though at a wake. MID network doors were locked, although there was a doorman on duty to admit technicians who were trying to find an answer to the problem. Some of the technicians who had been on duty the previous day had now spent over twenty-four hours without sleep.

George Bailey woke at noon, with only a slight headache. He shaved and showered, went out and drank a light breakfast and was himself again. He bought early editions of the afternoon papers, read them, grinned. His hunch had been right; whatever was wrong, it was nothing trivial.

But *what* was wrong?

The later editions of the afternoon papers had it.

EARTH INVADED, SAYS SCIENTIST

Thirty-six line type was the biggest they had; they used it. Not a home-edition copy of a newspaper was delivered that evening. Newsboys starting on their routes were practically mobbed. They sold papers instead of delivering them; the smart ones got a dollar apiece for them. The foolish and honest ones who didn't want to sell because they thought the papers should to the regular customers on their routes lost them anyway. People grabbed them.

The final editions changed the heading only slightly—only slightly, that is, from a typographical viewpoint. Nevertheless, it was a tremendous change in meaning. It read:

EARTH INVADED, SAY SCIENTISTS

Funny what moving an S from the ending of a verb to the ending of a noun can do.

Carnegie Hall shattered precedent that evening with a lecture given at midnight. An unscheduled and unadvertised lecture. Professor Helmetz had stepped off the train at eleven-thirty and a mob of reporters had been waiting for him. Helmetz, of Harvard, had been the scientist, singular, who had made that first headline.

Harvey Ambers, director of the board of Carnegie Hall, had pushed his way through the mob. He arrived minus glasses, hat and breath, but got hold of Helmetz's arm and hung on until he could talk again. "We want you to talk at Carnegie, Professor," he shouted into Helmetz's ear. "Five thousand dollars for a lecture on the 'vaders.' "

"Certainly. Tomorrow afternoon?"

"Now! I've a cab waiting. Come on."

"But—"

"We'll get you an audience. Hurry!" He turned to the mob. "Let us through. All of you can't hear the professor here. Come to Carnegie Hall and he'll talk to you. And spread the word on your way there."

The word spread so well that Carnegie Hall was jammed by the time the professor began to speak. Shortly after, they'd rigged a loud-speaker system so the people outside could hear. By one o'clock in the morning the streets were jammed for blocks around.

There wasn't a sponsor on Earth with a million dollars to his name who wouldn't have given a million dollars gladly for the privilege of sponsoring that lecture on TV or radio, but it was not telecast or broadcast. Both lines were busy.

"Questions?" asked Professor Helmetz.

A reporter in the front row made it first. "Professor," he asked, "Have *all* direction finding stations on Earth confirmed what you told us about the change this afternoon?"

"Yes, absolutely. At about noon all directional indications began to grow weaker. At 2:45 o'clock, Eastern Standard Time, they ceased completely. Until then the radio waves emanated from the sky, constantly changing direction with reference to the Earth's surface, but *constant* with reference to a point in the constellation Leo."

"What star in Leo?"

"No star visible on our charts. Either they came from a point in space or from a star too faint for our telescopes.

"But at 2:45 P.M. today—yesterday rather, since it is now past midnight—all direction finders went dead. But the signals persisted, now coming from all sides equally. The invaders had all arrived.

"There is no other conclusion to be drawn. Earth is now surrounded, completely blanketed, by radio-type waves which have *no point of origin*, which travel ceaselessly around the Earth in all directions, changing shape at their will—which currently is still in imitation of the Earth-origin radio signals which attracted their attention and brought them here."

"Do you think it was from a star we can't see, or could it have really been just a point in space?"

"Probably from a point in space. And why not? They are not creatures of matter. If they came from a star, it must be a very dark star for it to be invisible to us, since it would be relatively near to us—only twenty-eight light-years away, which is quite close as stellar distances go."

"How can you know the distance?"

"By assuming—and it is a quite reasonable assumption—that they started our way when they first discovered our radio signals—Marconi's S-S-S code broadcast of fifty-six years ago. Since that was the form taken by the first arrivals, we assume they started toward us when they encountered those signals. Marconi's signals, traveling at the speed of light, would have reached a point twenty-eight light-years away twenty-eight years ago; the invaders, also traveling at light speed would require an equal of time to reach us.

"As might be expected only the first arrivals took Morse code form. Later arrivals were in the form of other waves that they met and passed on—or perhaps absorbed—on their way to Earth. There are now wandering around the Earth, as it were, fragments of programs broadcast as recently as a few days ago. Undoubtedly there are fragments of the very last programs to be broadcast, but they have not yet been identified."

"Professor, can you *describe* one of these invaders?"

"As well as and no better than I can describe a radio wave. In effect, they *are* radio waves, although they emanate from no broadcasting station. They are a form of life dependent on wave motion, as our form of life is dependent on the vibration of matter."

"They are different sizes?"

"Yes, in two senses of the word size. Radio waves are measured from crest to crest, which measurement is known as wave length. Since the invaders cover the entire dials of our radio sets and television sets it is obvious that either one of two things is true: Either they come in all crest-to-crest sizes or each one can change his crest-to-crest measurement to adapt himself to the tuning of any receiver.

"But that is only the crest-to-crest length. In a sense it may be said that a radio wave has an over-all length determined by its duration. If a broadcasting station sends out a program that has a second's duration, a wave carrying that program is one light-second long, roughly 187,000 miles. A continuous half-hour program is, as it were, on a continuous wave one-half light-hour long, and so on.

"Taking that form of length, the individual invaders vary in length from a few thousand miles—a duration of only a small fraction of a second—to well over half a million miles long—a duration of several seconds. The longest continuous excerpt from any one program that has been observed has been about seven seconds."

"But, Professor Helmetz, why do you assume that these waves are *living* things, a life form. Why not just waves?"

"Because 'just waves' as you call them would follow certain laws, just as inanimate *matter* follows certain laws. An animal can climb uphill, for instance; a stone cannot unless impelled by some outside force. These invaders are life-forms because they show volition, because they can change their direction of travel, and most especially because they retain their identity; two signals never conflict on the same radio receiver. They follow one another but do not come simultaneously. They do not mix as signals on the same wave length would ordinarily do. They are not 'just waves.' "

"Would you say they are intelligent?"

Professor Helmetz took off his glasses and polished them thoughtfully. He said, "I doubt if we shall ever know. The intelligence of such beings, if any, would be on such a completely different plane from ours that there would be no common point from which we could start intercourse. We are material; they are immaterial. There is no common ground between us."

"But if they are intelligent at all—"

"Ants are intelligent, after a fashion. Call it instinct if you will, but instinct is a form of intelligence; at least it enables them to accomplish some of the same things intelligence would enable them to accomplish. Yet we cannot establish communication with ants and it is far less likely that we shall be able to establish communication with these invaders. The difference in type between ant-intelligence and our own would be nothing to the difference in type between the intelligence, if any, of the invaders and our own. No, I doubt if we shall ever communicate."

The professor had something there. Communication with the vaders—a clipped form, of course, of *invaders*—was never established.

Radio stocks stabilized on the exchange the next day. But the day following that someone asked Dr. Helmetz a sixty-four dollar question and the newspapers published his answer:

"Resume broadcasting? I don't know if we ever shall. Certainly we cannot until the invaders go away, and why should they? Unless radio communication is perfected on some other planet far away and they're attracted there.

"But at least some of them would be right back the moment we started to broadcast again."

Radio and TV stocks dropped to practically zero in an hour. There weren't, however, any frenzied scenes on the stock exchanges; there was no frenzied selling because there was no buying, frenzied or otherwise. No radio stocks changed hands.

Radio and television employes and entertainers began to look for other jobs. The entertainers had no trouble finding them. Every other form of entertainment suddenly boomed like mad.

"Two down," said George Bailey. The bartender asked what he meant.

"I dunno, Hank. It's just a hunch I've got."

"What kind of hunch?"

"I don't even know that. Shake me up one more of those and then I'll go home."

The electric shaker wouldn't work and Hank had to shake the drink by hand.

"Good exercise; that's just what you need," George said. "It'll take some of that fat off you."

Hank grunted, and the ice tinkled merrily as he tilted the shaker to pour out the drink.

George Bailey took his time drinking it and then strolled out into an April thundershower. He stood under the awning and watched for a taxi. An old man was standing there too.

"Some weather," George said.

The old man grinned at him. "You noticed it, eh?"

"Huh? Noticed what?"

"Just watch a while, mister. Just watch a while."

The old man moved on. No empty cab came by and Geroge stood there quite a while before he got it. His jaw dropped a little and then he closed his mouth and went back into the tavern. He went into a phone booth and called Pete Mulvaney.

He got three wrong numbers before he got Pete. Pete's voice said, "Yeah?"

"George Bailey, Pete. Listen, have you noticed the weather?"

"Damn right. *No lightning*, and there should be with a thunderstorm like this."

"What's it mean, Pete? The vaders?"

"Sure. And that's just going to be the start if—" A crackling sound on the wire blurred his voice out.

"Hey, Pete, you still there?"

The sound of a violin. Pete Mulvaney didn't play violin.

"Hey, Pete, what the hell—?"

Pete's voice again. "Come on over, George. Phone won't last long. Bring—" There was a buzzing noise and then a voice said, "—come to Carnegie Hall. The best tunes of all come—"

George slammed down the receiver.

He walked through the rain to Pete's place. On the way he bought a bottle of Scotch. Pete had started to tell him to bring something and maybe that's what he'd started to say.

It was.

They made a drink apiece and lifted them. The lights flickered briefly, went out, and then came on again but dimly.

"No lightning," said George. "No lightning and pretty soon no lighting. They're taking over the telephone. What do they do with the lightning?"

"Eat it, I guess. They must eat electricity."

"No lightning," said George. "Damn. I can get by without a telephone, and candles and oil lamps aren't bad for lights—but I'm going to miss lightning. I *like* lightning. Damn."

The lights went out completely.

Pete Mulvaney sipped his drink in the dark. He said, "Electric lights, refrigerators, electric toasters, vacuum cleaners—"

"Juke boxes," George said. "Think of it, no more God damn juke boxes. No public address systems, no—hey, how about movies?"

"No movies, not even silent ones. You can't work a projector with an oil lamp. But listen, George, no automobiles—no gasoline engine can work without electricity."

"Why not, if you crank it by hand instead of using a starter?"

"The spark, George. What do you think makes the spark."

"Right. No airplanes either, then. Or how about jet planes?"

"Well—I guess some types of jets could be rigged not to need electricity, but you couldn't do much with them. Jet plane's got more instruments than motor, and all those instruments are electrical. And you can't fly or land a jet by the seat of your pants."

"No radar. But what would we need it for? There won't be any more wars, not for a long time."

"A damned long time."

George sat up straight suddenly. "Hey, Pete, what about atomic fission? Atomic energy? Will it still work?"

"I doubt it. Subatomic phenomena are basically electrical. Bet you a dime they eat loose neutrons too."

(He'd have won his bet; the government had not announced that an A-bomb tested that day in Nevada had fizzled like a wet firecracker and that atomic piles were ceasing to function.)

George shook his head slowly, in wonder. He said, "Street-cars and buses, ocean liners—Pete, this means we're going back to the original source of horsepower. Horses. If you want to invest, buy horses. Particularly mares. A brood mare is going to be worth a thousand times her weight in platinum."

"Right. But don't forget steam. We'll still have steam engines, stationary and locomotive."

"Sure, that's right. The iron horse again, for the long hauls. But Dobbin for the short ones. Can you ride, Peter?"

"Used to, but I think I'm getting too old. I'll settle for a bicycle. Say, better buy a bike first thing tomorrow before the run on them starts. I know *I'm* going to."

"Good tip. And I used to be a good bike rider. It'll be swell with no autos around to louse you up. And say—"

"What?"

"I'm going to get a cornet too. Used to play one when I as a kid and I can pick it up again. And then maybe I'll hole in somewhere and write that nov— Say, what about printing?"

"They printed books long before electricity, George. It'll take a while to readjust the printing industry, but there'll be books all right. Thank God for that."

George Bailey grinned and got up. He walked over to the window and looked out into the night. The rain had stopped and the sky was clear.

A streetcar was stalled, without lights, in the middle of the block outside. An automobile stopped, then started more slowly, stopped again; its headlights were dimming rapidly.

George looked up at the sky and took a sip of his drink.

"No lightning," he said sadly. "I'm going to *miss* the lightning."

The changeover went more smoothly than anyone would have thought possible.

The government, in emergency session, made the wise decision of creating one board with absolutely unlimited authority and under it only three subsidiary boards. The main board, called the Economic Readjustment Bureau, had only seven members and its job was to co-ordinate the efforts of the three subsidiary boards and to decide, quickly and without appeal, any jurisdictional disputes among them.

First of the three subsidiary boards was the Transporation Bureau. It immediately took over, temporarily, the railroads. It ordered Diesel engines run on sidings and left there, organized use of the steam locomotives and solved the problems of railroading sans telegraphy and electric signals. It dictated, then, what should be transported; food coming first, coal and fuel oil second, and essential manufactured articles in the order of their relative importance. Carload after carload of new radios, electric stoves, refrigerators and such useless articles were dumped unceremoniously alongside the tracks, to be salvaged for scrap metal later.

All horses were declared wards of the government, graded according to capabilities, and put to work or to stud. Draft horses were used for only the most essential kinds of hauling. The breeding program was given the fullest possible emphasis; the bureau estimated that the equine population would double in two years, quadruple in three, and that within six or seven years there would be a horse in every garage in the country.

Farmers, deprived temporarily of their horses, and with their tractors rusting in the fields, were instructed how to use cattle for plowing and other work about the farm, including light hauling.

The second board, the Manpower Relocation Bureau, functioned just as one would deduce from its title. It handled unemployment benefits for the millions thrown temporarily out of work and helped relocate them—not too difficult a task considering the tremendously increased demand for hand labor in many fields.

In May of 1977 thirty-five million employables were out of work; in October, fifteen million; by May of 1978, five million. By 1979 the situation was completely in hand and competitive demand was already beginning to raise wages.

The third board had the most difficult job of the three. It was called the Factory Readjustment Bureau. It coped with the stupendous task of converting factories filled with electrically operated machinery and, for the most part, tooled for the production of other electrically operated machinery, over for the production, without electricity, of essential nonelectrical articles.

The few available stationary steam engines worked twenty-four hour shifts in those early days, and the first thing they were given to do was the running of lathes and stampers and planers and millers working on turning out more stationary steam engines, of all sizes. These, in turn, were first put to work making still more steam engines. The number of steam engines grew by squares and cubes, as did the number of horses put to stud. The principle was the same. One might, and many did, refer to those early steam engines as stud horses. At any rate, there was no lack of metal for them. The factories were filled with nonconvertible machinery waiting to be melted down.

Only when steam engines—the basis of the new factory economy—were in full production, were they assigned to running machinery for the manufacture of other articles. Oil lamps, clothing, coal stoves, oil stoves, bathtubs and bedsteads.

Not quite all of the big factories were converted. For while the conversion period went on, individual handicrafts sprang up in thousands of places. Little one- and two-man shops making and repairing furniture, shoes, candles, all sorts of things that *could* be made without complex machinery. At first these small shops made small fortunes because they had no competition from heavy industry. Later, they bought small steam engines to run small machines and held their own, growing with the boom that came with a return to normal employment and buying power, increasing gradually in size until many of them rivaled the bigger factories in output and beat them in quality.

There *was* suffering, during the period of economic

readjustment, but less than there had been during the great depression of the early thirties. And the recovery was quicker.

The reason was obvious: In combating the depression, the legislators were working in the dark. They didn't know its cause—rather, they knew a thousand conflicting theories of its cause—and they didn't know the cure. They were hampered by the idea that the thing was temporary and would cure itself if left alone. Briefly and frankly, they didn't know what it was all about and while they experimented, it snowballed.

But the situation that faced the country—and all other countries—in 1977 was clear-cut and obvious. No more electricity. Readjust for steam and horsepower.

As simple and clear as that, and no ifs or ands or buts. And the whole people—except for the usual scattering of cranks—back of them.

By 1981—

It was a rainy day in April and George Bailey was waiting under the sheltering roof of the little railroad station at Blakestown, Connecticut, to see who might come in on the 3:14.

It chugged in at 3:25 and came to a panting stop, three coaches and a baggage car. The baggage car door opened and a sack of mail was handed out and the door closed again. No luggage, so probably no passengers would—

Then at the sight of a tall dark man swinging down from the platform of the rear coach, George Bailey let out a yip of delight. "Pete! Pete Mulvaney! What the devil—"

"Bailey, by all that's holy! What are you doing here?"

George wrung Pete's hand. "Me? I live here. Two years now. I bought the *Blakestown Weekly* in '79, for a song, and I run it—editor, reporter, and janitor. Got one printer to help me out with that end, and Maisie does the social items. She's—"

"Maisie? Maisie Hetterman?"

"Maisie Bailey now. We got married same time I bought the paper and moved here. What are you doing here, Pete?"

"Business. Just here overnight. See a man named Wilcox."

"Oh, Wilcox. Our local screwball—but don't get me wrong; he's a smart guy all right. Well, you can see him tomorrow. You're coming home with me now, for dinner and to stay overnight. Maisie'll be glad to see you. Come on, my buggy's over here."

"Sure. Finished whatever you were here for?"

"Yep, just to pick up the news on who came in on the train. And *you* came in, so here we go."

They got in the buggy, and George picked up the reins and said, "Giddup, Bessie," to the mare. Then, "What are you doing now, Pete?"

"Research. For a gas-supply company. Been working on a more efficient mantle, one that'll give more light and be less destructible. This fellow Wilcox wrote us he had something along that line; the company sent me up to look it over. If it's what he claims, I'll take him back to New York with me, and let the company lawyers dicker with him."

"How's business, otherwise?"

"Great, George. *Gas*; that's the coming thing. Every new home's being piped for it, and plenty of the old ones. How about you?"

"We got it. Luckily we had one of the old Linotypes that ran the metal pot off a gas burner, so it was already piped in. And our home is right over the office and print shop, so all we had to do was pipe it up a flight. Great stuff, gas. How's New York?"

"Fine, George. Down to its last million people, and stabilizing there. No crowding and plenty of room for everybody. The *air*—why, it's better than Atlantic City, without gasoline fumes."

"Enough horses to go around yet?"

"Almost. But bicycling's the craze; the factories can't turn out enough to meet the demand. There's a cycling club in almost every block and all the able-bodied cycle to and from work. Doing 'em good, too; a few more years and the doctors will go on short rations."

"You got a bike?"

"Sure, a pre-vader one. Average five miles a day on it, and I eat like a horse."

George Bailey chuckled. "I'll have Maisie include some hay in the dinner. Well, here we are. Whoa, Bessie."

An upstairs window went up, and Maisie looked out and down. She called out, "Hi, Pete!"

"Extra plate, Maisie," George called. "We'll be up soon as I put the horse away and show Pete around downstairs."

He led Pete from the barn into the back door of the newspaper shop. "Our Linotype!" he announced proudly, pointing.

"How's it work? Where's your steam engine?"

George grinned. "Doesn't work yet; we still hand set the type. I could get only one steamer and had to use that on the press. But I've got one on order for the Lino, and coming up in a month or so. When we get it, Pop Jenkins, my printer, is going to put himself out of a job teaching me to run it. With the Linotype going, I can handle the whole thing myself."

"Kind of rough on Pop?"

George shook his head. "Pop eagerly awaits the day. He's sixty-nine and wants to retire. He's just staying on until I can do without him. Here's the press—a honey of a little Miehle; we do some job work on it, too. And this is the office, in front. Messy, but efficient."

Mulvaney looked around him and grinned. "George, I believe you've found your niche. You were cut out for a small-town editor."

"Cut out for it? I'm crazy about it. I have more fun than everybody. Believe it or not, I work like a dog, and like it. Come on upstairs."

On the stairs, Pete asked, "And the novel you were going to write?"

"Half done, and it isn't bad. But it isn't the novel I was going to write; I was a cynic then. Now—"

"George, I think the waveries were your best friends."

"Waveries?"

"Lord, how long does it take slang to get from New York out to the sticks? The vaders, of course. Some professor who specializes in studying them described one as a wavery place in the ether, and 'wavery' stuck—Hello there, Maisie, my girl. You look like a million."

They ate leisurely. Almost apologetically, George brought out beer, in cold bottles. "Sorry, Pete, haven't anything stronger to offer you. But I haven't been drinking lately. Guess—"

"*You* on the wagon, George?"

"Not on the wagon, exactly. Didn't swear off or anything, but haven't had a drink of strong liquor in almost a year. I don't know why, but—"

"I do," said Pete Mulvaney. "I know exactly why you don't—because I don't drink much either, for the same reason. We don't drink because we don't *have* to—say, isn't that a *radio* over there?"

George chuckled. "A souvenir. Wouldn't sell it for a fortune. Once in a while I like to look at it and think of the awful guff I used to sweat out for it. And then I go over and click the switch and nothing happens. Just silence. Silence is the most wonderful thing in the world, sometimes, Pete. Of course I couldn't do that if there was any juice, because I'd get vaders then. I suppose they're still doing business at the same old stand?"

"Yep, the Research Bureau checks daily. Try to get up current with a little generator run by a steam turbine. But no dice; the vaders suck it up as fast as it's generated."

"Suppose they'll ever go away?"

Mulvaney shrugged. "Helmetz thinks not. He thinks they propagate in proportion to the available electricity. Even if the development of radio broadcasting somewhere else in the Universe would attract them there, some would stay here—and multiply like flies the minute we tried to use electricity again. And meanwhile, they'll live on the static electricity in the air. What do you do evenings up here?"

"Do? Read, write, visit with one another, go to the amateur groups—Maisie's chairman of the Blakestown Players, and I play bit parts in it. With the movies out everybody goes in for theatricals and we've found some real talent. And there's the chess-and-checker club, and cycle trips and picnics—there isn't time enough. Not to mention music. Everybody plays an instrument, or is trying to."

"You?"

"Sure, cornet. First cornet in the Silver Concert Band, with solo parts. And—Good Heavens! Tonight's rehearsal, and we're giving a concert Sunday afternoon. I hate to desert you, but—"

"Can't I come around and sit in? I've got my flute in the brief case here, and—"

"*Flute?* We're short on flutes. Bring that around and Si Perkins, our director, will practically shanghai you into staying over for the concert Sunday—and it's only three days, so why not? And get it out now; we'll play a few old timers to warm up. Hey, Maisie, skip those dishes and come on in to the piano!"

While Pete Mulvaney went to the guest room to get his flute from the brief case, George Bailey picked up his cornet from the top of the piano and blew a soft, plaintive little minor run on it. Clear as a bell; his lip was in good shape tonight.

And with the shining silver thing in his hand he wandered over to the window and stood looking out into the night. It was dusk out and the rain had stopped.

A high-stepping horse *clop-clopped* by and the bell of a bicycle jangled. Somebody across the street was strumming a guitar and singing. He took a deep breath and let it out slowly.

The scent of spring was soft and weet in the moist air.

Peace and dusk.

Distant rolling thunder.

God damn it, he thought, *if only there was a bit of lightning.*

He missed the lightning.

IN THE ABYSS

BY H. G. WELLS

The lieutenant stood in front of the steel sphere and gnawed a piece of pine splinter. "What do you think of it, Steevens?" he asked.

"It's an idea," said Steevens, in the tone of one who keeps an open mind.

"I believe it will smash—flat," said the lieutenant.

"He seems to have calculated it all out pretty well," said Steevens, still impartial.

"But think of the pressure," said the lieutenant. "At the surface of the water it's fourteen pounds to the inch, thirty feet down it's double that; sixty, treble; ninety, four times; nine hundred, forty times; five thousand, three hundred—that's a mile—it's two hundred and forty times fourteen pounds; that's—let's see—thirty hundredweight—a ton and a half, Steevens; *a ton and a half* to the square inch. And the ocean where he's going is five miles deep. That's seven and a half——"

"Sounds a lot," said Steevens, "but it's jolly thick steel."

The lieutenant made no answer, but resumed his pine splinter. The object of their conversation was a huge ball of steel, having an exterior diameter of perhaps nine feet. It looked like the shot for some Titanic piece of artillery. It was elaborately nested in a monstrous scaffolding built into the framework of the vessel, and the gigantic spars that were presently to sling it overboard gave the stern of the ship an appearance that had raised the curiosity of every decent sailor who had sighted it, from the Pool of London to the Tropic of Capricorn. In two places, one above the other, the steel gave place to a couple of circular windows of enormously thick glass, and one of these, set in a steel frame of great solidity, was now partially unscrewed. Both the men had seen the interior of this globe for the first time that morning. It was elaborately padded with air cushions, with little studs sunk between bulging pillows to work the simple mechanism of the affair. Everything was elaborately padded, even the Myers apparatus which was to absorb carbonic acid and replace the oxygen inspired by its tenant, when he had crept in by the glass manhole and had been screwed in. It was so elaborately padded that a man might have been fired from a gun in it with perfect safety. And it had need to be, for presently a man was to crawl in through that glass manhole, to be screwed up tightly, and to be flung overboard, and to sink down—down—down, for five miles, even as the lietenant said. It had taken the strongest hold of his imagination; it made him a bore at mess; and he found Steevens, the new arrival aboard, a godsend to talk to about it, over and over again.

"It's my opinion," said the lieutenant, "that that glass will simply bend in and bulge and smash, under a pressure of that sort. Daubrée has made rocks run like water under big pressures—and, you mark my words——"

"If the glass did break in," said Steevens, "what then?"

"The water would shoot in like a jet of iron. Have you ever felt a straight jet of high-pressure water? It would hit as hard as a bullet. It would simply smash him and flatten him. It would tear down his throat, and into his lungs; it would blow in his ears——"

"What a detailed imagination you have!" protested Steevens, who saw things vividly.

"It's a simple statement of the inevitable," said the lieutenant.

"And the globe?"

"Would just give out a few little bubbles, and it would settle down comfortably against the day of judgment, among the oozes and the bottom clay—with poor Elstead spread over his own smashed cushions like butter over bread."

He repeated this sentence as though he liked it very much. "Like butter over bread," he said.

"Having a look at the jigger?" said a voice, and Elstead stood behind them, spick and span in white, with a cigarette between his teeth, and his eyes smiling out of the shadow of his ample hat-brim. "What's that about bread and butter, Weybridge? Grumbling as usual about the insufficient pay of naval officers? It won't be more than a day now before I start. We are to get the slings ready today. This clean sky and gentle swell is just the kind of thing for swinging off a dozen tons of lead and iron, isn't it?"

"It won't affect you much," said Weybridge.

"No. Seventy or eighty feet down, and I shall be there in a dozen seconds, there's not a particle moving, though the wind shriek itself hoarse up above, and the water lifts halfway to the clouds. No. Down there——" He moved to the side of the ship and the other two followed him. All three leant forward on their elbows and stared down into the yellow-green water.

"*Peace,*" said Elstead, finishing his thought aloud.

"Are you dead certain that clockwork will act?" asked Weybridge presently.

"It has worked thirty-five times," said Elstead. "It's bound to work."

"But if it doesn't?"

"Why shouldn't it?"

"I wouldn't go down in that confounded thing," said Weybridge, "for twenty thousand pounds."

"Cheerful chap you are," said Elstead, and spat sociably at a bubble below.

"I don't understand yet how you mean to work the thing," said Steevens.

"In the first place, I'm screwed into the sphere," said Elstead, "and when I've turned the electric light off and on three times to show I'm cheerful, I'm swung out over the stern by that crane, with all those big lead sinkers slung below me. The top lead weight has a roller carrying a hundred fathoms of strong cord rolled up, and that's all that joins the sinkers to the sphere, except the slings that will be cut when the affair is dropped. We use cord rather than wire rope because it's easier to cut and more buoyant—necessary points, as you will see.

"Through each of these lead weights you notice there is a hole, and an iron rod will be run through that and will project six feet on the lower side. If that rod is rammed up from below, it knocks up a lever and sets the clockwork in motion at the side of the cylinder on which the cord winds.

"Very well. The whole affair is lowered gently into the water, and the slings are cut. The sphere floats,—with the air in it, it's lighter than water,—but the lead weights go down straight and the cord runs out. When the cord is all paid out, the sphere will go down, too, pulled down by the cord."

"But why the cord?" asked Steevens. "Why not fasten the weights directly to the sphere?"

"Because of the smash down below. The whole affair will go rushing down, mile after mile, at a headlong pace at last. It would be knocked to pieces on the bottom, if it wasn't for that cord. But the weights will hit the bottom, and directly they do, the buoyancy of the sphere will come into play. It will go on sinking slower and slower; come to a stop at last, and then begin to float upward again.

"That's where the clockwork comes in. Directly the weights smash against the sea bottom, the rod will be knocked through and will kick up the clockwork, and the cord will be rewound on the reel. I shall be lugged down to the sea bottom. There I shall stay for half an hour, with the electric light on, looking about me. Then the clockwork will release a spring knife, the cord will be cut, and up I shall rush again, like a soda-water bubble. The cord itself will help the flotation."

"And if you should chance to hit a ship?" said Weybridge.

"I should come up at such a pace, I should go clean through it," said Elstead, "like a cannon ball. You needn't worry about that."

"And suppose some nimble crustacean should wriggle into your clockwork——"

"It would be a pressing sort of invitation for me to stop," said Elstead, turning his back on the water and staring at the sphere.

They had swung Elstead overboard by eleven o'clock. The day was serenely bright and calm, with the horizon lost in haze. The electric glare in the little upper compartment beamed cheerfully three times. Then they let him down slowly to the surface of the water, and a sailor in the stern chains hung ready to cut the tackle that held the lead weights and the sphere together. The globe, which had looked so large on deck, looked the smallest thing conceivable under the stern of the ship. It rolled a little, and its two dark windows, which floated uppermost, seemed like eyes turned up in round wonderment at the people who crowded the rail. A voice wondered how Elstead liked the rolling. "Are you ready?" sang out the commander. "Ay, ay, sir!" "Then let her go!"

The rope of the tackle tightened against the blade and was cut, and an eddy rolled over the globe in a grotesquely helpless fashion. Someone waved a handkerchief, someone else tried an ineffectual cheer, a middy was counting slowly: "Eight, nine, ten!" Another roll, then with a jerk and a splash the thing righted itself.

It seemed to be stationary for a moment, to grow rapidly smaller, and then the water closed over it, and it became visible, enlarged by refraction and dimmer, below the surface. Before one could count three it had disappeared. There was a flicker of white light far down in the water that diminished to a speck and vanished. Then there was nothing but a depth of water going down into blackness, through which a shark was swimming.

Then suddenly the screw of the cruiser began to rotate, the water was crickled, the shark disappeared in a wrinkled confusion, and a torrent of foam rushed across the crystalline clearness that had swallowed up Elstead. "What's the idee?" said one A. B. to another.

"We're going to lay off about a couple of miles, 'fear he should hit us when he comes up," said his mate.

The ship steamed slowly to her new position. Aboard her almost everyone who was unoccupied remained watching the breathing swell into which the sphere had sunk. For the next half-hour it is doubtful if a word was spoken that did not bear directly or indirectly on Elstead. The December sun was now high in the sky, and the heat very considerable.

"He'll be cold enough down there," said Weybridge. "They say that below a certain depth sea water's always just about freezing."

"Where'll he come up?" asked Steevens. "I've lost my bearings."

"That's the spot," said the commander, who prided himself on his omnisience. He extended a precise finger southeastward. "And this, I reckon, is pretty nearly the moment," he said. "He's been thirty-five minutes."

"How long does it take to reach the bottom of the ocean?" asked Steevens.

"For a depth of five miles, and reckoning—as we did—an acceleration of two feet per second, both ways, is just about three-quarters of a minute."

"Then he's overdue," said Weybridge.

"Pretty nearly," said the commander. "I suppose it takes a few minutes for that cord of his to wind in."

"I forgot that," said Weybridge, evidently relieved.

And then began the suspense. A minute slowly dragged itself out, and no sphere shot out of the water. Another followed, and nothing broke the low oily swell. The sailors explained to one another that little point about the winding-in of the cord. The rigging was dotted with expectant faces. "Come up, Elstead!" called one hairy-chested salt impatiently, and the others caught it up and shouted as though they were waiting for the curtain of a theatre to rise.

The commander glanced irritably at them.

"Of course, if the acceleration's less than two," he said, "he'll be all the longer. We aren't absolutely certain that was the proper figure. I'm no slavish believer in calculations."

Steevens agreed concisely. No one on the quarter-deck spoke for a couple of minutes. Then Steevens' watchcase clicked.

When, twenty-one minutes after, the sun reached the zenith, they were still wating for the globe to reappear, and not a man aboard had dared to whisper that hope was dead. It was Weybridge who first gave expression to that realization. He spoke while the sound of eight bells still hung in the air. "I always distrusted that window," he said quite suddenly to Steevens.

"Good God!" said Steevens; "you don't think——?"

"Well!" said Weybridge, and left the rest to his imagination.

"I'm no great believer in calculations myself," said the commander dubiously, "so that I'm not altogether hopeless yet." And at midnight the gunboat was steaming slowly in a spiral round the spot where the globe had sunk, and the white beam of the electric light fled and halted and swept discontentedly onward again over the waste of phosphorescent waters under the little stars.

"If his window hasn't burst and smashed him," said Weybridge, "then it's a cursed sight worse, for his clockwork has gone wrong, and he's alive now, five miles under our feet, down there in the cold and dark, anchored in that little bubble of his, where never a ray of light has shone or a human being lived, since the waters were gathered together. He's there without food, feeling hungry and thirsty and scared, wondering whether he'll starve or stifle. Which will it be? The Myers apparatus is running out, I suppose. How long do they last?"

"Good heavens!" he exclaimed; "what little things we are! What daring little devils! Down there, miles and miles of water—all water, and all this empty water about us and this sky. Gulfs!" He threw his hands out, and as he did so, a little white streak swept noiselessly up the sky, travelled more slowly, stopped, became a motionless dot, as though a new star had fallen up into the sky. Then it went sliding back again and lost itself amidst the reflections of the stars and the white haze of the sea's phosphorescence.

At the sight he stopped, arm extended and mouth open. He shut his mouth, opened it again, and waved his arms with an impatient gesture. Then he turned, shouted, "Elstead ahoy!" to the first watch, and went at a run to Lindley and the search-light. "I saw him," he said. "Starboard there! His light's on, and he's just shot out of the water. Bring the light round. We ought to see him drifting, when he lifts on the swell."

But they never picked up the explorer until dawn. Then they almost ran him down. The crane was swung out and a boat's crew hooked the chain to the sphere. When they had shipped the sphere, they unscrewed the manhole and peered into the darkness of the interior (for the electric-light chamber was intended to illuminate the water about the sphere, and was shut off entirely from its general cavity).

The air was very hot within the cavity, and the indiarubber at the lip of the manhole was soft. There was no answer to their eager questions and no sound of movement within. Elstead seemed to be lying motionless, crumpled up in the bottom of the globe. The ship's doctor crawled in and lifted him out to the men outside. For a moment or so they did not know whether Elstead was alive or dead. His face, in the yellow light of the ship's lamps, glistened with perspiration. They carried him down to his own cabin.

He was not dead, they found, but in a state of absolute nervous collapse, and besides cruelly bruised. For some days he had to lie perfectly still. It was a week before he could tell his experiences.

Almost his first words were that he was going down again. The sphere would have to be altered, he said, in order to allow him to throw off the cord if need be, and that was all. He had had the most marvellous experience.

"You thought I should find nothing but ooze," he said. "You laughed at my explorations, and I've discovered a new world!" He told his story in disconnected fragments, and chiefly from the wrong end, so that it is impossible to re-tell it in his words. But what follows is the narrative of his experience.

It began atrociously, he said. Before the cord ran out, the thing kept rolling over. He felt like a frog in a football. He could see nothing but the crane and the sky overhead, with an occasional glimpse of the people on the ship's rail. He couldn't tell a bit which way the thing would roll next. Suddenly he would find his feet going up, and try to step, and over he went rolling, head over heels, and just anyhow, on the padding. Any other shape would have been more comfortable, but no other shape was to be relied upon under the huge pressure of the nethermost abyss.

Suddenly the swaying ceased; the globe righted, and when he had picked himself up, he saw the water all about him, greeny-blue, with an attenuated light filtering down from above, and a shoal of little floating things went rushing up past him, as it seemed to him, towards the light. And even as he looked, it grew darker and darker, until the water above was as dark as the midnight sky, albeit of a greener shade, and the water below black. And little transparent things in the water developed a faint glint of luminosity, and shot past him in faint greenish streaks.

And the feeling of falling! It was just like the start of a lift, he said, only it kept on. One has to imagine what that means, that keeping on. It was then of all times that Elstead repented of his adventure. He saw the chances against him in an altogether new light. He thought of the big cuttle-fish people knew to exist in the middle waters, the kind of things they find half digested in whales at times, or floating dead and rotten and half eaten by fish. Suppose one caught hold and wouldn't let go. And had the clockwork really been sufficiently tested? But whether he wanted to go on or to go back mattered not the slightest now.

In fifty seconds everything was as black as night outside, except where the beam from his light struck through the scrap of sinking matter. They flashed by too fast for him to see what they were. Once he thinks he passed a shark. And then the sphere began to get hot by friction against the water. They had under-estimated this, it seems.

The first thing he noticed was that he was perspiring, and then he heard a hissing growing louder under his feet, and saw a lot of little bubbles—very little bubbles they were—rushing upward like a fan through the water outside. Steam! He felt the window, and it was hot. He turned on the minute glow-lamp that lit his own cavity, looked at the padded watch by the studs, and saw he had been travelling now for two minutes. It came into his head that the window would crack through the conflict of temperatures, for he knew the bottom water was very near freezing.

Then suddenly the floor of the sphere seemed to press against his feet, the rush of bubbles outside grew slower and slower, and the hissing diminished. The sphere rolled a little. The window had not cracked, nothing had given, and he knew that the dangers of sinking, at any rate, were over.

In another minute or so he would be on the floor of the abyss. He thought, he said, of Steevens and Weybridge and the rest of them five miles overhead, higher to him than the very highest clouds that ever floated over land are to us, steaming slowly and staring down and wondering what had happened to him.

He peered out of the window. There were no more bubbles now, and the hissing had stopped. Outside there was a heavy blackness—as black as black velvet—except where the electric light pierced the empty water and showed the colour of it—a yellow-green. Then three things like shapes of fire swam into sight, following each other through the water. Whether they were little and near or big and far off he could not tell.

Each was outlined in a bluish light almost as bright as the lights of a fishing smack, a light which seemed to be smoking greatly, and all along the sides of them were specks of this, like the lighter portholes of a ship. Their phosphorescence seemed to go out as they came into the radiance of his lamp, and he saw then that they were little fish of some strange sort, with huge heads, vast eyes, and dwindling bodies and tails. Their eyes were turned towards him, and he judged they were following him down. He supposed they were attracted by his glare.

Presently others of the same sort joined them. As he went on down, he noticed that the water became of a pallid colour, and that little specks twinkled in his ray like motes in a sunbeam. This was probably due to the clouds of ooze and mud that the impact of his leaden sinkers had disturbed.

By the time he was drawn down to the lead weights he was in a dense fog of white that his electric-light failed altogether to pierce for more than a few yards, and many minutes elapsed before the hanging sheets of sediment subsided to any extent. Then, lit by his light and by the transient phosphorescence of a distant shoal of fishes, he was able to see under the huge blackness of the superincumbent water an undulating expanse of greyish-white ooze, broken here and there by tangled thickets of a growth of sea lilies, waving hungry tentacles in the air.

Farther away were the graceful, translucent outlines of a group of gigantic sponges. About this floor there were scattered a number of bristling flattish tufts of rich purple and black, which he decided must be some sort of sea-urchin, and small, large-eyed or blind things having a curious resemblance, some to woodlice, and others to lobsters, crawled sluggishly across the track of the light and vanished into the obscurity again, leaving furrowed trails behind them.

Then suddenly the hovering swarm of little fishes veered about and came towards him as a flight of starlings might do. They passed over him like a phosphorescent snow, and then he saw behind them some larger creature advancing towards the sphere.

At first he could see it only dimly, a faintly moving figure remotely suggestive of a walking man, and then it came into the spray of light that the lamp shot out. As the glare struck it, it shut its eyes, dazzled. He stared in rigid astonishment.

It was a strange vertebrated animal. Its dark purple head was dimly suggestive of a chameleon, but it had such a high forehead and such a braincase as no reptile ever displayed before; the vertical pitch of its face gave it a most extraordinary resemblance to a human being.

Two large and protruding eyes projected from sockets in chameleon fashion, and it had a broad reptilian mouth with horny lips beneath its little nostrils. In the position of the ears were two huge gill-covers, and out of these floated a branching tree of coralline filaments, almost like the tree-like gills that very young rays and sharks possess.

But the humanity of the face was not the most extraordinary thing about the creature. It was a biped; its almost globular body was poised on a tripod of two frog-like legs and a long thick tail, and its forelimbs, which grotesquely caricatured the human hand, much as a frog's do, carried a long shaft of bone, tipped with copper. The colour of the creature was variegated; its head, hands, and legs were purple; but its skin, which hung loosely upon it, even as clothes might do, was a phosphorescent grey. And it stood there blinded by the light.

At last this unknown creature of the abyss blinked its eyes open, and, shading them with its disengaged hand, opened its mouth and gave vent to a shouting noise, articulate almost as speech might be, that penetrated even the steel case and padded jacket of the sphere. How a shouting may be accomplished without lungs Elstead does not profess to explain. It then moved sideways out of the glare into the mystery of shadow that bordered it on either side, and Elstead felt rather than saw that it was coming towards him. Fancying the light had attracted it, he turned the switch that cut off the current. In another moment something soft dabbed upon the steel, and the globe swayed.

Then the shouting was repeated, and it seemed to him that a distant echo answered it. The dabbing recurred, and the globe swayed and ground against the spindle over which the wire was rolled. He stood in the blackness and peered out into the everlasting night of the abyss. And presently he saw, very faint and remote, other phosphorescent quasi-human forms hurrying towards him.

Hardly knowing what he did, he felt about in his swaying prison for the stud of the exterior electric light, and came by accident against his own small glow-lamp in its padded recess. The sphere twisted, and then threw him down; he heard shouts like shouts of surprise, and when he rose to his feet, he saw two pairs of stalked eyes peering into the lower window and reflecting his light.

In another moment hands were dabbing vigorously at his steel casing, and there was a sound, horrible enough in his position, of the metal protection of the clockwork being vigorously hammered. That, indeed, sent his heart into his mouth, for if these strange creatures succeeded in stopping that, his release would never occur. Scarcely had he thought as much when he felt the sphere sway violently, and the floor of it press hard against his feet. He turned off the small glow-lamp that lit the interior, and sent the ray of the large light in the separate compartment out into the water. The sea-floor and the man-like creatures had disappeared, and a couple of fish chasing each other dropped suddenly by the window.

He thought at once that these strange denizens of the deep sea had broken the rope, and that he had escaped. He drove up faster and faster, and then stopped with a jerk that sent him flying against the padded room of his prison. For half a minute, perhaps, he was too astonished to think.

Then he felt that the sphere was spinning slowly, and rocking, and it seemed to him that it was also being drawn through the water. By crouching close to the window, he managed to make his weight effective and roll that part of the sphere downward, but he could see nothing save the pale ray of his light striking down ineffectively into the darkness. It occurred to him that he would see more if he turned the lamp off, and allowed his eyes to grow accustomed to the profound obscurity.

In this he was wise. After some minutes the velvety blackness became a translucent blackness, and then, far away, and as faint as the zodiacal light of an English summer evening, he saw shapes moving below. He judged these creatures had detached his cable, and were towing him along the sea bottom.

And then he saw something faint and remote across the undulations of the submarine plain, a broad horizon of pale luminosity that extended this way and that way as far as the range of his little window permitted him to see. To this he was being towed, as a balloon might be towed by men out of the open country, into a town. He approached it very slowly, and very slowly the dim irradiation was gathered together into more definite shapes.

It was nearly five o'clock before he came over this luminous area, and by that time he could make out an arrangement suggestive of streets and houses grouped about a vast roofless erection that was grotesquely suggestive of a ruined abbey. It was spread out like a map below him. The houses were all roofless enclosures of walls, and their substance being, as he afterwards saw, of phosphorescent bones, gave the place an appearance as if it were built of drowned moonshine.

Among the inner caves of the place waving trees of crinoid stretched their tentacles, and tall, slender, glassy sponges shot like shining minarets and lilies of filmy light out of the general glow of the city. In the open spaces of the place he could see a stirring movement as of crowds of people, but he was too many fathoms above them to distinguish the individuals in those crowds.

Then slowly they pulled him down, and as they did so, the details of the place crept slowly upon his apprehension. He saw that the courses of the cloudy buildings were marked out with beaded lines of round objects, and then he perceived that at several points below him, in broad open spaces, were forms like the encrusted shapes of ships.

Slowly and surely he was drawn down, and the forms below him became brighter, clearer, more distinct. He was being pulled down, he perceived, towards the large building in the centre of the town, and he could catch a glimpse ever and again of the multitudinous forms that were lugging at his cord. He was astonished to see that the rigging of one of the ships, which formed such a prominent feature of the place, was crowded with a host of gesticulating figures regarding him, and then the walls of the great building rose about him silently, and hid the city from his eyes.

And such walls they were, of water-logged wood, and twisted wire-rope, and iron spars, and copper, and the bones and skulls of dead men. The skulls ran in zigzag lines and spirals and fantastic curves over the building; and in and out of their eye-sockets, and over the whole surface of the place, lurked and played a multitude of silvery little fishes.

Suddenly his ears were filled with a low shouting and a noise like the violent blowing of horns, and this gave place to a fantastic chant. Down the sphere sank, past the huge pointed windows, through which he saw vaguely a great number of these strange, ghostlike people regarding him, and at last he came to rest, as it seemed, on a kind of altar that stood in the centre of the place.

And now he was at such a level that he could see these strange people of the abyss plainly once more. To his astonishment, he perceived that they were prostrating themselves before him, all save one, dressed as it seemed in a robe of placoid scales, and crowned with a luminous diadem, who stood with his reptilian mouth opening and shutting, as though he led the chanting of the worshippers.

A curious impulse made Elstead turn on his small glow-lamp again, so that he became visible to these creatures of the abyss, albeit the glare made them disappear forthwith into night. At this sudden sight of him, the chanting gave place to a tumult of exultant shouts; and Elstead, being anxious to watch them, turned his light off again, and vanished from before their eyes. But for a time he was too blind to make out what they were doing, and when at last he could distinguish them, they were kneeling again. And thus they continued worshipping him, without rest or intermission, for a space of three hours.

Most circumstantial was Elstead's account of this astounding city and its people, these people of perpetual night, who have never seen sun or moon or stars, green

vegetation, nor any living, air-breathing creatures, who know nothing of fire, nor any light but the phosphorescent light of living things.
know nothing of fire, nor any light but the phosphorescent light of living things.

Startling as is his story, it is yet more startling to find that scientific men, of such eminence as Adams and Jenkins, find nothing incredible in it. They tell me they see no reason why intelligent, water-breathing, vertebrated creatures, inured to a low temperature and enormous pressure, and of such a heavy structure, that neither alive nor dead would they float, might not live upon the bottom of the deep sea, and quite unsuspected by us, descendants like ourselves of the great Theriomorpha of the New Red Sandstone age.

We should be known to them, however, as strange, meteoric creatures, wont to fall catastrophically dead out of the mysterious blackness of their watery sky. And not only we ourselves, but our ships, our metals, our appliances, would come raining down out of the night. Sometimes sinking things would smite down and crush them, as if it were the judgment of some unseen power above, and sometimes would come things of the utmost rarity or utility, or shapes of inspiring suggestion. One can understand, perhaps, something of their behaviour at the descent of a living man, if one thinks what a barbaric people might do, to whom an enhaloed, shining creature came suddenly out of the sky.

At one time or another Elstead probably told the officers of the *Ptarmigan* every detail of his strange twelve hours in the abyss. That he also intended to write them down is certain, but he never did, and so unhappily we have to piece together the discrepant fragments of his story from the reminiscences of Commander Simmons, Weybridge, Steevens, Lindley, and the others.

We see the thing darkly in fragmentary glimpses—the huge ghostly building, the bowing, chanting people, with their dark chameleon-like heads and faintly luminous clothing, and Elstead, with his light turned on again, vainly trying to convey to their minds that the cord by which the sphere was held was to be severed. Minute after minute slipped away, and Elstead, looking at his watch, was horrified to find that he had oxygen only for four hours more. But the chant in his honor kept on as remorselessly as if it was the marching song of his approaching death.

The manner of his release he does not understand, but to judge by the end of cord that hung from the sphere, it had been cut through by rubbing against the edge of the altar. Abruptly the sphere rolled over, and he swept up, out of their world, as an ethereal creature clothed in a vacuum would sweep through our own atmosphere back to its native ether again. He must have torn out of their sight as a hydrogen bubble hastens upward from our air. A strange ascension it must have seemed to them.

The sphere rushed up with even greater velocity than, when weighted with the lead sinkers, it had rushed down. It became exceedingly hot. It drove up with the windows uppermost, and he remembers the torrent of bubbles frothing against the glass. Every moment he expected this to fly. Then suddenly something like a huge wheel seemed to be released in his head, the padded compartment began spinning about him, and he fainted. His next recollection was of his cabin, and of the doctor's voice.

But that is the substance of the extraordinary story that Elstead related in fragments to the officers of the *Ptarmigan*. He promised to write it all down at a later date. His mind was chiefly occupied with the improvement of his apparatus, which was effected at Rio.

It remains only to tell that on February 2, 1896, he made his second descent into the ocean abyss, with the improvements his first experience suggested. What happened we shall probably never know. He never returned. The *Ptarmigan* beat about over the point of his submersion, seeking him in vain for thirteen days. Then she returned to Rio, and the news was telegraphed to his friends. So the matter remains for the present. But it is hardly probable that no further attempt will be made to verify his strange story of these hitherto unsuspected cities of the deep sea.